BURNING

RAGE

To Kelly

Best Regards

September 29, 2021

Don Bonting

BURNING RAGE

RAGE

DON BANTING

Published by Don Banting, Edmonton, Canada

ISBN 978-1-77354-348-2

Publication assistance and digital printing in Canada by

PUBLISHING
PageMaster.ca

Emotionally neglected by her parents, bullied by her school peers and shunned by society, thirty- eight year old unappealing and lonely Jess embarks on a mission of revenge. It is now time for her to unleash decades of pent up anger.

"This isn't a high school thing or an age thing. It's a people thing. People cut other people down out of jealousy, because of something broken inside them, or for no reason at all. Just don't let them change you or stop you from singing or dancing around to your favorite song."
– Taylor Swift

"People are going to bring you down because of your drive. Ultimately, it makes you a stronger person to turn your cheek and go the other way."
– Selena Gomez

"I was bullied when I was younger and it would bring me down. You have to find a way to funnel those feelings into something proactive...Do something that is going to better yourself while you're trying to get over those resentments. Holding on to them only makes you sick."
– Demi Lovato

"You are not alone in this. There are so many people going through the same thing. Just know you are stronger than any voice that brings you down."
– Brittany Snow

"If someone attacks you because of who you are, know that there are millions of people who appreciate you living your own truth."
– Tyler Oakley

1

BONNIE DOON NIGHTCLUB BURNS

Edmonton Guardian
Laura Martin

Edmonton City Police are investigating a fire at the Doon-Boogie nightclub near Bonnie Doon Mall. Ron Baker, Chief of Police, said the call came in at around three in the morning on Saturday

"We are currently investigating a fire in the Bonnie Doon area," said Baker.

When asked if the Doon-Boogie fire was related to the previous two nightclub fires in the last month, Baker said they are currently still considering all possibilities in the investigation.

"There was so much smoke," said one nearby resident who did not wish to be named. "People were screaming and running. Thank God it was closed for the night. I can't believe this happened here."

Tony Rackerton, a spokesperson for the Cactus Club on Jasper Ave., said that nightclubs in the city are now on high alert.

He said that the police have urged owners to ensure their surveillance footage is working and to keep extra security outside of the club. "At this point, we are increasing our presence at all of the entrances. We will also be limiting the number of people we allow into our club each evening, for safety reasons," said Rackerton.

Anyone with any information regarding the Doon-Boogie fire or the two fires at the Oil Town Stomping Grounds and The Mighty Corral are encouraged to contact Crime Stoppers.

***

1990, eight years old:

The ponies were standing again, ready for the parade down the hall. Jess crawled along, making minor adjustments down the long train. It had to be right this time.

She crawled back to the first blue pony, her jeans dragging along the Berber carpet, making a swish, swish sound. Her mousy-brown hair hung lank in front of her as she moved the first one forward a foot.

Then she turned to move the next one, speaking their lines for them.

She could hear her mom's show in the living room and her brother making explosion noises in his room. It was her turn to play in the hallway today. Nathan had had the last two days in the hall, and that wasn't fair.

The ponies were almost at the linoleum when she remembered they needed a watering hole. "Oy yoy yoy," she said to herself as she made her way to the cupboard with the bowls. Her mom was right, she would lose her head if it wasn't attached!

The yellow Tupperware bowl had seen many years of use, and it wasn't kept for anything special, so it was perfect to water the ponies. She stood on her tiptoes at the sink and poured a little bit of water in and then set it in the centre of the kitchen. "No water on the carpet" was one of Mom's main rules.

"Jess. What are you doing?" She winced involuntarily at her mother's voice.

"Just playing ponies," she said, hoping to satisfy her mom. It worked; only a bit of grumbling came from the living room.

She made her way back to her ponies.

Then the bedroom door flew open and Nathan burst through with his transformers. Gun noises and spit erupted from his mouth as his toys smashed into her ponies.

"Stop it!" Jess screamed. Nathan ignored her and continued on down the line, stomping and kicking ponies. "Nathan!"

"Jessica Leanne, you stop shouting this instant!" Her mom's heavy stomps made the floor vibrate.

"What on Earth is going on?" Hands on her hips, Jess's mother, Lorraine, was glowering down at her.

"Nathan was wrecking my parade," said Jess. "It's not fair. It's my turn to play in the hall."

"Are you whining again, Miss Jess?"

"No, Mommy. It's just that-"

"Enough! Jess, I don't know what is wrong with you. I can't believe you won't share this space with your brother. You are a terrible role model right now. Did you know that?"

Jess felt a wave of shame and she realized her mom was right, she wasn't behaving very well with Nathan. He was only six and he would never learn to play nicely if she didn't play nicely with him.

"You apologize to your brother, right now."

Jess turned to Nathan who was sitting on the floor, flying his transformer through the air in front of him. "I'm sorry," she mumbled toward her feet.

"Pick up your toys and go to your room. I don't want to see you until supper, you hear me?"

It was hard to fit five ponies in her arms, but she managed it. In the room she shared with Nathan, she dodged GI Joe figurines, lego and other toys, making her way to her little box in the corner. She gently placed all five ponies inside before closing the lid. Then she crawled up to her bed on the top bunk, where she knew she would get to listen to Nathan play in the hallway for the rest of the day.

***

2019:

Laura looked at the police officer across the table, sipping his coffee. A coffee she'd paid for.

Give him a minute, Laura, she thought. Deadlines were looming and she needed this information. The guy knew it, too.

"So, Constable Jennings, were you able to get a copy for me?"

"Just call me Brian," he said. Then he reached into his pocket and pulled out a folded-up, crumpled piece of paper. "This was all I could get."

"That hardly looks official," remarked Laura. Still, it was better than she was likely to get otherwise. The Edmonton Police

Service and the Fire Rescue Services were being very tight-lipped about their information.

She grabbed the piece of paper and uncrumpled it. Then, without reading it, she folded it neatly and tucked it in her purse.

"I don't suppose you want to give a quote for my article, do you?"

Brian shook his head and lifted one palm up. "God, no! This is bad enough."

"Fair enough." *Well, this is done. On to the next.* Except she had to be polite. This guy had helped her before and he might help her again in the future.

"How's the little guy doing?" she asked.

"Growing like a weed," said Brian with a fatherly smile on his face. "The other day, Mel caught him climbing the bookcase."

Laura laughed and checked her Fitbit for the time. "He sounds like he's going to be quite a handful!"

"They always are," he sighed before licking some coffee off of his long moustache and then wiping his face with his hand. "Well, I'm guessing you have places to be. Thanks again for the coffee."

"Anytime, Brian, I appreciate your help."

It was two hours until her deadline. With traffic, she figured she could make it to the Guardian's offices in about half an hour. Maybe twenty-five minutes if she took the Henday. Either way, she was going to have to make some calls en route.

When she got to her car, she took a moment to pull the paper out of her purse and take a look at it. It was the summary sheet from the Fire Investigation Report on the last nightclub burning.

The cause for the fire was arson, again. The description of cause was an accelerant that had been poured into the roof of the building.

So, this was all likely the same person. Each of the nightclubs had had the same M.O. She wondered what the nightclub community would think of being targeted.

Arson was the leading cause of fires in Edmonton for the last decade. Fires in the city were always investigated jointly by the EPS and the FRS. Usually, though, it was abandoned warehouses and older buildings that were the targets. Harm to people was rarely the motivation for the arsonists. They just liked to watch things burn.

Laura felt there was something different about this one, though. These buildings were used every night. There was always a chance someone was inside when the fire started. This person, whoever he was, was after someone.

Maybe he was some fundamentalist who couldn't stand the unsavoury lifestyle of those who partied at the clubs? Or could it be a spurned employee who wanted to make the owners sweat?

She shook her head and tucked the report back into her purse. Figuring out who had done the deed was up to the police. Her job was to let the public know all of the information pertaining to the case.

The Guardian's office was on the east side of the city. She pulled into the parking lot, grabbed her purse and walked as fast as her pumps would allow her. Time was short and she had a story to write.

Mandy was busy taking a call when Laura came in, so she just gave a brief wave and headed to her desk in the back of the room. The air buzzed with conversations and the sound of keyboards. The deadline for the day was coming quickly and sometimes the sources waited until the last minute to call back.

"Laura," said a tall man in khakis and a polo shirt. "Did you get it?" Greg, her editor, jogged down the space between the cubicles to reach her.

"I did," said Laura. She dumped her purse on her desk and rifled through for the report.

"And?" he said eagerly.

"It's the same M.O. We've got a serial arsonist here."

"Excellent!" said Greg. "Do you need an extension or do you got this?"

"I'm good, I'll have it done by four."

"Great," he yelled over his shoulder as he trotted back down the cubicles. He was already on to the next story. "Aaron!" he shouted as he made his way to another desk.

Laura sat down and cracked her neck. Then after a quick stretch, she booted her laptop up and opened the program. Her coffee from that morning was still sitting on her desk. She took a quick swallow before settling in to write.

2

SERIAL ARSONIST HITS FOURTH CLUB

Edmonton Guardian
Laura Martin

A fourth nightclub has been reduced to rubble after a fire that happened Thursday night. Edmonton City Police, along with Edmonton Fire Services and the RCMP, are investigating the incident.

The blaze started at the Stockyard just before midnight on Thursday, said witnesses. ECS and EFS arrived on the scene shortly thereafter, but the fire was too far along to save it.

As with the other fires, there were no major injuries. One man was treated for smoke inhalation at the scene.

RCMP said they do believe the nightclub burnings are connected. They are asking for the public to be extra vigilant and to pay attention to their surroundings.

A source close to the investigation has confirmed that three of the four fires have started in the ceilings of the nightclubs. In

each case, an accelerant was used. Authorities
are not releasing any further details.

The other nightclub was believed to be set on
fire with a gasoline bomb, commonly known
as a molotov cocktail.

While there is still no known motive for
these burnings, RCMP said they are looking
for a caucasian male, between the ages of
25 and 40 for questioning. This individual
was seen on footage at more than one of the
crime scenes dressed in dark pants and a
dark hoodie with a ball cap on.

Anyone with information is encouraged to
contact Crime Stoppers.

***

1992, ten years old:

Her Dad's truck was at home when Jess got off the bus at their
trailer court. She had a feeling of dread as she approached
their blue trailer. She wanted to look inside the old Chev, but she
didn't dare.

Even outside, she could hear the screaming.

Nathan came bounding up behind her. "Dad's home!" he cried,
running up the porch stairs and into the trailer addition without
hesitation.

Jess wasn't so eager. She felt like someone had filled her shoes
with lead weights.

Suddenly, the yelling stopped and the screen door on the
addition banged open as her Dad stormed out.

"Daddy?" she asked from her perch on the bottom step. "What's
going on?"

"Jess, Daddy's going to be staying at Uncle Daryl's for a while, okay? I'll be by to see you this weekend."

"Can I come?" Her Uncle Daryl was her favourite, and staying at his cabin was always fun. Especially if Nathan didn't come.

"Not this time." He walked down the steps and tousled her hair. Then he walked to the truck, hopped in and backed out of the driveway. He didn't even wave goodbye.

Nathan stood in the doorway, watching him drive away, tears streaming down his cheeks. Jess rushed up to comfort him, wishing he didn't have to see that.

"Go away, Jess. This is your fault!"

He ran back into the house and Jess chased after him.

"Jessica! Leave him be," came her mother's command. She froze at her mother's voice.

"Mom, is everything okay?" Jess asked.

"What do you think? I swear, Jess, you were born with half a brain cell."

"Is Daddy coming back?"

"Doubt it, and good riddance, if you ask me. That cheating asshole can go live with his new family. We don't need him."

Her dad had a new family? Why hadn't he taken her with him? She didn't want to stay here with Nathan and Mom. Her mom might not need him, but Jess did. He was the only good thing she had in her life.

She hung her backpack on the peg inside her bedroom, trying her best to ignore Nathan's sniffles.

"Dad left 'cause of you," said Nathan.

"He did not," Jess sighed.

"Yeah, he did. I heard what he said to Mom. He said, 'Jess doesn't stand a chance and I can't stay here and watch it.'"

The words felt like blows to her stomach. Was it her fault? Was it because she wasn't pretty enough to get the boys to like her? Or because she wasn't smart? Had she driven him away?

Hot tears spilled down her cheeks, but she dashed them away with her hand. "Yeah, well, we don't need him anyway, Nathan. He's a cheating asshole and he can go live with his new family."

***

2019:

Staff Sergeant Hutchinson stalked the halls of his precinct. A promotion was riding on solving this case, he knew it. Yet none of the fucking idiots under him could find a clue. Literally and figuratively.

Now he had to sit down with the bigwigs to learn how he should be doing his job better. Fat lot of good that would do. Yet, here he was.

He slowed his step as he reached the conference room. He checked his navy blue tie, tugged on his shirt to remove any wrinkles and then proceeded at a casual pace.

There were four men waiting for him on roller chairs in a small room around an old oak table. A trestle table was on one side, filled with coffee and other goodies, including the stereotypical doughnuts.

The four men turned when he stepped into the room, each with a styrofoam coffee cup in hand.

"Hutchinson! Glad you could join us today," said Superintendent Miller.

"Of course, Sir," he said. "I wouldn't miss it." He was only missing his daughter's ringette finals. Lacey, his ex-wife, would be furious when she found out.

Miller gestured toward a short man with grey hair and a handlebar moustache. "This is Superintendent Grunnings with the RCMP." Grunnings raised his cup as a hello. A young blonde man leaned casually against the trestle table. "This is Inspector Young with the RCMP."

The other man, an overweight middle-aged man with a widow's peak was his boss, Inspector Kowalchuk. To Hutchinson's relief, Kowalchuk looked just as nervous as he felt.

Skipping the coffee, he pulled out a chair. The sooner this was done, the better.

Grunnings sat down and gestured for Young to join them. "We're here to discuss the nightclub arsons. I understand we've got next to nothing for leads."

Hutchinson pushed down the irritation that wanted to show on his face. "We have footage of a caucasian male in a dark hoodie and pants leaving the scene at two of the fires. We're currently looking at everyone with a previous record who fits that description."

Grunnings chuckled, "So, bupkis. That's what you've got."

"With all due respect, Sir," said Kowalchuk, "we all know that fires make it difficult to find much of anything in regards to evidence. We know that we're not dealing with an amateur. This guy's done this before."

"We've developed a profile we'd like to have your officers use," said Young. "In fact, we're not sure that this assailant is acting alone."

"It's gotta be gang-related," said Grunnings. "I want the books checked for those nightclubs. If they're cooking the books, then they're probably selling drugs and laundering money. I would bet my last penny that you're looking at a hostile turf war of some kind."

"I disagree," said Hutchinson. "We've been keeping an eye on those gangs and some of their ring leaders. We're not hearing any talk of this. This is someone who likes to watch fire burn. That's all."

"Then why target nightclubs?" asked Grunnings.

"We're working on that," said Hutchinson.

"That's why," said Miller, "we're going to go ahead and take a look at the profile Inspector Young has provided us. Maybe that will give us some insight into this pyro."

"Yeah, but you're basing your profile on gang relations," Hutchinson told him.

"We definitely did consider that," said Young, "but I think you'll find the rest helpful." He handed out four green Duotangs.

Hutchinson paged through the booklet, noting several differences between what he and his crew knew and what these guys thought they knew.

"You don't mention pyromania," Hutchinson pointed out.

"Because it's not about the fire," replied Grunnings. "It's about the message they're sending. Have you been listening?"

Hutchinson levelled the man with a flat look and closed the report. Then he looked at Miller. "I'll have these distributed to all of the units on Monday," he said.

Miller nodded at him. Hutchinson couldn't tell if Miller agreed with him or the RCMP, but he didn't care. His men could read this profile to their hearts' content, but it wasn't going to help solve the case, as far as he was concerned.

3

Ed Keller didn't mind working night shift most of the time. Lately, though, it was getting harder and harder to find the justification in the extra buck-fifty an hour he made to do it. He was too old to be doing building security.

Too many fires lately, and his ulcer was already bad enough. Not to mention his wife, Millie, worrying about him constantly. He'd had to turn his phone to silent so he didn't get in trouble for all of the texts she was sending him. She'd always been a bit of a worrywart, but this Rooftop Arsonist had her really riled up.

Although it was technically spring, there was still a bite to the air, especially in the wee hours of the morning. The Edmonton common was dead this time of night. There was the odd semi that came through, hauling supplies to Walmart and the Superstore, but other than that, traffic was limited.

As per routine, he picked up his mike and checked in with Cyrus, the guard inside the club. "Hey, Cyrus, just checking in. I'm outside on Ninety-ninth, I'm gonna make the circuit."

"Roger that!" came the voice through the walkie-talkie.

Normally, there was only one security guard at the club during the night. Now that everyone was on high alert, nobody was taking any chances anymore.

A city bus blew by, not even slowing for the bus stop. He made his way north on Ninety-ninth and then turned right, heading toward the theatre. Nothing in sight.

He pulled his phone out to check for texts. Nothing since midnight, Millie must have gone to sleep finally. He tucked his phone away into his pocket as he turned the corner to head east around the perimeter of the building.

There was a truck parked outside, its box backed up toward the building. Behind it, a ladder was leaned up against the wall.

He felt the hairs on the back of his neck lift up. For a second, he froze, unsure if he should call Cyrus first or check this out. Then he decided he would back around the corner before radioing it in.

As he was making his way back, he noticed a figure descending the ladder. It was a slender person in a dark hoodie, wearing a ball cap underneath. The man carried a jerry can, and he had a hatchet stuck through a loop in the toolbelt he was wearing around his waist.

"Hey, you!" Ed shouted before he could think. "What are you doing? You can't be up there!"

The figure never answered. It just continued until it reached the ground before tossing the jerry can into the back of the truck.

Ed started walking toward the truck, pulling his pepper spray out of its holster. Then he smelled smoke. He looked up at the roof, where he could see a trail of grey cloud dancing in the air.

There was a clang as the ladder was dropped into the truck and Ed shouted again. "Hey! The police are on their way!" He felt like an imbecile for saying that.

The figure turned toward him, hatchet in hand. Ed lifted the mike up to his mouth. "Cyrus we've got a sit-"

The figure was running at him, and Ed dropped the mike. Cyrus' voice was coming through, saying something, but Ed wasn't listening. He raised his hands over his head as the hatchet swung down.

It glanced off one wrist, and then slid down the arm, cutting his bicep.

He fell backward, holding the pepper spray up, but the person ran back toward the truck. It peeled out of the parking lot, leaving Ed holding his arm and watching the building start to burn.

***

1996, fourteen years old:

Jess pulled her ball cap low as she quickly strode across the school ground. Her toes ached with every step. Soon, they were going to bust through the end of her shoes.

"Hey, Jess!"

She picked up her pace. She wouldn't make the mistake of looking over her shoulder this time, it was best to just pretend they weren't there.

The chainlink fence around the bus stop was her safe point. It was only there that Matt and the others would leave her alone.

"Aw, Jess. You're no fun! Thought you might want to look at my dick again."

She stumbled over her shoelaces and nearly fell. One time. That was all it had taken. One time of her lingering by the boys' locker room, just to have a peek inside. She hadn't been trying to see a boy, just see what the room looked like. Alyssa had seen her and that had been that.

She would never live it down.

They gained on her after her stumble, and she could feel tears forming in her eyes. She started running. After this copse of trees, she would be in sight of the bus stop and safe.

Someone yanked on her backpack and she fell backward, landing on her ass on the cement sidewalk.

"Oops! Sorry, Jess," said Alyssa in her syrup voice. "I didn't mean for you to fall."

By then, Matt and his buddies had caught up to her and Alyssa walked on, giggling.

Jess pulled her knees to her chest and wrapped her arms around her legs, tucking her head down. Past experience had taught her that fighting back or even standing up would only end poorly. Maybe if she didn't give them the reaction they were wanting, they would go away.

Matt circled around in front of her and grabbed his crotch. "Is this what you were looking for?" He crouched down beside her and knocked her cap off her head. "Tell you what, rumour is you don't have any tits, so if you show me proof that you have them, I'll even let you touch it."

Shivers wracked her body and she did everything she could to keep sobs from escaping her lips.

"I bet she's only got mosquito bites," said a nasty voice behind her. His name was Jack.

Finally, Matt seemed to have enough. He stood up and spit on her. "Probably give us leprosy anyway," he said.

Someone behind her snorted loud and then she felt a loogie hit the back of her head and soak into her hair.

The guys all started laughing and then left her there. They had to go back toward the school, they lived in the area. All of them had gone out of their way to come find her and torment her.

Slowly, she got to her feet and tried wiping the spit out of her hair. All she could do was spread it around. Then she made her way to the bus stop, where Alyssa was talking to some friends and laughing.

A flush rose in her cheeks, but she held back the tears. She wouldn't give those fucking bitches the satisfaction of knowing how upset she was. One day, they would get what was coming to them.

***

2019:

The number of suicides in this country every day is huge. When you look at the demographics and see how many kids kill themselves, there's generally one cause: they were treated like shit.

I may be have been past that part of my life, but I was done watching as others had the life of their dreams and trampled others on the way there.

The parking lot was empty when I pulled up to the St. Thomas school. All these religious kids were all ready to graduate. Just the other day, when I was walking nearby, I saw some of them treating others like dirt. *Things really don't change.*

All of those social media whores trying to get people to stop bullying, they don't get it. There's only one way to deal with a bully. It's not by talking to them or about them. You have to scare them more than they scare you. Otherwise, they'll just keep coming.

I snuck around to the side of the building that was hidden by some nice foliage. I couldn't understand why they would cover up a window here, but it worked for me. It provided me with the perfect coverage to get in.

The screws on this security screen were Phillips. I put my flashlight between my teeth and pulled my screwdriver out of my tool belt and get to work. Once I'd got all of the screws out, I gently pulled the screen down, careful not to catch my latex gloves.

I didn't plan to leave any clues for the cops.

Next to come out was my handy roll of duct tape. I stretched a large X over the windowpane, and then an extra horizontal and vertical strip for good measure. I shrugged out of my hoodie and did my best to cover the window.

The hammer was aimed just so. I wanted the glass to break, but I didn't want it to shatter. Once I'd struck the glass through my hoodie, I dropped my hammer and pushed.

The glass broke, but the tape held it together, preventing the crashing sound of a smashed window. I picked out the pieces and repeated the process for the second pane of glass.

I shook my hoodie out and put it on before climbing through the broken window, sans glass.

My target was the gym. Earlier this evening, I'd driven by and saw several students and their parents hauling supplies in. Seeing all those smiling faces made me want to puke. Part of me wanted to rip through the parking lot and end them there. But that wouldn't be as satisfying.

The theme was Hollywood. Tacky cardboard letters were hung on the wall above a shitty city skyline that was made out of black paper. All they'd done was tape it to the walls.

Above me there were streamers going out from the centre to the outside edges. Dozens of tables lined the walls and a gaudy red carpet ran up the middle.

Silver stars with names written on them were stuck all over the walls. Each table had a cute little card that explained the seating arrangement.

To my left, there was a large sound system set up with a stand for a DJ. I could just picture them dancing in here, celebrating their perfect little lives.

Fury built up inside my chest until I was sure that if I didn't do something, I was going to explode. I ran toward the DJ booth and pushed the soundboard onto the floor. It made a satisfying crunching sound as it hit the hardwood.

Then I pushed the table over on top of it.

I was on a roll now.

I took my hatchet and punched in each of the speakers until they were unrecognizable. I took out my flask of lighter fluid out and dumped it all over that rug, weaving pretty lines back and forth. Each of the tables were smashed and all of the arrangement cards were shredded.

I ripped down each letter of Hollywood, tearing at the cardboard and stabbing holes into it with my screwdriver.

In a fury, I pulled down every single star and stabbed the names repeatedly with my screwdriver.

I didn't stop my rampage until I had worn myself out. My muscles were jelly and I felt… lighter.

My original plan had been to set everything on fire, but I changed my mind. I wanted the students to see what I had done. If I burned it down, there would be nothing to show, and maybe they wouldn't even know what had happened here.

That would be a shame. I put a lot of effort into this masterpiece.

With one final, satisfied smile, I left the same way I came in and made my way to the truck. I felt giddy and high as I made my way home. It had been a long time since I felt that good.

4

VANDALISTS DESTROY GRADUATION CELEBRATION

Edmonton Guardian
Laura Martin

Students at the St. Thomas Catholic School have had a graduation that they won't soon forget.

With Grad being held on Saturday night, several students from the Student Council and parent volunteers had decorated the gymnasium on May 23 for the celebrations. Sometime during the night, another person came in and destroyed their hard work.

"I just don't understand why someone would do this," said Brittany Bartlett, the head of the Student Council for St. Thomas. "We have earned our graduation. We've done nothing to deserve this."

Principal Sarah Claymore said she can't speak about the incident as it's currently under investigation. However, she said while they believe it was an isolated event, the school will remain closed on Monday for the safety of the students.

"Our counsellors are available to any students who are affected by this terrible act," said Claymore.

Authorities are investigating the incident, but are asking the public for help. Anyone in the area who witnessed any suspicious activity on the evening of May 23 are asked to contact Crime Stoppers.

In the meantime, St. Thomas will still celebrate their student graduation. Claymore said she's had multiple Edmontonians call and offer places for the graduates to come safely celebrate. She says the location they've chosen will not be disclosed to the public.

"We are not going to let this person get in the way of our night," said Bartlett. "We will still celebrate."

***

1998. sixteen years old:

She needed to get out of that trailer and away from her mom. If she had to listen to her mother tell Nathan how amazing he was one more time, she was going to lose it.

There was a small basement suite for rent on the south side of town. She almost had enough money for a deposit on it, but she'd just lost her job at McDonalds.

The customer was being an ass to her. She was tired of putting up with that shit and had told him where to go and how to get there. Management should have had her back.

Anyway, now she was going to move onto bigger and better things. Or at least a better job.

She'd picked up a special outfit for dropping off her resume at La Grille. She knew if she wanted to get a job there, she had to look professional, so she'd combed her hair and tied it back with a hair tie. Well, it was a scrunchy, but she had to go with what she had.

The hostess greeted her at the door.

"Welcome to La Grille, table for…one?" she asked. For a second, Jess almost lost her nerve. This woman was stunning in her little black dress and stilettos.

But she could do that too. So she would try.

"Actually, I'm here to drop off a resume with the manager," Jess said.

The hostess froze for a moment, her smile sitting stale on her face. "A resume?"

"Yes. I saw there was a job opening for a waitress."

"Oh, okay. Well, let me take you to Dan. He's the manager." Jess followed the blonde lady as she clicked her way through the lounge to the bar.

A middle-aged man in a button-up and jeans was leaning against the bar, talking to the bartender.

"Hi, Dan, this lady would like to give you her resume," the hostess said.

Dan looked down at the resume and then up at Jess. "I'm sorry, we're not hiring right now."

At that, the hostess quickly made her way back to her station.

"I just saw an ad posted yesterday for a waitress. You've already filled the position?"

"Oh, you're applying for a waitressing position." He hesitated and then set the paper on the bar top where it was quickly soaked through with water from melted ice cubes. "Listen, I'm gonna be honest here. You don't qualify for the position."

Jess felt herself flush with anger as she watched her resume get ruined on the bar top. "You barely looked at my resume."

"It's not your resume," he told her. "It's your…" he waved his hands up and down in front of Jess. "It's this."

"What do you mean?"

He sighed and rubbed his hand over his balding head. "Listen, sweetie-"

"Don't call me that," she said. How had he not noticed her name written in large bold letters at the top?

"Okay, well…" He glanced at the resume. "Jessica, take a look at Heidi over there." He pointed at the hostess. "She's a ten. You're not."

"Excuse me?" Jess couldn't believe what she was hearing. She looked down at the black button-up shirt and pressed pants she'd picked out. The cut had even been flattering on her; she thought it made her look like she had hips.

"Listen, no offence meant," he said with his hands in the air. "Our clients expect a certain experience when they come here. The staff is part of it. You'd need a push-up bra and a mini skirt."

"Are you fucking kidding me?" she asked.

"Woah! Watch your language!"

"You're telling me that you only hire the girls who are willing to whore themselves out for tips?" She reached for her resume and yanked it back. "You know what, fuck you! You're a Goddamn perv and I wouldn't want to work for you anyway."

Dan's mouth hung open, but he didn't seem to have anything to say. Jess turned her back, ignoring the stares of the patrons, and made her way out.

"Have a nice day," said Heidi in a shaky voice.

Jess held up her middle finger before slamming the doors open and running to her vehicle.

***

2019:

Hutchinson had a massive headache and was in desperate need of Advil. He rifled through his desk drawer, looking for the medication, then slammed it shut when all he came up with was some tums.

The corporal seated across the desk from him jumped at his anger. Jennings must've drawn the short straw because he was the one in here making the report. Of course, Hutchinson had already known about the shooting before he heard about it from his own squad. His daughter had tagged him in a post about it.

"Can you fucking explain it to me again?" asked Hutchinson. He was sure he was going to have a stroke one of these days. Maybe Lacey was funding the arsonist, hoping to put him in an early grave.

"Well, Sir, we have the profile that Inspector Young provided and we've been watching out for any gang activity."

"Yeah, I know that. Skip to the important part."

"Okay, well, we were responding to a complaint of suspicious activity at a nightclub. Someone had called in, saying there were fresh tags on the wall, so we went down to take a look. It sounded minor, so it was just me and Jacobs who went.

"When we got down there, we saw some dude in a hoodie spraying something on the wall of the club. Jacobs told him to stop what he was doing and raise his hands, but the guy didn't listen.

"So then Jacobs told him again and nothing. At this point, I was pulling out my gun and I told him to drop the paint can." He licked his lips, pulling his moustache into his mouth with the gesture. "Then he threw the can down and he ran right at us."

"And that's when you shot him?"

Jennings cleared his throat and wiped his hands on his pants. "That's when I discharged my weapon due to feeling threatened, Sir."

"Can you tell me what time of day it was, Jennings?"

The corporal shifted in his seat and looked down at his hands. "It was ten-thirty in the morning, Sir."

"Ten-thirty. In broad daylight," said Hutchinson. "And what was he painting on the wall of the club?"

"I didn't get a good look at it," said Jennings.

Fuck the Advil. He needed Aspirin. "It was fucking artwork, Jennings! He was working on a fucking assignment for school! For the goddamn university that he got into with a full fucking scholar-ship!"

Jennings flinched with each word, "Sir, I know-"

It wasn't really all on Jennings. That profile wasn't right and that was what it came down to. His guys were on high alert, especially after that security guard had been attacked. They were legitimately afraid for their lives.

He remembered what it was like to be working in the streets. It wasn't a cakewalk and sometimes the simplest decision could affect someone for the rest of their lives.

But this was still unacceptable.

"You are suspended, Jennings," he said in a softer voice. "With pay – for now. Someone will be in contact with you about the inves-tigation. But going forward, you and Jacobs need to cool your heels at home."

Jennings nodded numbly and handed over his badge and weapon. Hutchinson couldn't speak anymore, he just waved for him to leave. The man skulked out like a chastened child.

"Can somebody get me some fucking Asprin?" he shouted through the open door.

He was going to die young, he just knew it. And he was going to die without solving the case.

5

Laura Martin looked at the Post-It note beside her keyboard and counted the little marks she'd made. There were seven. That meant in the past three months, there had been seven nightclubs burned down.

Now there was a Wedding Boutique that had been lit up by a molotov cocktail. It wasn't necessarily related, but she couldn't shake the feeling that it was the same person.

What was going on?

The cops were scrambling, especially now Carter, a student at the University of Alberta, had been shot.

She said a small prayer for his recovery. The idea of any child suffering like that was awful.

"Martin, you're on the boutique, right? You got that insider?" asked Greg as he made his way past her desk.

"Uh, no," she replied. "That guy's not talking to me anymore."

"What'd you do?" Greg's voice was tinged with annoyance.

"I didn't do anything. He's just not talking."

"Okay. Then get the store owner and maybe some of the brides. Also, have we talked to the guy that was attacked?"

She looked at her computer and rolled her eyes. The calls had already been made. The pompous ass just wanted to sound important.

"You bet!" she said.

The article was already mostly put together. Police had responded to the scene on the night where a wedding boutique downtown had had a bomb thrown through the window. Nobody was hurt, no witnesses, blah, blah, blah.

It was nothing if the shop owner didn't call her back, just a re-gurgitation of the statement from the police.

She picked up the phone and dialled the woman's number again. Straight to voicemail.

"Hi, Tiara, this is Laura from the Edmonton Guardian again. Just looking for a quick quote from you about the fire. Can you give me a call? Thanks!"

As she set down her phone, one of her co-workers jumped up from his desk. "Holy shit, guys! There's been a bomb threat down at that fashion show at the Ag."

"What!" yelled Greg. "Who do we have down there? I want a report from them now! Laura, I want you on this."

She nodded, grabbed her jacket and jogged to the door. She couldn't believe this city right now. Nothing was safe.

When she arrived at the scene, it was organized chaos. Police had barricaded areas off and were calmly guiding evacuees away from the building.

They had the K9 unit here, too.

She pulled out her phone and snapped a couple of pictures of the waiting people. Then she made her way toward the knot of reporters talking to one of the officers.

"...at this point, we're taking all precautions. We have our dogs out and we will be sending in a bomb disposal unit once we've ensured everyone is evacuated."

One of the reporters shot her hand up. The officer nodded toward her.

"Do you think this incident is related to the Rooftop Arsonist? Or the boutique store?"

"We are not making any assumptions about this incident right now. Instead, we are focusing on the safety of the attendees and limiting damage to the building."

"When did the call come in?" asked a man.

"It came in around two p.m. from an anonymous tip."

"Do you think that's the person who planted the bomb?" asked Laura. She held up her phone to record his answer.

"Again, we have not yet been through the entire scene, and we are holding off on our thoughts about the incident until we've done our due diligence." He held up his hands and turned away from the reporters back to his car, where the schematics of the building were laid out.

"You'll have to wait for the press release for more information," said a young officer as he shooed the reporters away.

***

2000, eighteen years old:

Parties were not her thing, but Jess had been tired of her roommate whining about the party. Melissa was annoying when she wanted something and this party was going to be "ah-mazing!"

Of course, now that she was here, watching all of the gyrating bodies and listening to hip-hop, she regretted her decision. Especially because Melissa had fucked off as soon as she got out of the car.

She had a beer in her hand and was leaning up against the wall in the living room of some college kid's house. Or at least she hoped it was his house, because his parents were going to be pissed if it wasn't.

The living room floor had been cleared of furniture and a DJ was in attendance. The standard kegs were in the kitchen and the place was packed wall to wall. The reek of beer, body odour and vomit was revolting.

Her desire to leave was strong. Nobody spoke to her, or even noticed her, except to get her to move out of their way. She felt like a rabbit hiding from prey, too afraid to move and attract attention.

Still, she understood that this was what normal kids her age did. Who didn't want to get drunk and dance the night away? As strong as her urge to leave the party was, she had an equal feeling of loneliness. She wanted this kind of thing to be normal for her.

There was a cute guy talking to the DJ. He wasn't a jock or the preppy type. Just a normal guy in a t-shirt and jeans. The chances of rejection with him were much lower than with other guys.

Trying not to be creepy, she watched him out of the corner of her eye as he made his way through the room. He seemed to know everyone. There wasn't a person there who didn't smile at him or say hi.

KC and Jo-Jo came on and Jess had this weird feeling in her stomach. Like a person possessed, she walked toward the guy, blushing as she did.

"Hi," she said. He didn't hear her of course.

She pushed her way past a couple of girls dancing to get in his way. He drew up short when she stepped in front of him.

Just as she was about to speak, another dancer bumped into her back, shoving her forward. Her beer spilled on the guy's pants. She covered her mouth in embarrassment.

"What the fuck!?" he said. It looked like he'd had an accident.

"I'm so so-" she was cut off as someone shoved her to the side.

"Seriously? Who does that?" said a girl in heels. Her blue eyes were staring daggers at Jess. She put her hands on her hips and cocked one leg, accentuating the look of her skin-tight blue dress.

"I didn't mean-" said Jess, but the guy was shaking his head angrily.

"Come on, Billy, why don't we go see if we can find you some dry clothes upstairs?" The girl gave him a wink and held out her hand. Billy's expression instantly changed from anger to joy. He followed her off the floor and up the stairs like a lost child.

Jess stood on the floor, staring after them, wondering what had just happened to her. She looked around for Melissa and couldn't find her.

It was time to leave and she didn't give a damn what Melissa was doing. She could catch a ride home with someone else.

Making her way to the door was painful. She stepped out just in time to watch a guy puke over the side of the deck. It wasn't possible for her eyes to roll any further into the back of her head.

The driveway was jam-packed with vehicles. She realized, in dismay, that she was blocked in and there was no way of getting out.

Why did this party have to be in the country?

"Hey, little lady," came a voice behind her. The smell of vomit nearly made her gag. "Why so sad?"

She turned to see a man in cowboy boots and a stetson eyeing her up. He and puke guy seemed to be friends.

"Not sad. Annoyed."

"Well, why don't you come here and I can make you feel better?"

He reached over and grabbed her arm, guiding her over to him. "No thanks," she said, wrenching her arm out of his grasp.

"C'mon, me 'n Paul can show you a good time, right, bud?"

"Yeah!" came Paul, puke guy's, enthusiastic response.

"I said no!" *Fuck this night.* she would wait in her car until she could leave.

A hand grabbed her hair and pulled her back. "I wasn't done talking to you!"

"Let go!" she screamed. Paul reached out and groped at her chest. She slapped his arms away and stomped on the cowboy's foot.

"The fuck?" growled the cowboy.

"Right?" said Paul. "She's got no tits!" He turned to Jess, "Are you a dude? 'Cause that's not cool."

The cowboy still held her hair in his fist and he pulled it up to his nose. He wrinkled his face and spit to the side. "She smells gross, too." He pushed her away and she tumbled onto the deck in front of another girl who was coming outside.

"I said no!" said the cowboy. Paul gave him a high-five and they both went inside laughing.

The girl, who'd evidently been coming out for the same reason that Paul had, puked down her front and all over Jess.

"What the fuck are you doing, lying in front of the door? Now I've ruined my dress! Jesus," said the girl. She gave Jess a kick with her pointed pumps and then ran back inside, crying.

Jess stood and stared down at her body. There was a bruise forming on her arm, her scalp was sore, and she was now coated in somebody else's processed dinner.

Her phone chirped. It was Melissa. <Don't worry about me! Caught a ride with a friend. See you tmrw!>

***

2019:

I had been on such a high the last few months. I couldn't seem to screw anything up. That security guard could've got me, but he was too scared. *Nothing can top that feeling, when someone is scared of you.*

Or at least, if there was something that could top it, I hadn't experienced it yet.

But I was tired and I didn't want to be running around anymore. It was time for one last hurrah.

The bar I was outside of was no nightclub. People weren't going here to be with friends and have a good time. They were going here because they didn't want to go home. That suited me just fine.

It was called Whirls and Spurs. I would never understand how people think they could live in a city and still be a cowboy. It had baffled me for years, but since I was going in, I'd dressed the part.

I had my stetson on and some cheap boots that I found at Value Village. I stopped short at the cowboy shirt, instead opting for a plaid shirt. Even I couldn't put on a cowboy shirt without feeling tacky.

The room was dimly lit and not all that big. A hole in the wall would describe this place perfectly. There were a few patrons, though. Some had the sad sag of regulars, sitting on their lonesome at the bar.

A couple were having some brews with their buds after work, taking up the cracked leather seats in the booths.

It was a sad scene, as far as I was concerned. There wasn't even a T.V. running in here.

An old jukebox stood at the far left from the door, in front of a scuffed up hardwood dance floor. I wondered if people ever did dance in here. But there was no music playing.

As I made my way to the bar, I selected the man I wanted. He was older, wearing a stained t-shirt and crouched over the bar like it was his baby. I noticed that he had a couple of empty shot glasses in front of him. I counted that as a good sign.

"I'll have a Canadian," I said as I sat beside the man. He looked over at me right away, and though he seemed disinterested, I planned to change that. "And a shot of whatever he's having," I said.

Now I've got his attention.

"I'm Lyle," he said, reaching his hand across. I reached over and shook it. Then I wiped my hand on my pants. This man was nasty.

"Cathy," I said. He didn't need to know my real name.

"First time?"

"In here, yes. But this ain't my first rodeo," I said with a smile. He chuckled at my lame joke. *He's missing three of his front teeth.* "What brings you here?"

He shrugged his shoulders. "Beats being by myself at home." I knew it.

"I'm here to have some fun. What kind of music do you like?" I flashed some change for the jukebox.

"CCR, Haggard, Johnny Cash, that kind of stuff."

I smiled at him and took my change to the jukebox. I looked for old shitty music for him and selected a few songs. Then I gave out a whoop and walked back to the bar with a smile, just for him.

"That's the stuff!" he said as he bobbed his head to *Bad Moon Rising.*

I took a swig of my beer and touched his arm with my other hand. Then I touched him on his back and let my hand linger.

"Oh shit!" I said.

"What?" he asked.

"I was supposed to meet my friend after work. He was going to move some heavy boxes around in my truck." I set the beer down and look at my phone. "I better get going."

"I can do it," said Lyle.

"No, I can't ask you to do that. You're here to relax, not haul stuff around. I'll just head over to his place. "

"No, I'm serious," he told me. I stopped and looked at him, cocking my head to one side.

"Really?" I asked, layering surprise and sweetness in my tone. Hook, line and sinker.

"Yeah, let's get it done now..." He gave me a sly smile. "Then we can go back to relaxing."

I led him out to my truck in the parking lot, it was a dumpy, old, black extended cab and he didn't think anything of it. In my back seat, I'd loaded up some boxes of wood and other heavy camping supplies, including a jerry can, taped up inside a box with just the handle sticking out.

"I just want it in the box. I don't know what my brother was thinking." I stepped back from the door.

"No worries," he said, reaching in and grabbing the jerry can box. I smiled as he used the visible handle of the jerry can to move it. "He shouldn't have put all of the heavy stuff in the cab."

"Right?" I agreed.

I could see he was struggling with some of the boxes, but I didn't offer to lift so much as a finger. He worked up a good sweat by the time he was done. I wanted him thirsty.

When he was grabbing the last box, I crawled in the cab, giving him a good look at my ass. I dropped my phone on the floor, then I grabbed a lighter box that I'd stashed up front.

"I've got this one," I said with a smile.

When we were finally done, I had him move the stuff around a few times so I had easy access to the stuff I wanted, and we made our way back to the bar.

"Let me buy you a drink," I offered.

"I won't say no to another, I can say that!" He let out a loud guffaw as he sat down.

I lifted my finger to the bartender and he nodded, grabbing another two-ounce shot glass for Lyle.

As Lyle watched the bartender pour his whiskey, I slid my hand up his thigh, stopping just before his groin. He grinned and grabbed the glass, slamming it back like it was apple juice.

Then he turned to me and leaned in for a kiss. I obliged, though I had to go to my happy place to do it. He tasted like whiskey and cigarettes.

I leaned back and gave him my best imitation of a seductive smile. "Do you dance?"

He laughed uncomfortably and shook his head. I ran my hand up his thigh until I could feel his hard dick beneath my palm. "Are you sure?" I asked.

"Fine. Just one dance, though," he said. I grabbed his hand and pulled him onto the floor. It was a slow one, so he got to wrap his arms around me. I snuggled into him, breathing through my mouth as much as possible.

I managed to turn one into two with a pout. This was fun. I'd never been able to do this to a guy before. Before we sat down, I got the bartender's attention and asked for another.

I'd stopped drinking, pulling a trick I'd seen on a movie once. I pretended to hammer the shot and then chased it with my empty beer, spitting all the alcohol into the bottle. Lyle was getting smashed, I was feeling okay.

Now it was his turn to grope and he felt me up as I leaned against the bar. His touch was rough and unskilled.

"I need some air," I said. I grabbed his hand and pulled him outside with me. There was a bench beside the door and I took a seat. He sat next to me and lit a smoke. Then he pulled me under his arm and held me tight.

We sat like that for a while. He puffed away and flicked away his smoke. Then we made out and he felt me up. That was probably disappointing for him.

When he needed another smoke, he pulled the pack out again. I was wondering what time it was, I had to work in the morning, but my cell was in my truck.

"Should we have one more and then hit the road?" he asked, standing and heading to the door.

"I'm just going to grab my cell from my truck. I want to have it on me if we're going to your place tonight."

"Sure, sure." He went inside to order us another drink.

I pulled a Ziploc bag and some tweezers out of my pocket and picked up each of the butts he'd used. After shoving the bag back in my pocket, I dashed to my truck.

There was no way I was going home with him. I looked at my phone when I got in the truck and saw that it was nearly one in the morning. I didn't peel out of the parking lot like I wanted to. I wanted Lyle to completely forget about me.

6

2019:

As soon as I got to work this morning at six, I headed into the staff bathroom to wash out my mouth and splash water on my face. There wasn't anything to dry it with except the cheap, brown paper towel, but it was better than nothing.

I tied my hair back with a rubber band that I had in my pocket. Then with about two minutes to spare, I punched in.

I didn't even have a chance to go to my locker before I got in, so I just hung my hoodie on my cart. Two orders for parts had already been posted on the board. The paper tore easily as I pulled it from the board, too lazy to remove the tack.

Lance was behind me and snatched the list out of my hand. "Don't think you're qualified enough for that," he said.

"Fuck you. It's only four things."

"I got this," he said and pushed his cart away, burying the list in his pocket.

I snatched the other list off the board and shoved it in my pocket before someone else could steal it. If I didn't need this job so damn much, I wouldn't even care. Unlike most of the douches I worked with, I actually had a work ethic.

I was never late, rarely sick, and I busted ass all day long. I was pretty sure that was the only reason that Mike kept me around.

When I was away from the board and tucked away in a corner where I could see someone coming, I pulled the order from my pocket. It was a long one, full of heavy lifting and climbing the mobile ladders.

I cursed Lance under my breath as I made my way to the far end of the warehouse to start grabbing everything.

The order took me most of the morning to complete and by the time it was lunch, I was starving. I hadn't had a chance to bring any food, so I figured I would just get some spare change out of my locker and grab something from the vending machine. It would be enough to get me through to punching-out time.

The lunchroom was empty, and for good reason. It smelled like something had died in there. I gagged when I first walked in, and then I started breathing through my mouth. I could eat outside, I just needed my change and I'd be on my way.

I dashed over to my locker and pulled it open. The source of the nasty smell greeted me at the bottom of my locker. An open can of sardines had been dumped over my work boots, my name tag and all the other stuff I had kept there, including some cash and change.

I slammed the door shut and stormed out of the lunchroom. Lance, Evan and Dave were all doubled over, laughing.

Rage boiled through me and I didn't even think, I charged over there and punched Lance in the stomach as hard as I could. He stopped laughing when the air was knocked out of him.

"What the fuck?" said Dave.

Evan threw up his fists like he was in a boxing match and backed away from me. "We thought you'd like the fish smell. Ain't that what you're used to eating?" asked Evan.

"I'm not a fucking dyke!" I shouted at them.

"What the *hell* is going on?" boomed a voice from behind me. Mike had heard us.

I whirled around and took a breath. "These guys thought it would be funny to dump a can of sardines all over my stuff in my locker."

"It was a fucking joke," wheezed Lance. "She's always bitching that she doesn't fit in and no one likes her, and then when we include her she gets violent. I'm going to fucking HR for this."

"Nobody's going to HR!" Mike raised his hands up, and I could see the vein in his forehead pop out. Then he took a breath and said in a calm voice. "HR doesn't need to hear about a stupid prank."

I opened my mouth to protest but Mike fixed me with a glare. "Just like no one needs to be written up for workplace violence."

"That's bullshit!" said Evan.

"Is it?" asked Mike. He took a step toward Evan, and the lanky man backed away quickly. "Because I'm not going to dock you for the money it's going to take to replace her work boots. That saves you about two hundred bucks." Then he turned his attention to Dave.

"You're going to clean that Goddamned locker out. Right now. That lunchroom better smell like roses in the springtime when you're done." Dave swore and pushed past me. The guy had it coming as far as I was concerned. He was twenty-something and thought he was King Shit of Turd Mountain.

"Lance, go home, you're done for the day."

"What? Why do I have to go home?"

"Because I also saw you steal that list from her this morning. And then I watched you fuck the dog on the order. So if you don't want to be fired, I suggest you get the hell out of my sight."

Lance lumbered off toward the lunchroom, muttering under his breath.

Only me and Mike were left standing there. I was waiting to be fired. HR would fire me if they knew what happened.

"Next time, Jess, you come talk to me," he said. Then he put his hand on my shoulder and gave it a squeeze. "You can expense the boots and whatever else needs replacing. Take the rest of the day off and go get some new ones. Do you have the money to get some?"

"Yeah…" I said. Why was he being so nice to me? Now I wouldn't rest until the other shoe dropped.

"Good." He gave me a clap on the back. "Don't worry about clocking out. I'll take care of that later."

***

2019:

Laura tapped her fingers on her glass anxiously as she waited at the Olive Garden. Garett, her boyfriend of six months, was supposed to be here ten minutes ago. It wasn't like him to be late.

"More water?" asked the server.

"Please."

"And are you still waiting to order?"

She looked at her phone. At this rate, she was going to have to take her lunch to go. *Thank God for unlimited breadsticks and salad.* "No, I'll wait, thanks."

Thankfully, she didn't have to wait long, Garett came in shortly after the waitress left. He was filthy.

"I am *so* sorry. Had to run over to the kid's place and change her tire for her." He looked at the time and sighed. "I should've texted."

Laura wasn't used to dating someone who had kids. Well, at least not kids that were still dependent on their parents. She'd never had kids herself, so it was taking time for her to get used to it.

"Is she getting settled, then?"

"Yeah, I think so. We've moved most of her stuff from the house to the apartment. But, you know, change is hard on kids. I have a feeling she'll be a little more needy in the next few months as she settles in."

"Or maybe she'll run in the other direction and never talk to you," said Laura with a laugh.

Garett gave her a sad smile, "Maybe. I hope not."

He was a widower and he'd only had one child in his marriage. Laura suspected that part of the reason he'd put his profile up online was because he didn't want to be lonely after his daughter moved out.

She hadn't even met the girl yet. She wondered if it was the equivalent of meeting his parents.

"I'm sorry about tonight," Laura said. "This event dropped in my lap last minute and I couldn't say no."

"Hey, no, I get it. If you don't prioritize your work, no one will."

This was a strange feeling for her. No man had ever prioritized her career over time spent with them. Normally she had to apologize for everything. Especially at her age when everyone around her seemed to expect her to slow down.

She wasn't ready for that yet. She would slow down when she was good and ready.

"Have you ever taught her to change her own tire?" asked Laura.

Garett blushed. "No. I haven't." He put down his breadstick. "Don't get me wrong, I know she needs to know that, but it's nice that she still needs me every now and again, you know?"

"I get it." She'd been a Daddy's girl right up until he'd passed from lung cancer. Garett's daughter would probably always find an excuse to ask her dad for help.

"So what's new in the news world?" he asked, clearly trying to change the subject.

"There's been another arson," said Laura. She'd been assigned the story as soon as she'd walked in that morning. As terrible as it sounded, it was starting to get boring to write about it. But she was the one who was the most knowledgeable about the situation, so she got the stories.

"Wow! When are they gonna catch this guy? He's begging to be caught."

"Well, last night they found some evidence for the first time, so that's exciting for them," said Laura.

"What kind?" asked Garett.

She shrugged. "Beats me. I'm not privy to that information, but I'm willing to bet there will be an arrest soon."

"Wouldn't that be something," he said. "That guy'll get put away for years. They'll make documentaries out of him."

"Probably."

She was starving by the time the waitress came to take their order. And she realized she was having a nice enough time with Garett that she would extend her lunch by those fifteen minutes. What was Greg going to do? Fire her?

***

2019:

The office of Inspector Miller was just as full of Miller as Miller was of himself. The walls were covered in different course certificates and honours. Whenever Hutchinson was in there, he made a point of not noticing them.

But that meant noticing the desk, which was filled with knick-knacks that Miller had acquired over his career.

"I want an arrest as soon as we get an ID on those fingerprints."

"I don't think it's our guy," said Hutchinson. "There's never been a jerry can left behind at any of the other cases. Why start now?"

"Maybe he dropped it. Maybe he's tired and wants to get caught. Maybe he always does this drunk and this time he forgot the jerry can. I don't really care. We have evidence that links this guy to the fires, so we're going to arrest him. End of story."

Hutchinson felt bad for the poor schmuck who had the sorry luck of dropping a jerry can in the wrong dumpster on the wrong day. He was going to get nailed with this case and if he was proven guilty, which Hutchinson doubted he was, he'd be in prison for the next twenty years.

"And I want those cigarette butts analyzed, too," said Miller. "I know they'll take longer, but send 'em off and have the techs check the DNA. We might just get lucky."

"Lucky? Is that how police work is supposed to go?" Hutchinson asked.

"You and I both know that luck plays a role in solving any case. And for this one, we need every drop we can get."

Hutchinson left the meeting feeling sick to his stomach. Arresting the person who'd dumped the jerry can was the wrong move. This whole crime scene felt staged.

Miller just wanted to appease the public. As much as Hutchinson disagreed with the move, he understood the necessity of appeasement. Heads were going to start rolling soon if it didn't look like they were moving forward.

Besides, Hutchinson had been wrong in the past. Maybe Miller was right, maybe they'd finally got the evidence they needed to catch this son of a bitch.

Rather than dwell on that, he decided he would read over the transcripts from Ed again. Ed had provided a statement for the police and then when he was well enough, he had come in to do a more detailed interview, with the hope of giving more insight.

While Hutchinson himself did not interview Ed, he was definitely privy to the conversation.

He had a large binder on his desk full of the evidence they had so far managed to put together on the case. It looked silly with the small stack of paper inside, but the hope was to fill it one day.

He flipped over to the section with the interviews of witnesses and found the one he was looking for easily.

> *Detective Badiuk: Can you please state your name for the record?*
>
> *Ed Keller: I'm Ed Keller, a security guard with the Game Room.*
>
> *Detective Badiuk: Thank you. We have your statement here from the other night, can you please reiterate in your own words what happened?*
>
> *Ed Keller: We'd been told that we had to up our surveillance due to the many issues that nightclubs were facing. As part of that protocol, we made sure to do a walk-around every fifteen minutes.*
>
> *Cyrus had done the last walk-around, so it was my turn. We both had our radios out and kept in constant contact. I had let him know that things were good until I rounded*

the North East corner, when I spotted a pickup truck backed up to the building.

Someone was descending a ladder from the roof. I hollered at the person to stop and then pulled my radio out. I managed to say something and then the person came at me. [Pause] I don't recall what happened afterward. My understanding is that I was attacked and I fell back and hit my head.

Detective Badiuk: *Do you think you can describe the assailant?*

Ed Keller: *He was small, shorter than I am, and not very big. It had to have been a young man. He was wearing dark clothing, I think a hoodie, and a tool belt.*

Detective Badiuk: *Are you certain he was working alone?*

Ed Keller: *No, I can't be certain. There may have been someone in the truck, but like I said, my memory about the time is a bit foggy.*

Detective Badiuk: *But you're certain that you remember the assailant?*

Ed Keller: *Yes. He was short and thin, he was a small man, potentially quite young.*

Detective Badiuk: *And later you gave a description to one of our sketch artists, correct?*

Ed Keller: *I did. Again, I can't be certain of the exact details. Everything happened so fast and I hit my head, but I'm certain that it was a small man.*

Detective Badiuk: *Is there anything else you can remember that you would like to share with us?*

Ed Keller: No. I've tried to recall other things, but I can't seem to do it.

Detective Badiuk: Okay, thank you for taking the time to talk to us, Ed. I know it wasn't easy for you to revisit that night.

From his conversation with the arresting officer, Hutchinson knew Lyle Walker didn't fit this description even remotely. Walker was a big guy, tall and round. He likely had to shop at Big and Tall just to find clothes that would fit him.

The only other thing that Hutchinson could think was that Walker was only an accomplice, and he wasn't the brains of the operation, either.

***

2002, twenty years old:

Jess stood in front of the card section of the drug store, looking at the wide variety of flashy cards displayed before her. This was not her thing and she resented her mother for forcing her to get Nathan a card. Who cared if he was eighteen? It wasn't that big of a deal.

Finally, she decided to choose a card at random. She closed her eyes and reached out to grab one. Once she had it she didn't even glance to look at it, she just grabbed the envelope and made her way to the counter.

"Is this everything?" asked the cashier.

"I'll get a scratch ticket, too. Just a five-dollar one is fine. Doesn't matter which."

When she was back out in her truck, she took a deep breath and looked at her phone. She'd missed a call while inside. It looked like it was Nathan.

Frowning, she punched in his number and gave him a call. He rarely reached out to her and she was fine with it. If he was calling her, he most likely needed her to pick something up on the way to his party. A lecture from her mom wasn't what she had in mind today.

"Hey," said Nathan. "I want to run something by you before you come tonight."

"What is it?" She couldn't imagine a single thing her brother would want to run by her. They were barely on speaking terms at the moment and she wasn't eager to encourage a relationship.

"I wanted to talk to you separately because I don't think it will make Mom happy."

"What?" Jess said, irritated that he wouldn't just get to it.

"Now that I'm eighteen, I'm thinking about finding dad."

Jess nearly dropped her phone. There was a sudden ringing in her ears and she felt her heart begin to race. "Why would you do that?" she asked. The words came out as a whisper.

"Don't you want to confront him? Ask him why he did it?"

"We already know why he did it, Nathan. He started a new family, away from us." *Away from me.*

"You aren't even a bit curious? We might have a brother or sister that we don't know about."

Jess had thought of that possibility her whole life, but in her experience up until that point, siblings weren't everything they were made to be. Nathan had been nothing but a thorn in Jess's side her entire life and the idea of having another one of him in it was ridiculous to her.

Besides, she'd vowed to herself that she wouldn't reach out to her dad anymore. He'd disappointed her too many times, promising to show up and then never being there. She needed him years ago, when she was little and couldn't take care of herself.

I'm an adult now and I don't need to rely on anyone, least of all him.

"I don't want to meet anyone from his family. I also don't care if I never see him again," Jess said.

"So if I found him, you wouldn't want to come with me?"

"No. You're on your own with this one. I'm not interested." He was silent for a moment. Jess wasn't sure what he expected her to say. "Are you seriously going to be stupid enough to bring this up to Mom?"

"Well, I think she has a right to know," Nathan told her.

"She'll disown you, just like she disowned Uncle Daryl. Can you handle that?" He was silent again, then Jess heard a sigh.

"I don't know why I even bothered calling you, Jess. You never think of anyone except yourself. You've decided your life is shit and you're not willing to do anything to make it better."

"Well, fuck you, too," she retorted.

"Whatever." Then the line went dead.

She sat in her truck for a moment, contemplating what he had said. There was no way she was interested in meeting her dad again. *Why does Nathan need my permission for it? I couldn't care less what he does in his spare time.*

When Jess finally left the parking lot, she was on the phone with her mom, telling her that she wouldn't be able to make it to the party tonight. Jess knew her mother would give her shit, but she didn't want to be present for the big dramatic scene when Nathan told their mom what he was doing.

Besides, she didn't really want to go, anyway.

7

Nathan picked his way through the shit-strewn yard to the back of his sister's trailer. He didn't understand how her neighbours hadn't complained about the smell. Jess needed to either shovel shit or get rid of the damn dog.

He couldn't believe she'd been selfish enough to avoid their mom's calls for the past month or so. If he had Jess's phone number, he would have called her himself, but he didn't want her to have his.

So instead he'd gotten the address from their mother and decided to drive down to her place and check to see if there was a dead person inside. He thought his mom had been ridiculous when she suggested it, but now that he was here, he realized no one would be able to smell a rotting body over the smell of dog shit.

He couldn't find the spare key. That was fine, though, Thrasher, her Doberman, had been growling fiercely when he tried to look through the kitchen window. He wasn't interested in dealing with that.

He leaned his face up against the back patio door, trying to peer inside. Gauzy curtains made it hard to see anything.

Thrasher leapt at the window and Nathan jumped back. *The dog is a fucking psycho. How does she live with this thing?*

Well, that's enough reconnaissance for today. He couldn't see a body and if his mom wanted to know more, she could come down here herself.

"Nathan?"

He jumped again. "Jesus, Jess! Warn a guy."

"You're standing in my backyard, peeping through my window. Why should I warn you?" she asked.

"Yeah, well I wouldn't be here if you'd answer your damn phone sometimes." She looked rundown, he thought. Her mousy brown hair hung lank and stringy around her face and there were puffy bags under her eyes.

"I don't want to talk to her," Jess said with a shrug.

"Well, she's going to come down here and check on you herself if you don't start talking to her."

"Hopefully, I won't be home," said Jess. "I'm going to let Thrasher out. Can you go to the front? He doesn't like strangers."

"Are you gonna grab a shovel, too? Because this is disgusting."

Jess looked out over the yard and shrugged her shoulders. "I'm not kidding about him. I would get moving if I were you."

Nathan tried to casually make his way through the gate and out to the front, but as Jess put her hand on the handle, he picked up the pace and dashed out.

The dog came barreling out and straight to the fence where Nathan stood. It snarled and barked, snapping its teeth. *Is it rabid?*

"Thrasher," Jess said in a soft voice, "it's okay. I'm safe." The dog stopped barking and restrained itself to growling.

She let herself out the gate and stood there with her hands on her hips. "So, I'm alive. Is there anything else?"

"Why are you home in the middle of the day? Did you get fired again?" he asked.

"That's none of your business."

"Of course it is," he said, throwing his hands in the air. "Only, who do you think Mom goes to when she needs help with money? It's me, every damn time. Why can't you get a real job or something?"

"Mom's never been able to manage her money. Don't know why that's a surprise to you."

"That's not the point, Jess. You're living in a dump. I mean, I know your standards are low, but this?" He shook his head. *What's the point? She's never cared to try to be less than an annoying burden.* "Just forget it. Call Mom."

He hopped in his car and left the trashy place, thinking that he'd gotten lucky that she was the one who got their low-life dad's genes. He wasn't okay letting their mom starve and he didn't like to make her worry. *Jess doesn't care about anyone except herself. And maybe that damn dog.*

***

1998, sixteen years old:

She couldn't do it anymore. With each passing year, she thought things might get better, that she would make a friend. Just one. She wasn't asking for miracles.

Now she was sixteen years old and looking at another year of hell. Being tormented daily at school and reminded that she wasn't good enough when she got home after school.

Her grades weren't bad, they weren't honours, but she was smart enough to make it through most of the classes just fine. She loved the idea of being an honours student, but she knew she wasn't smart enough for that.

So what's the point, then?

Any university program she'd ever considered required honours in all of the top-tier classes. That was never going to happen.

Even more laughable was the thought of how she was going to pay for it all. Her mom wasn't going to help out and her dad hadn't even tried to talk to her since he left. She couldn't count on him.

She'd ditched the day and gone to Whyte Avenue instead. It had been wonderful. The last time she'd enjoyed herself that much had been when her dad had taken her to Uncle Daryl's cabin.

When she got home, though, her mother was furious.

"Do you know what it's like to get a call at work that your child couldn't be bothered to show up for school?" She stood in the addition, blocking the entryway for Jess. "I have half a mind to send you on your way!"

"I'm not going back," said Jess. She didn't know where this bravery had come from, but she knew it was the truth. She was sixteen and she was done with school.

"Jessica Leanne, you will finish school. You're not going to be like your good-for-nothing dad."

Nathan poked his head out of the door long enough to grin at Jess and then he disappeared again.

"You can't make me," said Jess.

"Pardon me?"

"You. Can't. Make. Me," Jess repeated. "I'm sixteen and it's my choice."

Her mother narrowed her eyes at her. "Is that so?" she said quietly. That scared Jess more than the shouting did.

"Y-yeah. I'm done with being treated like shit at school."

"Maybe if you took care of yourself and made yourself less of a target, school would be easier for you. I've talked to the principal, you practically bring it on yourself, Jess. Stop acting like the weirdo and you'll have no problems."

"You're supposed to have my back!" screamed Jess.

"It's kind of hard to do that when you're skipping school and punching kids, isn't it." Her mom backed up, leaving space for Jess to pass. "You know what, forget it. If you wanna quit, then do it. It's not like you were going places anyway."

Jess shoved past her and went to her room. Some of Nathan's stuff was still in the closet, but the room was technically hers now that he'd moved into the master bedroom. Her mom had decided that Nathan needed privacy now that he was going through puberty. For the moment, the living room was her mother's room.

She slammed the door and threw her backpack across the room. Her mother's words kept repeating in her head. *"It's not like you were going places."*

That was the simple truth of it. Jess knew she wasn't destined for anything more than a life spent struggling to survive. She couldn't even count on winning a rich husband, not with her looks.

She turned on her music, cranking the stereo and ignoring her mother's shouts to turn it down. Part of her wanted her mom to burst into the room and give her more shit.

Instead, the worst consequence was a couple of bangs on the door and unintelligible yelling. Then it went away.

She sniffled and realized suddenly that she was crying. Angrily, she swiped at her eyes, trying to wipe away the tears.

How could her own mother not have her back about this? *The bitch blames me for all of the bullying I've had to endure over my life.*

She caught her reflection in the dresser mirror. Her face was puffy and red. *I have to be an ugly crier, too.*

Before she realized what she was doing, she was across the room and punching the mirror. The splintering sound it made was satisfying and the physical pain on her knuckles distracted her from the pain she felt inside.

She studied the knuckles on the back of her hand. A small piece of glass was stuck between two of them and blood poured down over her wrist. With a wince, she pulled the chunk of glass out of her hand and looked at it.

Almost as though she was in a trance, she pressed the shard to her arm until blood sprang from a wound. Then she pulled it down to make a neat line of red on her forearm. She brought the glass up to her wrist again and made a second line.

Now the blood was running to her elbow and dripping onto the floor. The way it ran in rivulets down her arm was fascinating. For the first time in recent memory, she wasn't feeling any pain inside. Only the pain in her wrist.

The door burst open like her mother had used a battering ram. "What did I-" Then her mother screamed and yelled for Nathan to call 911.

She rushed over to Jess, "Oh my baby, what have you done? Why would you do this to me?"

***

Jess didn't remember the trip to the hospital. She'd been awake but felt like she was floating. She'd never experienced astral projection, but she wondered if that was what it felt like.

When she was finally able to focus again, she was in the hospital. Her arm was bandaged up with gauze. It hurt like a son of a bitch when she lifted it.

"Hey, honey," said her mom. "Don't move that hand, okay? It needs to heal. Just let it rest."

"Mommy," she whispered. "I'm sorry."

"I know, baby. I know."

"Where's Dad?" Jess asked weakly. "Did you call him?"

Her mom froze in her seat. "Is that why you did this? So your dad would come see you?" Her expression was soft, like Jess remembered from when she was little. "Honey, he doesn't want to see you. He was annoyed that I called him. I'm so, so sorry."

It was almost like Jess could feel her heart grow smaller inside her chest. He didn't love her, never had. But maybe her mom did.

"He's just a cheating asshole, anyway, right?" Jess said.

Her mom smiled and squeezed her hand. "Yeah, he's a good-for-nothing cheater."

***

2019:

I hated that I couldn't get Nathan's lecture out of my head. I didn't owe my mother a damn thing. She'd screwed me up good and well.

But maybe I could have been something. Maybe if I'd just pushed through those final years in high school I would be able to live a more comfortable life. Possibly even a happy life.

Nathan had got that with his wife. I was surprised he didn't rub that in my face, too.

I pet Thrasher absently as I watched the news. I liked the paper articles better. They seemed more permanent than what played on the T.V. I had a scrapbook of all of the articles and pictures of my work.

That was how I thought of it. It was my work, my portfolio. It was something that I was actually passionate about.

Now that I'd set Lyle up for the fall, it would be wise to just lay low and let it blow over. A repeat would only confirm what he was no doubt telling them. He'd been framed.

I wondered if he remembered me from that night. Did he connect the dots with me? I doubted it. The guy wasn't exactly the brightest bulb in the showroom. He wouldn't remember grabbing the handle of the jerry can as he moved all the boxes around.

I wish I could've been there to see him arrested.

Being a police officer could be fun. People would treat you with respect, at least. And it would feel pretty badass to be able to boss others around. Bust up some people who were being assholes to those around them.

"Sorry, Your Honour," I said out loud. "He resisted arrest." Thrasher cocked his head and looked at me. I rubbed his head and gave him a kiss on the snout.

I'd rescued Thrasher from a kill shelter a couple of years ago. I had thought I would get a cat because they were less needy than dogs, but it was love at first sight. Especially when they told me that he was going to be euthanized because he was too aggressive.

It was clear he'd been beaten and traumatized. He had a scar down the back of his head where the fur grew in white and one of his ears was missing the tip.

There were other lumps and bumps on him, too. Scar tissue, I suspected.

Even the volunteers at the shelter wanted nothing to do with him. When I'd approached though, he'd only whimpered and licked my hand. No cat was going to be good enough after that display.

I'd had to sign some liability forms and everything before I left. The discount I got on him was insulting to him as far as I was concerned. Were animals truly worth less if those around them treated them badly?

But then I looked at myself. Those around me would argue that my life was worthless despite my scars and my willingness to survive.

Still, here I was at thirty-eight, a spinster who lived with a dog. I had no friends, a minimum-wage job and a rented trailer. Was this the best I could expect?

Lyle's picture on the news distracted me from my thoughts.

"...the man authorities have brought in for questioning in relation to the Rooftop Arsonist. The blazes causing fear in the city have been happening since March, earlier this year. There has been a total of eight million dollars in damage caused by the fires. EPS and Fire Services estimate their cost has been an additional two million."

That was it. They weren't going to say anything else? Annoyed, I turned it off.

It was anti-climatic after all of the effort I had to put into getting Lyle to fall. It was disappointing.

And then suddenly it dawned on me that with Lyle in custody, the world would happily move on. No more would they look at my work with awe.

My time in the spotlight was over.

Suddenly the itch was back. The one that told me this couldn't be it. That there was more for me out there if I only looked for it. I hated that feeling because it always led to more disappointment for me.

Still, it couldn't be ignored and I decided I would go for a drive to distract myself.

I grabbed Thrasher a half-pound of raw ground beef from the fridge. He drooled as he watched me dump it into his bowl.

"Good boy," I said as I set the bowl down. He waited for me to step back before he dove in. I had trained him well.

"I'm going out for a bit, bud," I said.

It wasn't late as I headed out for a cruise. At least there wasn't much traffic. I hated driving in rush hour.

I had no particular destination in mind, I just drove wherever my whim took me. I ended up down on Whyte Ave. Big surprise. There was something about this street that helped to calm the itch. Maybe it was sheeple-watching and realizing that I wasn't one of them. I was unique.

Instead of feeling better, though, I watched couple after couple walk down the street hand in hand. They were always laughing or had smiles on their face. Sometimes they kissed.

Kissing Lyle hadn't been a picnic, that was for sure. He wasn't my type at all. Yet… I still felt comforted when he had tucked me under his arm outside the bar. Like he was going to take care of me and I didn't have to look out for myself anymore.

Looking back, I realized that if someone had tried to do anything to me, Lyle would have stood up to them and defended me. Maybe even got into a fistfight over me.

So much for the distraction from the itch. I parked my truck in the Timmie's parking lot and decided to wander for a bit. Maybe I could go into another bar and find someone else?

I looked at the pretty people passing me by and decided I was wrong. I didn't know what had overcome me that night at Whirls and Spurs, but that girl was not coming out tonight.

Eventually, my feet took me to the University at the end of Whyte. There were fewer couples here, the students didn't even notice me as I walked into the dorm. Belatedly, I realized that this dorm was for the nursing students, so there probably wouldn't be many guys here.

I still wanted to people-watch, though. I could have been a nurse if I would have applied myself. If I wouldn't have dropped out of school. I could still be a nurse if I wanted to.

There was a stand of pamphlets in the foyer. I grabbed a couple and then sat down on one of the couches. I pretended to be reading them in depth as I watched everyone come and go.

One young couple walked in and over to the bulletin board where all of the announcements were posted. The girl, a voluptuous blonde, gave her boyfriend a kiss and then he left. She pulled a yellow piece of paper out of her bag and tacked it onto the board.

I watched as she left, greeting some friends on the way. Then I stood and walked over to the poster to see what it said.

Big bold letters were centred on the page: NURSING PARTY, SHOOTING STAR NITE CLUB, STUDENTS $5 GUESTS $10.

I looked both ways to see if anyone was looking at me, then I tore the poster down. Maybe I could get that girl from Whirls and Spurs to make an appearance at this party.

8

Hutchinson walked to the front desk of the precinct, trying to tell himself that someone was there to thank him for doing an outstanding job of catching the arsonist. It would be a small miracle if that happened, but he still hoped for it.

Instead, he found the security guy that had been attacked waiting for him. He couldn't remember his name and hoped he wouldn't need to use it.

"Hey, bud, how're you feeling?" Hutchinson asked.

The man didn't have a sling anymore, but Hutchinson could see that the pain wasn't completely gone. The blow from the hatchet that had cut him had nearly severed his tendon. It would be years of physical therapy before he got the full use of his arm back. If he ever had full use of it again.

"Sergeant," he said. He had a deeper voice than his small frame would suggest. "I've been better."

"Yeah," said Hutchinson. "Doc give you a return to work date yet?"

He ushered the man in behind the desk. Denise was a busy girl and didn't need two men gossiping over her.

"Milly and I've decided I'm not going back," the man said, shaking his head. "It was too close a call, that's for certain. Do you mind if I have a word with you?"

They headed back to Hutchinson's office, stopping by the lunchroom for a coffee. The man – *his name is Ed!* – declined politely.

"So what can I help you with?" asked Hutchinson once they were settled in his office with the door closed and the blinds drawn.

"I saw the picture of the guy you guys brought in on the news the other night," said Ed.

Hutchinson only nodded and took a sip of his coffee. It was stale and no amount of cream and sugar could change that, but it would keep him awake.

"I don't have too much of a recollection of what happened that night. I hit my head when I fell down, but I don't recall my assailant being that big."

Of course this was the reason for the visit. Someone here to confirm his hunch, and yet, he couldn't let on that he was aware. "Oh?" he said.

"Yeah, I mean it was hard to see and everything happened so fast-"

"And you hit your head," Hutchinson added.

"And I hit my head. But, the guy wasn't taller than me. He definitely wasn't fat."

Hutchinson set his cup down and steepled his fingers in front of him. "Ed, first of all, I would like to thank you for coming down here to speak to me about this. It says a lot about your character."

"But…"

"But, we have strong evidence to suggest that this man is responsible for those fires. I'm sure you're aware that we can't share all of the details of the investigation with the public."

Ed waved his good hand at Hutchinson, "I know how it goes, but I'm telling you-"

"This is the man who did it, Ed." He hated saying that out loud, but to admit they'd possibly made a mistake would be career-ending for him. "We have proof. We don't just go picking people up willy-nilly."

"Well, didn't you guys get the sketch of the perp?" Ed asked.

Hutchinson fought back the urge to sigh. He wanted Ed gone, but at the same time, he felt like he owed him something.

"I didn't see it personally, but I know we received it. Listen, the problem is that we have physical evidence that puts this man at the crime scene. Unfortunately, we have to go with that. It would be too easy for the defence attorney to point out that you'd hit your head and it was dark."

"So you guys don't believe me."

This was not going the way he had hoped it would go. He had better things to do than reassure some old man that they did take his statement seriously.

"That's not what I said."

"Wow, it's good to see where my taxes are going." Ed stood and opened the door. "You're putting an innocent man in jail for a long time."

Then he left and Hutchinson just sat there, sipping his coffee. He knew in his gut that Ed was right, but there was nothing he could do about it.

Six more years until retirement. He could do this.

***

2019:

I didn't own any makeup and I didn't have any fancy clothes. I couldn't afford brand names, anyway. I shopped at Wal-Mart or Goodwill. So, I wasn't entirely sure what I was going to wear to this party.

Sure, I'd had a couple of days to hit the store, but I hated shopping. Nothing ever fit properly and I hated looking at my body in the mirror. Worse yet were the bubbly sales ladies, or guys, that would come around telling you how everything looked so cute on you even though you knew it didn't.

I flip-flopped about whether I was even going to go in the first place. If Thrasher could talk, he would tell me he was tired of me talking about it.

In the end, I decided the best thing I could do was just be myself. That was how I'd gotten to Lyle. Besides the cowboy getup, anyway. No makeup, nothing fancy with my hair. Just plain ol' me.

Maybe my personality would shine through, whatever that meant.

I was both excited and nervous about this. I knew that I was going to be older than most of the people there, but so what? People started university or college at different ages all the time.

Rather than take my truck, I took the bus to the club. I knew I might need a few drinks to loosen up. Also, what if I ended up going home with someone? I didn't want to worry about my truck.

It was weird heading into a nightclub without any plans to burn it to the ground. And ironic, if I was thinking correctly. This place was where happy people went to celebrate. I hated happy people.

Maybe if I was happy, though, I wouldn't hate happy people. It bothered me to admit it, but it was most likely that I was just jealous of all of the popular kids.

But kids were different these days. When I grew up, they were brutal. Now there was all this talk about stopping bullying and treating each other kindly. So it was likely that this generation would treat me better than my own did.

As soon as I handed my cover over to the doorman, I felt self-conscious. I was at least ten years older than he was and he looked much older than the dancers in the club.

Grow a set, I told myself. I didn't ask myself what the worst that could happen would be. I'd experienced enough bad to know that it could get worse, and usually, it wasn't something you ever imagined it would be.

I was also underdressed in my black tank top and jeans. I'd never seen so many shiny girls before. These ladies had on shirts that shimmered and sparkled. Their makeup also glowed under the lights.

I could not have been more out of place if I'd tried. Still, I was going to see this through.

I sat at a table off to the side. The server, with cat-eye makeup nearly to her eyebrows, took my order of a Canadian and then I sat back to watch.

Before long, I felt myself shaking. The adrenaline was coursing through me. Lyle had been a piece of cake. This was completely different.

There were no desperate men here. Only confident young men with their whole futures ahead of them. They didn't yet know what it was like to hit rock bottom. They were just learning to fly on their own.

The beer went down easily and I was ordering a second before long. Already I was feeling a bit of a buzz.

I'd never understood popular music, even when I was young. I always listened to the angriest music I could get my hands on. This hip-hoppy music was irritating and I was annoyed to catch myself bobbing my head.

Then I remembered that was why I was here, to expand my horizons and step outside of my comfort zone. It was time to try something new.

When my second beer came, I pounded it back and then picked a random table to approach. All of the guys here were cute, so it didn't really matter who I talked to.

My destination was a round table at the corner of the dance floor. There were three guys sitting there, all wearing tight shirts and necklaces. I decided to talk to the blond.

I sat down at the table and all three of them went silent.

"Hey," I said to the guy. "Would you like to dance?"

"Uh, no thank you," he replied. His friends were grinning like idiots, but I did my best to ignore them. "I don't dance. Sorry."

Okay, one down, like thirty to go. It was his loss. I fought down my embarrassment when I heard them all break out into laughter when I left. I didn't want to hear what they said about me. Confidence was key here.

The next table I hit had a couple of girls at it and the guy, an Asian man this time, was quick to grab the hand of the nearest one. "I would love to, but I'm sort of involved with someone," he said.

After that, some guy assured me he was gay. When I said he would probably know how to dance then, he told me that he couldn't.

Every excuse under the sun was muttered to me. Some didn't say anything, only stared at me. Others burst into laughter as soon as I asked.

With each rejection, I felt myself grow colder and less confident. I was getting more angry as the night went on. There was a reason I'd burned all of the other clubs. I fantasized about burning this one with everyone in it.

By the time my fourth beer joined me, I was in quite the mood. It was time to leave. I chugged the beer, too cheap to leave it behind then started to make my way out.

That was when I saw her.

It was the same blonde girl from the foyer the other night, only this time, she wasn't there with her boyfriend. She was dancing by herself on the floor in a bright red halter top with short shorts on. Her legs seemed to go on forever.

I was so busy watching her that I didn't notice I was holding up traffic as I stood there. I moved out of the way and stood against the wall.

When the song ended, she headed off toward the bathroom. I followed her in.

The music seemed muted in the bathroom, which I was thankful for. I could barely hear myself think out there.

I waited until I heard her flush the toilet, then I went to one of the sinks and pretended to wash my hands. She came out with a sigh, tugging her shorts down. When she stepped up to the sink, I adjusted my clothing. Finally, I forced myself to speak.

"I saw you dancing out there. You're really good," I said.

"Oh? Thank you," she responded with a genuine smile.

"I'm Cathy." I didn't know why I'd chosen Cathy, it just slipped out when I was with Lyle the other night, and for some reason, I didn't want her to know my real name either.

"Brandy," she said.

"Would you like to dance?" I asked.

She hesitated before she spoke, so I knew what the answer was going to be before she said it. "Sorry, Cathy, I'm all danced out. And I really should go see my friends. Thanks, though."

I couldn't stop staring as she walked away. It was unnerving.

Now that I knew Brandy was here, I wasn't as eager to leave. I decided to head back to my table and watch her for a bit. I ordered another beer so I didn't look suspicious, but I didn't have more than a sip.

On impulse, I waved the server over. "I would like to buy that table a round of drinks," I said.

"Okay," she replied with a bright smile. "Anything in particular?"

"Whatever they're having works."

I watched as the server went to the bar and ordered the drinks. I hoped they weren't expensive, but I was feeling oddly giving right now.

I pushed my beer away from me.

When the server dropped the drinks off at the table, she pointed at me. I was sure they couldn't see me in the dim light. They would have no idea who'd bought them the drinks.

To my delight, Brandy made her way to my table.

"Hey, Cathy, thanks for the drinks. You didn't have to do that."

"You're welcome," I said with a shrug.

She sat down and I was thrown for a moment. Nobody ever willingly sat with me unless they were about to make fun of me.

"Do you come here often? I don't think I've seen you before."

"No," I said, my brain zooming around for an excuse. "I was supposed to meet my boyfriend here, but he couldn't make it."

"That's too bad. You guys should try again next Friday. The nursing program always gets discounts on Fridays."

"Oh, I'm not in the program.".

"Sorry, I just assumed," she said. "I am. It's my second year. I'm going to be an RN."

"You'll be great," I told her. "You've got the personality to pull it off."

"Thank you." She blushed.

"So how is it you can dance all night and not break a sweat?"

She laughed and touched her hand to her face for a second. "I exercise a lot. I especially like to run."

That was interesting to me. I'd never met someone who actually enjoyed running. My itch hit me then. Hard. It nearly took my breath away.

"I run, too," I blurted. That was the biggest line of bullshit I'd fed anybody all night. I didn't know how I kept a straight face doing it. "I'm looking for a new route, though. I'm getting bored."

"You should try the Marigold Path in the River Valley. It's a nice mixture of grass and concrete. It's better for your knees."

"Huh, I didn't realize that. I've been running on sidewalks this whole time. I'll have to give it a shot."

"Awesome!" she looked over her shoulder at her friends. "Well, I better head back. Thanks again for the drink."

"No problem. I hope you have a great night."

"You, too, Cathy. It was nice meeting you."

I watched her walk away and felt my itch get worse. I had enjoyed talking to her. It wasn't awkward and it wasn't forced, it had been genuinely...nice.

Coming here had been a mistake. I wasn't leaving this place feeling better. I was leaving here realizing what I had been missing all this time.

9

Laura checked her make-up one more time before she left the bathroom. She was working late again, but this time it was about a man donating money to a family who'd had their house burn down. All of the negative news had been wearing on her lately. Sometimes it was too much.

Tonight it was especially important that she get out of here on time. Garett was picking her up and taking her to dinner. She would get to meet his daughter tonight. The only thing throwing her off about the evening was the butterflies in her stomach.

Garett was starting to mean a lot to her and she wanted this dinner to go well. It wouldn't be easy for this girl to watch her dad be with another woman. And Laura had no experience with kids herself.

When she was satisfied with her look, she headed down to the front door of the office. Garett had said he would just pick her up and they would be on their way.

Garett was waiting for her at the curb. She picked up her pace, as much as she could in her heels, and got into the car.

"Hi, you're early," she said.

"No, right on time," he said curtly.

She looked down at her watch. He had said he'd be there at six to pick her up and it was quarter to right now.

He was dressed nicely and he smelled nice. He'd had his hair cut and he'd shaved off the ridiculous beard. But his eyes weren't as warm as they usually were, and his posture was stiff. His hands were wrapped so tightly around the steering wheel that his knuckles were turning white.

"Everything okay?" she asked.

He didn't answer at first. "Well, I'm a little frustrated that we're late. Brandy's there by herself right now."

"What do you mean? You said six."

"No," he said. "I said dinner was at six, but the show starts earlier."

She'd forgotten that it was a dinner and a show. So much for the good first impression. "Why didn't you call me when you got here?"

"Why would I bother you when you're working?"

"I wasn't. I was sitting there chatting for the last half an hour."

"So this is my fault?" he asked.

She closed her eyes and willed herself to breathe deeply. This was supposed to be a good night. It shouldn't start off with an argument.

"That's not what I meant," she said. "Look, I'm sorry. I didn't mean to make us late." She put her hand on his knee, but instead of grabbing it like he normally did, he kept his hands on the wheel.

Dinner was a quiet affair, even though there was a live play happening around them. They made introductions and small talk at first, but Laura soon ran out of things to say. Garett did little to help the conversation along.

From the brief amount of time they had together, Laura thought she and Brandy would get along. Brandy was nice, polite and respectful. She was also good at small talk.

Around dessert, Laura decided she would give up on Garett and focus only on Brandy. Clearly, he couldn't get past their earlier argument and they were going to have to talk about it later.

"So why nursing?" Laura asked.

"It was because of the experience I had with nurses when Mom was in the hospital," Brandy said.

"Honey," interrupted Garett. "Not tonight. You don't have to talk about it tonight."

Laura looked over at him as he spoke, but he wouldn't look her in the eye. *What is going on?*

"It's fine, Dad." Brandy had a concerned frown on her face, but she went back to explaining. "There was one nurse there who was really kind to me. She took me on walks, brought me snacks and listened to me. Dad was so distraught, I didn't want to bother him. I mean, it happened so suddenly, he barely had time to register what was going on."

"It was a hard time for both of us," he said. He still wouldn't look at Laura. "I'm grateful they were so kind to you."

"Yes," said Laura. "It's times like that when it's most important to be surrounded by kindness. It must have been terrible for you both."

"It was," he replied.

After that, the conversation stalled and they ate their crumble in silence.

By the end of the evening, Laura was exhausted. She'd attempted to make conversation again, but Garett had been downright rude. Now she had to sit with him in the car to go get her vehicle.

"What was that all about?" she demanded when they got in the car.

"What do you mean?"

"You were unbelievably rude to me. And not overly nice to Brandy either. Was it because I was late?"

"How do you think I felt, listening to my daughter tell my girlfriend about my wife?"

He couldn't have shocked her more if he slapped her. His wife? She had been gone for five years. Laura felt tears forming in her eyes and looked up at the roof of the car, willing them to go away.

"Would you rather we didn't talk about it? Pretend it didn't happen?" she asked. She needed a tissue. *Damnit!* Her mascara would run.

"Forget it," he said. Then he reached over to the radio and turned it on.

She stared out her window for the remainder of the trip. He was not allowed to see how much he was hurting her right now. This was why she didn't like to date. It was hard being so vulnerable.

When he stopped the car at the office, she didn't say a word to him. She unbuckled and got out of the seat, closing his door as gently as possible.

She wanted to slam it so hard the glass broke. But she wasn't going to let him bring that out in her.

***

1995, thirteen years old:

Her birthday was coming up. She was going to be thirteen. Officially a teenager.

Her mom didn't have anything planned. Maybe a cake, if she remembered. Jess had no friends to invite over, so really, it was a pointless effort anyway.

The only thing she was looking forward to was spending the day with her dad. Her mom had called and made arrangements the month before.

"Every girl should spend that kind of special day with their dad," she said. "Grandpa bought me roses when I turned thirteen."

The sudden maternal attention from her mom had been unexpected. Since their dad had left a couple of years ago, she had been more than distant with Jess. As far as she could see, everything was the same with Nathan, but it was like she had disappointed her mom somehow.

Whenever she thought about it, she remembered Nathan's words, "It's all your fault."

Her parents had been fighting about her when they split. She didn't know what she had done, but she didn't doubt that she had screwed up somehow. Like her mom said, everything she touched just fell apart.

Part of her was hoping that her mom would want to come with her. Maybe her parents would talk to each other and like each other again. Then one day, they could come to love each other.

She always had to remind herself that her dad had a new family now. He'd left his wife and his kids for a new life with a new wife and kids.

It was a forgivable trespass, she had decided. This wasn't a very happy home and maybe he just wanted to be happy. She couldn't help but think that if her mom could find someone to love, she would be happier, too. But her mom was uninterested in meeting anyone else. She said she was wrecked for any other man.

The entire day at school went basically without incident. Molly had called her a dyke, but names were nothing. If all they did was call her names, she would be fine with it.

Nothing could dampen her spirits. She hadn't seen her dad since the day he left and she couldn't wait to hug him.

After the last bell rang, she raced to her locker. She had shoved all her homework in her bag before most students had even left their classrooms.

She wove her way through the students, making her way to the front entrance. A wide face-splitting smile was stuck on her face and it got her a couple of odd looks, but she ignored them.

When she got outside, she scanned the parking lot for her dad. She didn't even know what he drove, but he would probably walk up to the doors to meet her.

While she waited, she sat on the red bench by the parking lot. A few people called out to her, but she barely noticed them. Any minute now, he would pull in and they would go for supper.

After the last of the buses left, she started to get a little worried. Maybe he didn't know when school was over. Everybody was late sometimes.

Twenty minutes later, the secretary for the school was approaching the bench. "Jess, did you miss the bus today?" she asked.

"My dad is picking me up," Jess said. She tried to inject enthusiasm into her words, but she was feeling hollow inside.

"Well, it's twenty after four. Why don't you come on inside and we'll give him a call?"

"I don't know his number," Jess mumbled.

Mrs. Abraham's lips dipped into a quick frown. Then she forced the smile back onto her round face. "That's fine. Your mom will know it. Come on," she said. She reached a hand out for Jess and gave her a pat on the shoulder when she reluctantly went with her.

"My mom's still at work."

"That's fine," said Mrs. Abraham. "She won't be mad. This is out of your control."

The secretary could not have been more incorrect. Her mother was furious at being called at work. Even more angry that she would have to leave early to come pick Jess up.

When she pulled up, she gave Mrs. Abraham a smile, pretending nothing was wrong. For a moment, Jess nearly clung to the secretary and asked her to take her home. Instead, she walked toward the car while tears made tracks on her cheeks.

"I can't believe the nerve!" said her mom when they got in the car. "I was at work! I can't just drop everything and leave, I'll lose my job!"

"I'm sorry, Mom. Why didn't Daddy come get me?"

"That's what I'm most angry about. I called him and he told me that he'd changed his mind. What kind of man does that to his child?"

Jess physically felt the sobs as they made their way up her throat. Her Dad didn't even want to spend time with her on her birthday. What had she done? What was wrong with her?

"Stop it, Jessica," snapped her mom. "I'm already irritated. I don't need to hear you boohooing on top of everything."

For the next fifteen minutes, Jess worked to rein in her grief. She vowed that she would never wait on her dad again. Never would she allow that man to have such a hold over her feelings again.

When they got home, her mother got out of the car and stormed into the house without a word.

There was no cake that night.

***

2019:

I couldn't get her out of my head. In my mind, I replayed our conversation over and over again. Brandy was easily the most beautiful girl I'd ever met. And the nicest.

And she'd been kind to me.

I don't understand the feeling that I have. There is a... lightness in my step. It's indescribable. I can't remember feeling this way before.

When I was burning the buildings, it was close. Even closer still when I destroyed that graduation ceremony.

This was different, though. I was humming as I worked.

Worse, I was distracted. My mind was sitting next to Brandy instead of focusing on my job. The guys had been much better since the last incident. They still didn't talk to me, but that was preferable to the way they'd been treating me before.

Mike had been good on his word and replaced my steel-toed boots for me. And the hoodie I had in there, too. It was an act of kindness that had been unexpected, even though he'd told me he would do that.

How did I repay him? By dancing down the aisles. I forgot items on my list and was constantly running back and forth in the warehouse. It was such a waste of time.

On the third day, Mike pulled me into his office.

"Hey, Jess, you seem different. What's going on in your world?"

There was no way I was telling him about Brandy, so I told him that nothing had changed. I could tell he didn't buy it, but it was none of his business.

"Okay, well, are the guys being better?" he asked.

"Yeah, it's been fine. We don't even talk, really, which is probably for the best."

"Is that what's put you in such a good mood?"

"I don't know… Maybe? Why do you ask?"

"It's just that it's affecting your work. You're my superstar and you're starting to worry me," he said.

I'd never been anyone's superstar before, so that was nice to hear. But mostly what I heard was that I was disappointing him. My weird joy was disappointing my boss.

"What do you mean?"

"Well, the last two days, Lance has pulled in more orders than you have. And they were larger ones." He leaned forward over his desk. "I'm not giving you a hard time, I'm just concerned. Times are tough right now. If we can't justify every employee then we have to replace them."

Was he threatening to fire me? I hadn't even noticed that Lance was running circles around me. That meant Dave and Evan were, too.

I had been wrong about nothing dampening my mood. This conversation was like a wet blanket over a fire.

"I'll be better," I said hastily. I didn't like the way I sounded, but I really didn't have a choice. I needed the job. "I'm sorry."

"No, it's all good," he said with a smile. "Like I said, I'm not giving you a hard time. I just thought I would bring it up now before it gets too bad."

I left his office in a foul mood. It must have been palpable because every time one of the guys had to grab a part near me, they did it as quickly as they could and left.

This was no good. The last time someone had such control over how I felt, I'd been crushed. I wasn't going to do that again.

Rather than moon over Brandy for the rest of my shift, I started making plans. When we were together, it would be me who was in control of the relationship.

10

Laura hadn't spoken to Garett since the night of the argument. He'd texted her and left her voicemails, but she'd ignored them all.

If Garett still considered Emily to be his current wife, then maybe there wasn't room in his life for Laura. Either way, she needed room to breathe. She'd never seen him act that way before and it was unsettling.

She busied herself at work, volunteering for as many assignments as she could. Her lunch break was spent at her desk and she always made sure to go straight home every night.

He knew where she lived; that was where they had spent the majority of their time. The hope was that he had enough decency to leave her alone at home.

Now that she looked back, it was odd that Garett always wanted to stay at her place. Was it because of his memories of Emily? Did he feel like he was cheating on his wife when he was with Laura?

She couldn't play second fiddle in this relationship. She'd done the whole married man thing and it didn't turn out well for her. The conversation they'd had after dinner had left her feeling like she was a homewrecker again and she didn't need that.

When Brandy showed up at her office one day, she didn't know what to think. Clearly, she was skipping school to be here.

"Brandy? Is everything okay?" For a moment, she had a feeling of dread.

"Yeah, I was just wondering if you wanted to go for lunch. I'll buy," Brandy said with a smile.

Laura wanted to say no. This was a bad idea. Garett hadn't yet forgiven her for speaking about his late wife with Brandy. She couldn't even imagine how he would react when he found out they were meeting behind his back.

There was something about Brandy's expression, though. She looked both concerned and hopeful and Laura found herself accepting the offer. She grabbed her coat and told the receptionist she would be on her cell and they left.

Laura had insisted on driving, not wanting a repeat of the evening with Brandy's father. This time she wanted to be able to leave the situation when she was upset. It had been awful to sit there listening to the radio in angry silence.

When they sat down, Laura wasn't sure what to say. Brandy wasn't being forthcoming and she dreaded the awkwardness of a silent lunch. Finally, she decided to be the bigger person.

"So, how's school go-"

"I'm sorry," blurted Brandy. She wrung her hands together on the table. "Dad isn't normally like that. Did he blow it with you?"

Laura had even less to say now, but what had she expected? She and Brandy had nothing but Garett in common. How could their conversation be about anything else?

"I recognized that he wasn't acting like himself," Laura said cautiously.

"You're the first one he's introduced me to. I don't know if there have been others, but I've been waiting for it."

Silence was preferable to this conversation. "Does that mean you're ready to see your dad with someone else?"

Brandy nodded and bit her lip. "I am. Really," she said. "It's just that I don't think he was ready to talk about Mom with you."

"Well, he's talked about her before."

"Then maybe he wasn't ready to see us getting along and talking about Mom. I don't know. I just know that he's been a mess since that night."

"I haven't been feeling great, myself," said Laura. Their salads arrived and she wondered how fast she could scarf it down without embarrassing herself.

"I just..." Brandy started. "You've been really good for him. He's come out of his shell again. It's really nice to see him finally moving forward with his life."

More guilt, that was what she needed. "Brandy, I'm sorry that you're feeling so put out, but this is really between your Dad and me."

"I know, I just didn't want you to think that I was the issue. I hope you two are able to work things out."

Laura realized she hoped for that as well. Unfortunately, that would involve talking with Garett, something she was dreading. In all of her past relationships, the breakdown had been in communication. Except with the married man; he'd just flat-out refused to leave his wife.

"I understand, but I'm not making any promises or commitments here," said Laura.

"I get that. I don't know why I thought it was a good idea to come see you." Brandy picked at her salad, moving it around more than eating it.

Had Laura had kids, she would probably know the right thing to say to this girl. As it was, part of her wanted to tell her to grow the hell up and the other part of her wanted to comfort her and make her whatever promises she needed to hear.

"I think it was brave of you to come see me," she said finally. She saw Brandy blush and worked to keep a smile off of her face. "I wouldn't have been brave enough to go see some woman my dad had pissed off."

Brandy laughed at that. It was a bright tinkling laugh that Laura loved as soon as she heard it.

"Seriously, though," said Laura. "Tell me about school. Is it everything you'd hoped it would be?"

As Brandy launched into a detailed description of the school year thus far, Laura felt herself relax for the first time since the disastrous dinner. By the end of the meal, she realized that she could come to really like Brandy.

Maybe it was time to give Garett a call. She hoped it wasn't too late.

***

2019:

Mike didn't have reason to call me into the office again. I doubled down and even beat my previous record, completing six orders in one shift. He didn't talk to me about it, but I could tell that he was happy with my performance again.

It also helped to clear my head. I threw myself into work and was able to block all other thoughts as I did. Brandy only haunted my thoughts when I had downtime, or when I was planning.

I didn't know how, yet, but Brandy and I were going to be together.

The planning part is always the most fun for me. The possibilities are infinite and the only limit is your imagination.

I happened to have a very active imagination.

I enjoyed drawing maps, making lists and covering my walls with all of the information I had. I was able to find Brandy on social media. I was annoyed that she had such strong privacy settings, but I still printed her profile picture. I cut her boyfriend out of the image.

I tried to creep her friends, but she had that blocked as well. I debated adding her as a friend, but I didn't want to scare her off. It was best if she thought our running into each other was purely coincidental.

The only major annoyance I had was my mother. Nathan was right, she was worried about me. I didn't know what her sudden interest was. For most of my life, she could barely be bothered to keep in touch. Now she was calling every few days.

I lived a very boring life. I didn't have that much to talk about. Coming up with conversation was exhausting.

"And how's Thrasher?" she'd asked the night before. That was scraping the bottom of the barrel, even for her. We all knew she didn't give a rat's ass about my dog.

"Fine," I had said. I didn't know what she wanted me to say.

"Yeah? Is he calming down a bit?"

My mom had made the mistake of coming to visit shortly after I had brought Thrasher home for the first time. He's a loyal dog and when she started yelling at me, he took exception to it. He had only growled at her. It wasn't like he bit her or anything. Now she was afraid to come visit, which was fine with me.

"He's never been a problem for me," I said. "He's a gentle pup."

She didn't have anything to say to that. I stood there by my sink, waiting for her to get to the point so I could go watch T.V. or do some more planning.

"I miss you," she said finally.

"What?"

That was probably not the response she was looking for, but she caught me off guard. She'd never said that kind of thing to me before.

"You heard me," she snapped. "I worry about you, Jess. You're all on your lonesome with that dog. You didn't even come out to Nathan and Jenny's baby shower."

I rolled my eyes so hard, I was surprised she didn't hear it. I hadn't gone to that damn thing because I didn't want to. I couldn't care less about Nathan and Jenny. I would be perfectly happy if they never spoke to me again.

"We both know that wouldn't have gone over well," I said.

"What do you mean?" Now she sounded offended. This was the woman I remembered.

"Nathan and Jenny don't like me, Mom. And I don't like them. Why should we pretend otherwise?"

"How can you say that? Your brother loves you. He's looked up to you his entire life."

No. He had not. He had gone out of his way to add to my misery every single day. Why she thought otherwise was beyond me.

"Yeah, well he has a funny way of showing it," I said. I whirled my finger through the air, willing her to wrap it up.

"Since you missed Mother's Day, too, I thought maybe we could get together for a dinner in the next couple of weeks."

I had not forgotten Mother's Day. I had ignored it. There was a huge difference there that my mother was having a hard time putting together.

"Like go out to eat?" I asked with fingers crossed.

"No, I'll cook something. I'll make ham, your favourite."

"That's Nathan's favourite."

"Whatever, you love it too. You don't always need to pick a fight with me, you know, Jess?"

Getting her riled up was easy. If I pressed on, she would get mad enough to hang up on me and then I could carry on with my night. I debated the best way to do that in my mind as she proceeded to lecture me on all of my faults.

She petered out after not too long, which was a bit of a relief. "I would really like it if you could make an effort to come."

Would she never stop talking? Even Thrasher was starting to feel sorry for me. He laid at my feet, looking up at me with sad puppy eyes.

"I'm not making any promises," I said. "But text me when you're having the dinner and if I'm not working, I'll try to make it."

"Try?" she whined.

"Oh my God, Mom!" I snapped. "Fine! I'll come if I'm not working. Can we talk about anything else now?"

It turned out that was all I needed to do. *Raise my voice once and my mom has a meltdown.* She hung up on me and I sighed with relief. I turned my phone off so I couldn't hear her calling me again. Undoubtedly there would be a sad-sounding voicemail waiting for me in the morning.

That or she would call Nathan, who would also call me to give me a lecture.

Why did family have to be such a huge pain in the ass?

11

Garett answered her call on the first ring. It was a bit unnerving to think that he'd been sitting on his phone all this time, just waiting for her to call.

"Hey, Laura," he said. She could hear the relief in his voice.

"Hey. I think we need to talk, do you want to come over tonight?"

"Yes. I'll grab us some takeout."

After she hung up, she wondered if she was making the right decision. Garett was a nice guy, but if he wasn't over Emily then there wasn't anything there for her.

The rest of the day was spent making phone calls and taking notes. Now that the arsonist was arrested, there were more fluff pieces for her to do. Which was a nice break for sure, but it made the day seem longer. Especially longer because she was nervous about seeing Garett that night.

True to his word, he brought them some Chinese food. She pulled out plates and they dished up. Not much was said for the first while; it was mostly spent on small talk and eating.

By the end of the meal, she knew she had to bite the bullet.

"I have to know if we're a long-term thing or if I'm just a fling you're having as you try to figure things out."

Garett took a sip of his coke before answering her. "Laura, I have strong feelings for you. It's scary for me. I loved Emily, she was my saviour. I don't ever want to forget her or dishonour her in any way."

"What do you mean she was your saviour?"

"She wasn't my first serious relationship. I'd been in one before and it ended terribly. My world stopped turning and I wasn't sure how I was going to continue. I was pretty messed up and I was looking at taking the wrong road."

"I get that she has a special place in your heart, Garett. And I'm not looking to be her replacement. But if we stay together, we can't decide that certain subjects are off-limits for Brandy and me to discuss."

"I know. I overreacted," he said. "You're the first woman I've had feelings for since Emily and this is all new territory for me, too."

Laura placed their plates into the dishwasher and then beckoned him to the living room so they could settle in for a long talk.

"I've been with a married man." She lifted her hand when he raised his eyebrows, "I know. I'm a homewrecker, blah, blah, blah. But here's the thing. I fell for this guy head over heels. I thought he was the one.

"He was going to leave his wife. He was just waiting for the right moment. For three years. I think he's still with her. So technically, I'm not a homewrecker, but I was wrecked." She still felt hurt when she thought of him.

"So when I started talking about Emily like that…" said Garett.

"Yeah. The conversation we had, made me feel like I was getting in between a husband and wife yet again. I'm not interested in that."

"I need to be more upfront with you about things that I'm uncomfortable with," he said.

"Yes, please. You also need to understand that if I'm with you, I have to have a relationship with Brandy. I'm sure we'd both prefer it to be a positive one."

He leaned back in the chair, flipping the bottom of the Lay Z Boy out. "Well, now that you've met her once, the second time should be a little easier."

"Twice, we've met twice," corrected Laura.

"What do you mean you've met her twice?"

"She didn't tell you that she came to see me the other day?" Laura crossed her arms in discomfort. Now she felt like she was betraying Brandy.

"No, she didn't," he said. Then he sighed and ran his hand through his greying hair. "I don't think I've been the greatest father since Emily passed. She feels like she needs to take care of me."

Laura watched him stand and pace across her living room. His shoulders were slumped and he looked like he hadn't shaved in days. He was exhausted.

"That's not the sense I got," said Laura. "She just didn't want me to misunderstand what had happened."

"Maybe…" he said. Then he walked over and sat beside her on the couch. "Laura, you are very important to me. Sometimes I can be a real dumbass, and I'm sorry. I just… I just can't take losing anyone else."

She could sense there was more to his words than she understood, but she didn't want to interrupt him and get him to clarify. Laura could feel something shift inside her, and she realized she was falling for this man.

She lifted his arm up and put it around her. Snuggling into his chest, she sighed and said, "I'm not going anywhere, Garett. I'm going to be right here with you."

***

1992, ten years old:

Her Dad was taking just her to see her Uncle Daryl this weekend. She couldn't wait to hang out with the two of them. He had promised they would go fishing both days and she'd been up all night, packing her tackle box.

She didn't like to say it, but it was a relief that Nathan and her mom weren't coming. Sometimes it was just too hard with them, so it was nice to have the time with her dad all by herself.

"Don't forget your rubber boots," he said as he passed her room in the hallway. He blew her a kiss and winked, too. "Remember what happened to your shoes last time?"

A giggle escaped her, and she covered her mouth to prevent more. Her mother had not been happy when her shoes had come back all covered in mud. She'd been in really big trouble and had to wear boy shoes for a whole month.

She lugged her bag out into the hall. She'd packed all of the essentials she would need; hat, sunscreen, bug spray, clothing, everything she could think of. Her rubber boots would be on her feet when she got in the truck so she wouldn't forget them.

"Are we going to have smores again?" she asked.

Her dad put his finger to his lips and glanced around, looking for the rest of the family. "Maybe, but remember, that's our little secret. Otherwise, Nathan will want to come."

She liked that he didn't want Nathan to come, too. It made her feel even more special.

Her dad was always away working and when he was gone, she never had the chance to feel special. She was always disappointing her mom and annoying Nathan.

Her dad, though. It was like he completely understood her.

Her Uncle Daryl was just as fun. He was her mother's brother, which was weird because they weren't alike at all. While her mom was mean and always made her feel bad, her uncle was always laughing and trying to cheer her up. That was probably why he and her dad got along so well.

She followed her dad out to the truck, hauling her bag with her. "If we catch some whitefish, can we have it for dinner?"

"Of course. If we don't catch any then we're going to go hungry. I don't think Uncle Daryl ever has healthy food out there."

"Can we stop and get ice cream, too?" she asked.

"Let me guess? Tiger?"

"Yup!" The orange and black licorice was her all-time favourite and she'd only ever had it at the ice cream shop by Pigeon Lake.

The drive out to the lake was a peaceful one, filled with outrageous hair metal that was never allowed any other time. He played their usual game with the radio.

"Do you know who this is?"

"Is it… Twisted Sister?"

"Bingo!" he said. Then they headbanged to the music before the next one came on and the ritual was repeated.

The cabin itself wasn't really on the lake. It was set back off the highway on a small acreage. There were little pockets of communities around the lake, but Uncle Daryl's cabin was all by its lonesome.

"The isolation suits me," he said. "I come out here to get away from people, not to chat strangers up."

Every summer, Daryl would spend as much time out at the lake as he possibly could. If she was lucky, she would get to spend a week out there, but her dad didn't always have days off. And if Nathan came, it was not as fun.

Jess loved being out in nature. She would wake up with the birds and sneak outside to see the sunrise. Usually, her dad would be right behind her with a cup of tea with honey and milk. He always had a mug of hot coffee in his favourite old tin cup.

This weekend was no different. Uncle Daryl slept in, not being a morning person, but she and her dad found some walking sticks and set out to the lake. They weren't going fishing just yet; they always waited for Uncle Daryl.

Instead, they were going out to check if the lake was calm. If it was choppy, with the white crests topping the grey water, then they couldn't fish from the aluminum boat her uncle had. On those days, they would set up on the dock and try to fish there.

Today, the water looked like a mirror of the sky. The only thing marring the surface was the tiny ripples the water beetles and dragonflies made.

The frogs croaked and in the distance, she could hear the chickadee serenading the morning sun.

"We're definitely going out in the boat today," he said. Then he sighed and leaned on his stick, taking in the beauty of the morning. "You know the best part of something this beautiful, Jess?" She shook her head and looked out to see if she could see it. He reached over and ruffled her hair. "The best part is sharing this beauty with someone you love."

He was right, she realized. There was no one else she ever wanted to see the sunrise with. Not her mom, not her brother and not even her uncle. The sunrise belonged to her and her dad alone, as far as she was concerned.

After the oranges and pinks had faded, her dad turned around and head back to the cabin. It was time to start making breakfast and getting ready to go out.

The fish were hungry that day. Jess caught two whitefish, enough for her to make her own dinner. Her dad and her uncle sat at either end of the boat, beers in hand and relaxing.

Very little was said while fishing. It wasn't a good idea to be too loud because it would scare the fish away. But also, fishing was a peaceful thing that was best enjoyed when everyone was relaxed.

When they pulled the boat back in, though, the conversation didn't stop. They parked the boat at the back shed and made their way to the picnic table behind the cabin.

"Here, Jess, this year you get to clean your own fish, okay?" He handed her the knife.

"Really?"

"Yeah," he said with a grin. "Just remember, the knife always faces away from you. And if you aren't careful, you'll cut away the good stuff."

She set to work quickly, slicing the belly of the fish and pulling out the insides. It was stinky business, cleaning a fish, but worth it. The next step was to descale it and then cut off the head and tail.

She pushed the knife against the scales and then gasped as she nicked herself with it. "Ouch!"

"You get yourself? Here, let's wash it real quick. Uncle can take care of the rest," said her dad. He hadn't left her side while she was doing it. "You did a great job," he told her as he poured some water over her thumb. "You just have to watch where you put your other hand, right? But don't worry, I still nick myself sometimes, too. It's all part of learning."

To her, it looked like she had a pretty good slash in her thumb, but she put on a tough face and barely winced as he wiped it down with iodine and then put a bandaid on it.

By the time the fish was ready to eat, she didn't even feel it anymore. They ate their feast of fish with some cheesies, making it hands down Jess's favourite meal ever.

She was quiet as they sat around the fire. Her dad and her uncle chewed the fat, as they always said, and she just snuggled into her blanket in her little fold-up chair. It was a She-Ra blanket that her uncle had bought especially for her and she loved it.

It wasn't long before she felt herself drifting off to sleep. She woke only as her dad was carrying her to bed.

"... damn shame is what it is," said her uncle.

"It is," replied her dad as he gently tucked her into the cot her uncle had set up for her. "But we both know that Lorraine will fight me tooth and nail for them, so I don't know what to do."

"And she'll get them."

"I know. That's why I'm still here."

The door closed and Jess laid there for a while, trying to make sense of what she'd overheard. It didn't make sense, but her dad had sounded so sad. Eventually, she drifted off to sleep, dreaming of watching the sunrise again.

***

2019:

I was back in Mike's good books. I didn't let him see that I was still distracted. Like normal people everywhere, I separated my work and home life at the door.

To a certain extent. There were some things I needed and if I happened to come across some of those necessary items, like plastic zip ties, I helped myself to them. It wasn't like anyone would miss them.

I think it was good for my soul to be working toward something again.

Not that I was really into that hippy-dippy shit.

It just felt nice to have a purpose in life.

Thrasher was my everything, but I could only get so excited about spending time with him. He couldn't give me the affection that a real person could. And who was I kidding, I needed human interaction.

Well, besides the jack-asses I had to work with every day.

Since Mike had told the guys off they'd mostly avoided me, which I appreciated. Being by myself was not the punishment many seemed to think it was. The less I had to interact with losers, the better.

It was hot in the warehouse. I was sweating buckets and wishing I'd thought to put on deodorant before I left. We were having an Indian Summer and the warehouse, being centrally controlled, already had the furnace turned on.

Even Mike who sat in his office doing nothing was dying a little.

I threw my hair up in a rubber band and pushed my cart forward with my hips for a moment as I walked. I wasn't going to slow down for anything. I didn't want to bring Mike's attention down on me again.

Just as I was coming to the end of the aisle, another cart came hurtling down the main corridor. Dave's cart smashed into mine and there were parts everywhere.

"Watch where you're going!" I snapped.

He lifted his finger, but didn't say anything. I grumbled under my breath and picked up the stuff that had fallen off my cart. One of the boxes was making noises it shouldn't, which likely meant it was broken.

Great, add a few more minutes to my order time as I run to put it in the returns bin and then back to grab a working part off of the shelf.

"Thanks a lot," I said as I set off at a jog toward the back.

"Fuck you!" The words trailed after me and I didn't bother to grace them with an answer. It was his damn fault for not paying attention.

It turned out he wasn't far behind me. Some of his stuff must have been broken too.

There was a pallet in the back that we had to place all damaged items on. Then we had to write down our names and the date. The worst part was we had to fill out whether the part had been damaged on arrival or if it had been damaged due to "human error."

If we had too many human errors, our pay could be docked. I'd heard rumours that some workers had been written up.

I wasn't taking that risk. I scratched out *human* beside my name and wrote *Dave* overtop of it. Dave error. That was better, because it sure as fuck wasn't my error.

I handed the clipboard to Dave when I was done.

"Seriously? Why do you gotta be such a bitch?" he asked.

"You ran into my cart. It's your error. Not mine."

I started pushing my cart again. I had six more items on the list and then I had to hit the exact opposite corner of the building to get that part again.

Something struck my foot and I fell forward, pushing the cart with my chest and slamming my chin on the handle bar. I immediately fell to my knees, woozy and tasting blood. I wiped my hand over my mouth and it came back with some red saliva.

I stood and turned to see what I'd tripped over. There was nothing there. Only Dave whistling as he filled out the paperwork.

Fury tore through me. I felt my fists clench and my jaw set. Then I took a deep breath. Now was not the time. I couldn't afford to be reported to HR, and I had no proof of anything, unless I wanted to look through security footage.

Nothing would get done about it anyway.

I spit at Dave, missing him by a foot or so, which only made him chuckle. Then I turned my back and stalked away.

Thankfully, nothing else had come off the cart. It had only careened off to the side of the corridor and the items just needed some minor readjusting. My steps were not as quick now. I felt a headache coming on and my mouth was aching.

It took me the rest of the morning to get the order completed. That meant that the other three were basically able to lap me with their own stuff. At lunch, I warmed up my hoagie and then cursed as I tried to eat with a cut on the inside of my mouth. I only got a few bites into me before I called it quits. Water would have to do.

That afternoon, I picked an order that needed the forklift. Every employee had training in running the machine. It was a mandatory health and safety thing.

So were the bright vests we were supposed to be wearing, but Mike never replaced them as they fell apart. Most were in the garbage now except for the brand new shiny ones that hung in Mike's office, waiting for a visit from Management.

I liked using the forklift. It added an extra cushion of privacy to my space. The guys all respected the machine enough to stay away and obey the little hazard signs I set out at the end of the aisle when I had to use it.

There was a feeling of power when I could make them change what they were doing simply because I wanted to. I liked the feeling of control.

Unfortunately, we were only allowed to use the forklift if there were objects on the order that were high on the shelves and over a certain weight. Otherwise, we just used the mobile ladders to get to things.

Today, though, I'd hit the motherload. I had five things on this list that needed to be removed from the top shelf. That meant I would be spending the afternoon toodling around the place in my own little bubble.

For every aisle I went down, I had to set up barriers at the beginning and end. The rule was that nobody used the area until the person operating the forklift had placed their items on their cart. Once there was no danger of falling objects, it was generally considered safe. However, everyone was still supposed to wait until the hazard signs were removed.

It was such a pain to follow that rule. Especially when you knew the person operating the lift was only killing time and that one thing you needed was on aisle twelve, where the forklift was. I knew they did it just to annoy me sometimes, but I did my best to hide my anger.

Today it was my turn to pull the stall tactics and delay everyone.

Gleefully, I headed toward the second aisle, making sure I wasn't going too fast. I didn't need Mike to give me shit for this either. No stunting for me.

Once I arrived, I got out and placed the sign down. Then I carried the other sign over to the other side of the aisle. It felt good to extend my bubble. No one could come near me now.

As I climbed into the forklift, I saw something move out of the corner of my eye. I sat up tall and twisted around to see what was going on. There shouldn't have been any movement.

Behind me, Dave was pushing his cart casually down the aisle.

My hands clenched into fists again and dropped down into my seat while I tried to breathe through my white-hot rage. *What the fuck is he doing here?*

Technically, I wasn't supposed to move the forklift if there was anyone in the aisle, but I decided that if Dave was going to be a dick, so was I.

I backed up the forklift and was satisfied to see Dave jump forward quickly. The siren was even louder if you were directly behind the machine.

Carefully, I turned the machine so I could head down the aisle.

I moved the gear into place and started forward. I had to slam on the brakes because Dave pushed his cart in front of me.

Hitting the brakes jarred me and reminded me of my sore chin and mouth.

That was all it took.

He had his back to me, pretending not to notice the forklift. Instead of moving forward, I turned the machine to the left.

The feeling of collision as one of the tines struck his calves was amazing. I couldn't really feel it because he was too small. And I didn't actually hear the sound of his nose and face crunching as he plowed into the cement floor, but I filled those minor details in myself for my memory.

He'd obviously shouted as I knocked his feet out from under him because everyone came running to see what had happened.

I climbed out of the forklift, shaking from the adrenaline rush. There was blood pooling around Dave and I ran over to him, kind of hoping he was dead.

Mike got there first and checked his pulse. "Call nine-one-one!" he shouted. Lance had his phone out and was babbling to the dispatcher.

"There's been an accident. My coworker is hurt." He looked like a little sissy girl with his big googly eyes and white face. I hoped he would faint.

I didn't listen as he rattled off the address and then started pacing.

There wasn't much to be done. Mike said Dave's pulse was still strong and he was still breathing. It was too bad he'd landed face-first instead of smashing his skull on the cement. Then maybe he could've drowned in his own blood.

For now though, this would do.

12

Hutchinson didn't appreciate losing sleep over a case that was already solved as far as his superiors were concerned. In fact, it pissed him off that he was too tired to focus completely on his daughter's chatter as they headed to Dairy Queen for ice cream before he dropped her off with her mother.

A case that had been solved should have been a burden lifted from his shoulders. The Rooftop Arsonist was behind bars and the nightclubs of the city were once again safe.

Yet there was a niggling feeling in the back of his mind that told him it wasn't right. That niggling feeling was often referred to as gut instinct on the force. Or a hunch. And it was a poor police officer that ignored that feeling.

Things just didn't line up.

The Rooftop Arsonist was not a careless person. Even when Ed had confronted him, the man had kept his cool enough to leave no physical evidence behind.

What was the difference this last time? Why would he suddenly be so forgetful as to leave cigarette butts laying around? And why ditch the jerry can basically at the scene of the crime?

It didn't make sense.

He knew he wasn't the only one who felt that way. Ed had made that clear, and so had some of the guys on his team. But the strings were being pulled from up top and there wasn't a lot he could do about it.

Besides, it was considered bad form to not support the forces' decisions in public. The last thing he needed was to be disciplined for raising doubts.

"... so Elaine and I are thinking we'll just go together," said Crystal.

"Go where?" he asked as he turned into the drive-thru.

"To the dance," she said. "Are you even listening to me?"

"I am." He held up his hand as the voice came over the intercom.

"Welcome to Dairy Queen! May I take your order please?"

"Hi, can I get two medium skor blizzards, please?" he asked.

When he looked back over, Crystal had her arms crossed and was glaring out the passenger window. The speaker came to life and the server told him the price, but he didn't listen, just pulled ahead.

"Honey, I'm sorry. I'm just a little distracted with work."

"You're always distracted with work." She still wouldn't look at him.

He pulled up to the window where a cashier patiently waited. He handed her a twenty and then turned his attention back to Crystal.

"Why are they having a dance in September?" he asked, digging in his memory for anything that would show he'd caught some of what she'd said.

She let out a sigh and shrugged her shoulders in annoyance. "Because they want all of the new kids at the high school to get to know each other? I don't know. It's some kind of introductory thing."

"You didn't go last year?" he asked.

"No, Dad. I didn't go last year. I wasn't in high school, remember? I was at the junior high for all of Grade Nine."

Right, yes, that was stupid of me. Crystal hadn't been ready to move up to a high school last year. Lacey had moved her to a school that kept students until Grade Nine and then started her in the high school at Grade Ten instead.

He hadn't agreed with the decision. Crystal needed to learn how to face her fears and not let intimidation from someone else get in her way.

But Lacey was the primary caregiver, so all she had to do was inform him of her decision.

When the cashier handed him the blizzards, he passed one over to Crystal right away. "You're upset that you'll be one of the few Grade Tens at the dance, right?"

"That's what I've been saying."

Now that he'd pieced it all together, he had a hard time pretending that he cared. He hated the teenage stage. They seemed to think that all of their problems were the worst in the world and no one else's existed.

"And who is Elaine?"

"Oh. My. God," she said. "Nevermind, Dad. Just forget it."

He couldn't just forget it, but no amount of pestering got Crystal to speak. She just methodically ate her blizzard, savouring each bite while staring out the window. His ice cream melted in the cupholder beside him.

The plan had been to stop at the park and enjoy the evening outside, but he'd changed his mind. Crystal's demeanour was so icy, he didn't even want the ice cream anymore.

As much as he hated to admit it, it was a relief to drop her off at her mother's house. The cold shoulder was something she'd learned from her mom and he resented it in her. Then he felt guilty about resenting her. It was a vicious cycle he couldn't seem to escape.

The problem, he knew, lay with his work. He needed, desperately, to explain the factors that told him things weren't right with the arson case. He needed them to understand his gut feeling. The problem was, he didn't know how he was going to do that.

He drove around the city for a while, trying to think of what he could do to shake it. In the end, he could only come up with what he'd done in the past. Try to work through it.

Unconsciously, he ended up near Whirls and Spurs, the bar that Lyle Walker had said he'd been at the night of the fire. He shut his car off and stared at the doors for a minute before he decided he was actually going to go in.

The bar was disgusting, the kind of place he wouldn't want to be seen in on his roughest day. The dank interior and the rancid smell, like rotting vegetables, made him vow to himself that he would never, ever get to the point where he would grace a similar establishment.

He made his way to the bar, surreptitiously taking a look around him. The few patrons wore worn-out jeans and shirts with sweat stains. Or at least he hoped they were sweat stains. It was hard to tell with the low-watt bulbs.

The bartender was hardly dressed any better. His button-up shirt looked like he'd slept in it for the past few days and his beard had gone from a stylish scruff to the look of a homeless man.

"Hi, what can I get you?" the guy asked.

"I'll take a sparkling water if you have any," said Hutchinson.

"Nope. We aren't that fancy. I can probably grab you a club soda, though."

"That would be great." He drummed his fingers on the bar top and then immediately regretted it as his thumbs touched some kind of sticky substance.

"Do you want any appies?" asked the bartender as he dropped off the soda.

"No," said Hutchinson. "I'm actually kind of here for work."

"Work?"

"Yes, I'm Sergeant Hutchinson of the EPS. I was wondering if you had a few minutes."

The bartender took a step back and raised his hands to waist level with his palms out. "Is this about the fight here last night? Because we cut that guy off at two drinks. I don't know what his problem was. Do you want to see my ProServe?"

"No. No, that's not what I'm here about. Listen, no one's in trouble, I was just wondering a few things if you don't mind."

"Whatever I can do to help."

"Can I start with your name?" Hutchinson asked.

"Paul Jensen."

"Great, thank you, Paul. I'm actually here about a patron that used to come here often. His name was Lyle Walker."

"The arsonist? Yeah he was always in here. Super nice guy, never pictured him as the type to pull something like that off."

"Yeah, well, you can never tell with those people," said Hutchinson. "I'm just curious about how he was behaving the last few times you saw him."

Paul shook his head and shrugged. "Just like normal. He always came in and sat down at the end. His orders varied but normally it was hard liquor. Always seemed like he was getting right down to business when he was drinking."

"Did he ever cause a fuss?"

"Nope. Very quiet, kept to himself mostly."

"What do you mean 'mostly'?"

"Well, there was the odd time that he was here with someone."

"A buddy from work?"

"Nah, and now that I think on it, it was really only one time, but there was a girl."

This was new, Walker hadn't mentioned any women. "He had a girlfriend?"

"I don't think so. I think she just came in looking for a good time," Paul mused.

"When?"

"I don't know." He looked over Hutchinson's shoulder and nodded at one of the guys in the back booth. "A while ago. I'll be right back." He grabbed a beer out of the fridge and popped it open before heading out to serve it.

When Hutchinson thought back on Walker, he didn't think he looked like the type that most women would want to have a good time with. He prayed Crystal would always have the good sense to avoid men like that, anyway.

"Can you give me a ballpark?" he asked when Paul came back.

"I don't know, a few weeks ago?"

"Was it during the time when the nightclubs were being burned?" Hutchinson asked.

"Yeah, toward the end of it, I think. It wasn't long after that that he was arrested, I think."

This was very interesting news indeed. There was no way this bar had any security footage going that far back, but he would bet dollars to doughnuts that this was an important development.

"Walker never mentioned a girl," Hutchinson told Paul.

"I doubt he remembered much about that night. He even danced with her."

"If we were to get a sketch artist in here, could you give a description of this girl?"

"Probably. I mean, I see a lot of people through here, but I think I can remember what she looked like."

That feeling in his gut was flaring like a supernova. He was onto something here. That girl was important. Now he just needed to track her down.

***

2019:

The downside to my temper tantrum was that we were now short a person at the warehouse. Mike said Occupational Health and Safety was all up his ass after Dave's incident.

When he called me into his office, I was sweating pretty good.

"How are you doing, Jess?" he asked after I had taken a seat. No bigwigs, just him, for which I was thankful.

"I'm fine," I said. He was asking how I felt about Dave's incident and that really didn't bother me. The only thing I was worried about was my job.

"Fine? You just watched Dave get his face smashed in."

"Yeah, well, what do you expect me to say? I can't take time off work because I'm upset, so, I'm fine."

"I wanted you to know that we've reviewed the security footage." He flipped his computer monitor around so I could take a look. "I don't know what the fuck Dave was doing there. You clearly had everything marked off. You didn't see him there?"

"I was focused on getting the stuff. When I put up the signs, the aisle was empty. I didn't expect anyone to be near the machine."

Mike nodded and pressed play on the footage. I watched as Dave snuck into the aisle after I got into the forklift. You could see me turn around, but they couldn't see what I was looking at.

As I backed up, Dave darted ahead of me and then pushed the cart in front of the lift.

I leaned forward to take a closer look at the screen. It looked as though I was looking at the cart when I turned the machine to the left.

Mike stopped the footage as the tine came into contact with Dave.

"Why'd you turn the forklift?" he asked.

"The cart startled me. It was a knee-jerk reaction," I said.

"I checked your file, your training is still up to date. Barely. We're going to have to get you in to renew it in the next couple of weeks. I don't know what else they'll want me to do. Probably suspend you for a bit."

"What?" I snapped.

"At the very least, you won't be going near the forklift any time soon." He held up his hands placatingly. "Listen, Jess. I can't afford to have you take off any more than you can afford to take time off. This whole situation is just… It's going to take some time to sort out."

"That's fine if I don't use the forklift. I can always ask Lance or Evan if I need to. Or just grab orders that don't need it."

"I can't guarantee anything," he said. "But I'll do what I can, alright?"

That was really the best that I could ask for out of the situation. It was reckless of me to let my emotions take control like that. That was what happened when there was no plan.

As much as it killed me, I decided I should probably send Dave some flowers or something, too. I had to appear somewhat regretful of the accident. Even though he knew that he had it coming.

When I left work, I went to a flower shop on my way to the hardware store. I talked to the lady inside for way too long, but we eventually decided on some carnations. I didn't want to drop large amounts of money on this, but I also didn't want to appear cheap. I bought a card to go with it and just signed my name inside.

The very act left me feeling vile.

The hardware store was much more fun. I wandered up the aisles, looking for some plywood, ratchet straps and other goodies. I'd taken what I dared from the warehouse, but that was only going to get me so far.

In reality, zip ties were never a permanent solution. They worked well in the moment, but if I wanted to keep anything in place for any length of time, I would need something different.

I left with a heavy bag of tools and a light heart. I had looked at the price of lumber and decided I would wait on the plywood.

My phone buzzed just as I was pulling up to my trailer. It was my mother. I hit ignore and made my way to the front door. I could hear Thrasher inside whining. He always recognized the sound of my truck.

The phone buzzed again as I was unlocking the door. "Yeah," I answered, not even bothering to look at the Call-ID this time.

"Is that any way to greet your mother?"

"I'm kinda busy, Mom. What's going on?"

"I'm just checking in on you. Nancy told me that she heard that there was a workplace accident at your warehouse. Are you okay?"

I heaved a big sigh and dropped my bag on the table. It annoyed me that she even knew where I worked. I had let it slip one time and I would never forgive myself forever after.

"Yep, it wasn't me that got hurt."

"Well, you know, after something like that, it's usually a good idea to check in with your family."

"If I was hurt, I would have checked in." I pulled some hamburger out of the fridge for Thrasher and put it on a plate. He usually preferred it warm, but he was just going to have to deal for now.

"How nice of you," she said. I could just see her sitting in her armchair, tapping her foot on the floor as she spoke to me. "So I was thinking we'd have that dinner this weekend. Does that work for you?"

"Depends what time. We're short-staffed now."

"How about you check with your boss and let me know what works for you? Nathan and Jenny said they're flexible."

Fuck. Just what I needed – family time. That meant I would have to meet Nathan's kid, too. So much for my weekend plans.

"Okay, I'll give you a call after I talk to him," I said.

I waited for her to say goodbye, but she didn't. "So how have things been otherwise? Been seeing any boys?"

I groaned loudly. "Mom, if I were seeing any guys, I sure as hell wouldn't tell you about it."

"It sounds to me like your attitude stinks too much to attract anyone, Jess. I've been trying to tell you for years, you're one of those people that have to attract others with the beauty inside of you. That means you have to put in more effort."

She had been telling me that for years. Unfortunately, most people didn't get past my actual looks to give me a chance. I doubted anyone would ever look that deeply at me.

"Sure thing, Ma," I said.

"You are so rude sometimes. Did you know that?"

"Hey, I've gotta go. I've got some errands to run." I hung up the phone before she could get in another word. I debated whether to call Mike right now or just wait until the morning to talk to him.

In the end, I decided I'd wait for the morning. I didn't want to ruin my evening by having him tell me that it wouldn't be a problem for me to take an evening with my family.

I wondered if I was still good at lying.

The phone buzzed again and this time I saw Nathan's name.

"Yeah?" I said again.

"Why do you have to treat Mom like that?"

"Like what? I told her I was busy!"

"And then you hung up on her."

"Jesus, Nathan! Why are you the one calling me to give me shit if she's so offended?"

He sighed and then he said something to Jenny. I could hear the baby crying in the background. Even over the phone it was awful. "Jess, she just wants to get together this weekend. Would it kill you to do that for her?"

"It might," I said.

"You're so dramatic. All the time. Why do you have to be that way?"

"Look Nathan, I'm busy so…"

"You gonna hang up on me now?"

"Is there a point to this conversation?" I asked. "Because if that's all you were calling for then yes, I'm hanging up."

He snuck in a "Whatever," before I hit the button.

Thrasher looked up from his bowl. He had burger on his lips, but he'd licked the bowl clean. "Hey, bud, why don't we go to the dog park? See if you can scare off some more poodles?"

My evening was going to be spent with someone I loved, and not worrying about what my family thought of me.

After the dog park, I decided to swing by the university to see what I could see. I hoped that I would catch a glimpse of Brandy, which was a stretch and I knew it. Still, one more look at her would buoy my mood for the next little while.

It was reckless to drive by in my vehicle with my dog with me, but it was a risk I couldn't help but take.

Unfortunately, there was no sign of her that evening. By the time I was finished, though, I'd decided that I would be making another visit. I needed to gauge her size, anyway. I wanted to be completely prepared for what was to come.

13

This time, Laura made sure to triple-check the time of dinner with Garett. Ever since they'd had their talk, the two had been closer than ever. In fact, she was sure the next step in their relationship wasn't far away.

She basically lived at his house anyway. Which was a nice difference from before they spoke about Emily.

Before that, Garett came to her place more often than not. He'd never said anything, but she felt like she was intruding on a sacred space.

Brandy had come over one weekend and helped him to pack up the last of Emily's stuff. The last that remained were a few sentimental items in an ebony box on his nightstand.

Each night after they turned out the lamps, he blew a kiss to the box, which had thrown Laura off at first. She'd talked to her sister about it, though, and Randy had suggested that maybe she look at it a different way.

"If it weren't for the relationship he had with Emily, he wouldn't be the man he is today. So, in a way, you owe Emily your thanks," she'd said.

It wasn't a terrible way to view things. Since then, she'd also taken to saying a thank you to Emily every night when she was at Garett's place.

Her stuff was gone, but there was still a feeling of her in the house. She knew that Garett would never be able to part with the house where he'd been so happy, so she'd decided that when the time came, she would move in with him.

While her house was her home, it didn't hold the sentimentality that Garett's held for him. Laura had never had a family of her own, much to her mother's disappointment. Instead, she'd been what millennials now termed a Serial Monogamist, flitting from one serious relationship to the next.

It felt different with Garett. For one, she actually liked Brandy and could see herself being close with her.

The second was the way that she felt with Garett. She'd thought she'd felt love in the past, and maybe she had, but she'd never felt the love of another the way she experienced it from Garett.

They weren't a perfect couple by any means. There were disagreements from time to time and the odd argument. But for the most part, Garett never treated her with anything except respect. He was understanding if she had to work late and made her a priority whenever he could.

In return, Laura treated Garett the same. She understood that Brandy would always top the list for him, and all she had to do was crook her finger and her daddy would come running. Some would say that made Brandy spoiled, but Laura only saw it as a measure of Garett's love for his daughter.

Tonight marked a milestone according to Garett. For the first time in her adult life, Brandy was introducing them to a boyfriend.

"She rarely even tells me their names," he said when he'd invited Laura one morning. "Usually, it's just this guy she's seeing or hanging out with. Things must be getting pretty serious with Austin if we get to meet him."

"Is he a student, too?"

"You know, I'm not sure. She's really avoiding answering any questions about him. I don't know if she thinks I'll judge him or what it is."

"Well," Laura said as she sipped her coffee, "your opinion probably matters more than you think and she's a little bit nervous about saying too much."

They'd taken to having a sit-down breakfast every Saturday with all of the fixings. Today, it was waffles with berries and whipped cream. And bacon. Garett had insisted it wasn't breakfast if there was no bacon.

"I guess. I never really worried about what my parents thought," he said.

"I'm sure they loved Emily," said Laura.

"Well, Emily isn't the only girl I've ever been with."

"I never talked to my parents, either. I think they would have liked you, though."

She felt a pang at the thought that Garett would never meet her parents. She thought that for once her mother wouldn't have worried about who she was seeing. And her dad would have wanted to get to know Garett.

Instead, she'd only introduced them to a string of men who weren't actually committed to her. She'd wasted so many years with her parents. She wished she could get some of them back.

"We would have got on famously from what you've told me," he said.

***

Now that the big night was upon them, Laura felt nervous for Austin as much as Brandy. There was no show tonight, only a small dinner for the four of them.

"You hungry?" he asked when she got in the car.

"Starving. Haven't eaten anything all day," she said.

"Saving up for the cheesecake?"

"I might skip supper and go straight for dessert."

Brandy and Austin were waiting for them in the restaurant when they got there. A bottle of wine and sparkling cider was waiting at the table and Brandy was already halfway through a glass of the Merlot.

"Daddy! Laura!" she said as they walked up. She gestured to Austin, "I'd like you to meet Austin Jacobsen. Austin, this is my dad, Garett, and his girlfriend Laura."

"Hi, Mr.-"

"Please, call me Garett."

Austin nodded. "Garett, then. It's nice to meet you. Brandy has told me so much about you."

"You have us at a disadvantage then," said Laura. "You are quite the mystery for us."

Brandy blushed slightly at Laura's words. "I wanted to be sure before I introduced you guys to anyone."

Seeing the warmth in Garett's eyes at the statement made Laura feel giddy inside. For once, she felt like she was part of a family of her own.

"That's good to know. So, Austin, tell us everything," Laura said.

She reached for the bottle of wine and poured herself some. Garett lifted his glass of cider and said, "Cheers!"

Austin was a student, but he was in his last year at the University. He was going to be a teacher and he already had some offers from the school where he'd done his practicum.

Brandy had met him at a house party the year before, which meant she'd been keeping the relationship to herself much longer than Laura had thought. This made the night all the more special for Brandy and Laura felt herself warming even more toward the girl.

She was surprised at how much relief she felt as she talked to Austin. With no previous experience in the parenting department, Laura hadn't realized that she had some maternal instincts. She'd chalked her stress up to worry for Garett, not even thinking that she might be worried for Brandy, too.

Something about Austin set her at ease. He was funny, candid, and clearly in love with Brandy.

It was even more obvious that Brandy felt the same about him.

Garett and Laura left the restaurant that evening feeling jubilant. They held hands the entire way back to his house.

She was planning to spend the weekend there. She had some work to do, but her laptop was already charging in his office.

"So, what did you think?" she asked when they had settled onto the couch.

"I think that I'm both happy and a bit sad," he said. "I'm happy that Austin isn't a loser and that he treats her well, but I'm sad that she's growing up."

"You'll always be part of her life, Garett. You don't have to worry about that."

He put his arm around her and pulled her tight. "I know. I just..."

"And I'll be here for you, too. You won't be alone."

He smiled down at her and kissed her softly on the nose. "Thank you. I don't know what I'd do without you."

She grabbed the remote and turned on the television. "You never would have watched Scrubs, and that would have been a pity."

He laughed and kissed her again then grabbed a blanket off of the arm of the chair.

As Laura settled against him, she wondered if Brandy was feeling what she was right now. He was The One. There wasn't much she wouldn't do for this man.

***

2019:

I'd taken the afternoon off, disappointing Mike immensely, but now I had an excuse to do it and I wasn't going to pass up the opportunity. After everything with Dave, it was natural that I would still be a bit shaken up, who wouldn't? So it made sense for me to take some time to myself.

He didn't realize that I wasn't at all upset about Dave, but I wasn't going to let him in on that little secret. As far as I was concerned, he could think what he wanted about me, so long as I got the time off that I wanted.

During my time off, I made my way down to the university area again. I had zipped home and changed out of my work clothes. My hair was still tied back with a band, but I had put on some jeans and a t-shirt. I hoped that my choice would help me to blend in with the students in the area.

I knew Brandy would have to take lunch at some point, so I waited outside of the doors, trying to look like I was waiting for someone. I was, so I didn't have to do much acting.

There were so many people coming and going that it seemed impossible for me to catch her, and I worried that she would potentially leave by a different entrance, but if that was the case then I would have to find her another day.

My luck was with me though. I saw her come out, chatting with her friends, headed over to the parking lot.

I intentionally stepped in front of her and pretended to drop my purse to the ground. I'd never carried a purse around, so it wasn't difficult to act awkward with it.

Brandy and her friends stopped, but when she recognized me, she sent them ahead.

"Cathy, right?" she said.

"Yes…" I replied, pretending that I didn't recognize her. It was brilliant acting if you asked me.

"It's me, Brandy. We met at the nightclub a while back," she said. I wasn't sure if she bought my pretense or not.

"Right! Yes, you were the awesome dancer," I said.

She blushed and bent down to grab my purse. "What brings you here? I thought you weren't a student."

"Well, after meeting you and seeing all of the students at the club, I started thinking that maybe it was time for me to get some more classes." I tried to gauge her size carefully. She was wearing some tight, black leggings and a long t-shirt that clung to her voluptuous body in an alluring way.

"That's exciting, what did you pick?" she asked.

"Uh, well, I'm still looking into my options. Probably some upgrading first," I said.

"Yeah, that's always a good start," she said. She looked over my shoulder and waved at someone. "Well, it was good to see you again, Cathy! Maybe we'll see each other on the paths?"

"Sounds good! See you," I said, pretending I also had some place to be.

I watched her leave with a sense of disappointment in me. All of that effort for only a few seconds of time with her. It had been worth it, but it wasn't enough for me. I was looking forward to spending all of my spare time with her.

For now, the best I could do was ensure that everything was ready for her homecoming.

1993, eleven years old:

After her dad disappeared, her mom got even more weird than she'd been before. Jess was surprised to see that sometimes Nathan got into trouble now, too. That wasn't very common before.

She had cried every night for the first few months, but then she felt like she had no more tears in her. Like she'd used up all of the water she had crying over him.

Her mom had made her and Nathan talk to some adults. Then she pestered them about the cost of the adults. It didn't make sense to Jess, but she did everything she could to stay in her mother's good graces.

Now that they were a "one-income family", her mom had to work longer hours than she did before. That meant that Jess was mostly responsible for Nathan after school. Babysitters were a huge expense and her mom was broke.

Every now and then, she would hear her mom on the phone. It wasn't that hard to hear through the paper walls of the trailer. And her mom didn't try to keep her voice down, either. The rules were different for her, she said.

"Daryl, I don't know what to tell you. He isn't helping out and I have bills," she heard one night.

Jess had asked if she could sell some of her toys to help her mom with the bills, but that just got her laughed at. Apparently, the stuff she owned wasn't worth much of anything and there was no point even trying.

At least she'd been willing to sell some of her stuff. Nathan had clung to his toys like his life depended on them and had refused to help Jess.

Now that she could hear the phone conversation, she was even more worried than she had been before. If they couldn't pay the bills, they would end up on the streets. They would be hobos.

"I can't come help with Mom. I have to work and gas isn't cheap. And what would I do with the kids? Cart them along with me to the hospital? I don't think so."

Grandma was in the hospital again. Jess couldn't remember exactly what was wrong, but her mom said it was something to do with her heart. It had been broken somehow. She didn't understand.

Nathan was always asleep for these late-night conversations, but Jess always sat awake listening for them. She missed her uncle Daryl, too.

When she was really sad, she tried to think of watching the sunrise with her dad. She wasn't allowed to leave the trailer too early in the morning, but sometimes, if she was really quiet, she would sneak out of the room and watch it from the kitchen window. Maybe her dad was watching it, too.

She had been shocked when her mother had come home and said she was seeing a doctor for her mind. Lorraine had never thought much about those who had to see those kinds of doctors, and she'd told her kids about it several times.

"They're just feeling sorry for themselves and looking for an excuse to have a pity-party," she said when Jess told her someone at school had been talking to one. "And those quacks will take all of the money you have just to pat you on the shoulder and say 'There, there.'"

But maybe her mom was sad, too. Jess couldn't recall seeing her cry, mostly her mom just acted angry. Sometimes, though, people acted angry when they were really feeling sad. Or, at least, that was what the adults had told her.

It took a long time before her mom went to see the doctor though. Jess had long since stopped crying. She'd wanted to call her dad more than once, but she didn't know if he had a phone number. And he wouldn't be listed in the phone book they had just yet, so there was no point looking there.

Plus her mom would be so mad if she racked up the phone bill just to say hi to her dad.

Now that she was seeing a doctor though, her mom was doing all kinds of weird things. She carried a diary with her everywhere. No one was allowed to look at the diary, but she made notes in it all the time.

Sometimes she would hang up the phone and write for half an hour in the book.

She also started exercising more. Whenever she could, she would throw in one of the tapes with the girls in bathing suits. Then she would dance in the living room. When she'd worked up a sweat, her mom would come into the kitchen and grab a coke from the fridge before telling Jess that she should probably exercise, too.

One day, her mom was late coming home from work. She had to work late because of an appointment with the doctor. Jess had fed Nathan some hotdogs and Kraft Dinner for supper, carefully putting the leftovers in a Tupperware container for her mom. "Waste not, want not" was the new motto in their house.

When her mom came home, she was too agitated to speak. Instead of having a coke, she went into the cupboard above the fridge and pulled out the grown-up drinks.

"Kids," she said as she poured an amber liquid into a glass. "My doctor told me today that I have some homework to do."

Homework was never any fun and Jess felt sorry for her. She watched her mom drink the liquid and then pour another.

"My homework involves you guys," she said. Now she sat at the table with them, holding the cup with two hands. "I'm supposed to get you two to write a letter saying what it is you love about me. In that letter, I need you to tell me how you feel about your dad finding a new family and leaving us behind. Do you think you can do that for me?"

Lorraine looked so miserable when she asked that Jess thought her heart would never stop hurting for her. "You know we love you, Mommy!" she said.

"I know, Jess, my love. The reason the doctor wants you to write it down is so that I can look at the letter whenever I'm sad."

For once, Jess and Nathan didn't fight as they worked together on the letter. Jess had to write it out, of course, because Nathan's writing wasn't neat. It took about two hours to get everything just right, but they were happy with the result.

Dear Mommy,

Me and Nathan love you all the way to the moon. You take care of us and work extra hard just to keep a roof over our heads and shirts on our back.

You make the best lazanya we've ever had.

We love listening to you sing and talk to the actors on the T.V.

We're sad that Daddy didn't love us enough to stay. He made you laugh and smile lots, and now you don't do that very much.

Daddy should never have left us for a new family. WE are his family.

You are the most pretty woman in the world and he should have loved you like you deserv.

You love us so much that we know we don't need Daddy here with us. You're a mom and a dad, and so we will be just fine.

Thank you for always buying us food and doing our londry. We make a lot of it!

Please don't forget any of this. You'll be happy again one day.

Love:

Jess and Nathan

Jess was disappointed that her mom didn't cry when she read it, but she was happy that it made her smile. Her mom tucked it into her diary right away and then heated up her supper before sending them to brush their teeth and go to bed.

That night, her mom spoke on the phone again, but this time it wasn't to Uncle Daryl. Or at least, Jess didn't think so.

"The retainer is only good for ten hours. After that, it's by the minute… It better not take months, I don't have that kind of money… You think?… Yeah, I've been writing everything down."

The television came on and Jess couldn't hear anything except the late-night news.

For the first time in a long time, Jess didn't think about her dad that night. Instead, she thought about her mom and what she could do to make her life a little bit happier.

She fell asleep to the lull of her mother's voice and the weatherman's forecast.

***

2019:

My mother still lived in the same trailer we'd had when we grew up. Which essentially meant that it was still a piece of shit.

Sure, she'd updated a few things. Appliances mostly as they'd gone the way of the dodo. There were new couches, too, I thought. It had been a while and I tried to make my stay as brief as humanly possible.

I was surprised today to see that she'd put new siding on the trailer. Gone was the drab yellowish tan of all seventies trailers, replaced with a cheery blue that didn't seem right. It was a wolf dressed in sheep's clothing.

There wasn't room for my truck and Nathan's Equinox in the driveway, so I parked on the road. I wondered if I was late. A lecture would be a grand way to start the evening.

Inside there were improvements as well. There was new laminate throughout the place and a new television. The ham did smell good, even though I would have preferred lasagna.

"Jess! You made it, we were beginning to worry," said Mom.

Jenny stood behind Mom with a smile plastered on her face. The baby (Simon?) was in her arms and chewing on his thumb. Even with the smile, her narrow face still looked pinched. The woman was perpetually unhappy.

"You said supper was at six," I said. I'd made sure I was on time.

"It's usually courteous to show up an hour before." My brother came from the hall and wrapped his arms around Jenny. "You know, to visit."

"Oh." The awkwardness had already descended. I crossed my arms and then uncrossed them, unsure what to do with myself. "The ham smells good," I said finally.

"I don't think you've met Sebastian yet, have you?" said Mom. She pulled the baby out of Jenny's arms and brought him over to me. "This is your nephew. Would you like to hold him?"

"No-" I tried to pull away, but Mom didn't give me much of a choice. She shoved the kid into my arms and backed away.

"A baby looks good on you, Jess," she said with a coy smile.

It wouldn't stop wiggling around in my arms. Then it started to cry and I held it out at arm's length. Nathan pushed past Mom and grabbed him from me.

"And you have great maternal instincts…" he muttered.

"Did you remember your gift for Sebastian?" asked Mom.

I stared at her blankly for a second before remembering that I was supposed to bring a gift to the baby shower that I never went to.

I pulled my wallet out of my pocket and grabbed a twenty. "Here, you can put it toward his education or something," I said as I handed Nathan the money.

Jenny snatched the bill out of Nathan's hands and gave me a gracious smile. "That's so kind of you to think of his future, Jess. Thank you very much." She gave Nathan a nudge with her elbow.

"Yeah, Jess, thanks. Appreciate it."

As per usual, Mom had a list of stuff for us to do while we were there. I felt I got off light this time, I just had to set the table. Nathan was stuck looking at her wash machine and seeing if he could do anything about it.

Jenny nursed Sebastian and then put him down on a blanket before she came to help me. He made gurgling and cooing sounds that I did my best to ignore. On the plus side, it made small talk difficult.

Supper was tasty enough. Ham, scalloped potatoes and peas were always tasty. Especially when you didn't have to cook it yourself.

For whatever reason, Mom wasn't herself while we ate. She only picked at the food on her plate and pushed the peas around. Twice she excused herself to go to the washroom and when she came back the second time, I could see she'd been crying.

I wasn't going to ask. There were many reasons Mom could be in the bathroom crying, not the least of which was that I hadn't gotten Sebastian a proper gift.

Nathan, on the other hand, recognized her distress and asked her what was wrong.

"Everything okay, Mom? You seem upset."

She set her utensils down and then clasped her hands in front of herself on the table. "Actually, I asked you all here so I could tell you something," she said. "Recently, I haven't been feeling well, so I went to the doctor and he ran some tests." Now the tears flowed freely. "The diagnosis is stage three lung cancer."

The atmosphere in the room felt even more suffocating once Mom stopped talking. I was frozen with a piece of ham halfway to my mouth.

"Cancer?" I said at the same time that Jenny burst into tears. She got up from the table and ran to the bathroom. Nathan didn't chase after her though. He sat at the table, frozen as well.

"Yes. Cancer," Mom said quietly.

My appetite disappeared and I felt like I couldn't breathe. I set my fork down and closed my eyes, focusing on taking deep breaths.

"Wha-Are... Are there treatments?" Nathan finally asked.

"There are. All kinds of pills and radiation therapy. There's even the option of surgery, I think."

"So you'll be okay?" I asked.

She shook her head slowly and, to my surprise, reached out to hold my hand. "I don't think I want to go through any of the side effects that come with it."

"You're just giving up?" I thought I was going to choke on the words. My heart was racing and my breath was coming in short gasps. I didn't understand what was happening to me. "You're just going to go?"

A cry tore through the silence and Nathan jumped up to grab Sebastian. The baby was suddenly howling so loud that I couldn't think.

"Mom!" I shouted. "You're going to leave us?"

She didn't respond, only cried. I stood up from the table, knocking my drink over, but I didn't stop. I ran out of the trailer without looking back.

14

Hutchinson slumped in his desk and rubbed his temples. In front of him was the sketch of the suspect from the night Ed was attacked and the sketch of Walker's mystery woman.

Many factors came into play when considering the sketches. First was that Ed was attacked at night and he didn't have anything to see the face of the attacker besides the nearby streetlights. And then he'd struck his head.

Witnesses were notoriously unreliable when it came to passing along information. You could have two people standing side by side, watching the exact same scene playing out and they would still tell two slightly different versions of the story.

From what he understood, differences in versions were the result of the separate life experiences each witness had experienced.

One would notice that the attacker had a handlebar moustache because they'd had bad experiences with someone who'd had similar facial hair. The other would tell you about the tattoos on the backs of his hand in detail.

When you considered Ed's head injury then his perspective had likely altered.

As for Paul, when the girl had come in, the lighting had been low. He had a feeling Paul was the type to have a joint on his break, which meant that his perception might be dramatically altered from what the girl actually looked like.

The one thing that bothered him, though, was how certain Ed had been when he came to talk to the precinct.

"... the guy wasn't taller than me. He definitely wasn't fat."

Was it possible that Walker had been set up? Hutchinson had to be careful. He couldn't bring forward damning evidence unless he had something concrete that proved that Walker wasn't the guy. Anything less would make them look like they were just a bunch of fools.

The press already had enough fun with that.

He picked up the phone, hesitating only a moment before he dialled.

The phone rang for a while before a woman answered. "Hello?" she said.

"Hi, this is Sergeant Hutchinson from the EPS, I was wondering if your husband was home."

"You want to talk to Ed? Is everything okay?" The worry in her voice made him wince. This poor woman had had her share of scary news lately. He didn't like adding to her plate.

"Everything's fine. I'm just calling to see how he's doing. We've been thinking about him here," he said. The lie left his mouth without a thought. He wasn't going to stress Milly out any more than necessary.

"Oh, well, that's very kind of you. He's just in the garage. I'll go get him for you." He heard her call out Ed's name as she carried the phone to him.

"Hutchinson," he said curtly when Milly gave him the phone.

"Ed, hey, I was wondering if we could go for coffee in the next couple of days. I have some thoughts that I want to run by you if you don't mind."

"You're second-guessing yourself, aren't you?"

"I'm being thorough," said Hutchinson. Ed had every right to be upset with him and the job they had done, but he wasn't going to play games with the man. He wouldn't tolerate rudeness either.

"Yeah, I can swing by this afternoon."

"Not here. I'll meet you at the Starbucks around the corner at two."

"I'll be there."

Hutchinson didn't have to kill much time before meeting Ed. Between meetings and filling out reports, he kept himself busy. Part of him wished he could have brought Ed into the precinct. It might have been easier to go over events with the guard if he had the file in front of him.

But he wasn't going to risk anyone becoming suspicious about what he was getting up to.

He was out the door fifteen minutes early, telling the receptionist that he would be taking a late lunch. She barely noticed him going, giving him a quick smile before answering the ringing phone.

He hurried down the street, choosing to walk rather than drive. It was unseasonably warm out and he figured the fresh air would do him good.

Ed was waiting for him at a table in the corner with two black coffees. Hutchinson was glad to see that Ed seemed to be moving a bit better. He still wore the sling, but there wasn't as much pain in his body as there had been before.

"Hey," Hutchinson said as he sat down. "You didn't have to buy, thank you."

"I would have put something extra in there if they allowed it in this place, but something tells me the barista would be upset if I broke out a flask."

Hutchinson chuckled at the bad joke and took a sip of his drink. The coffee was a marked improvement over what he'd had that morning at the office. If it didn't go against every fibre of common sense that he had, Hutchinson would grab a coffee here every morning.

Instead, it was a luxury for him.

They talked for a minute, exchanging pleasantries and asking about families. He hadn't known Ed until the incident, but the more he talked to him, the more he liked the guy. He figured they might one day be friends.

"But you didn't bring me here to talk about my grandkids," Ed said finally.

"No," said Hutchinson. "I've actually given some thought to what you were saying the last time I saw you. You're right, Walker doesn't fit, but I can't fight the higher-ups on this one. I'd be putting my job on the line."

Ed nodded in agreement, he'd been there, too.

"But I can't shake the feeling that something isn't right. It's like the puzzle piece is just a little bit off. At first, it looks like it fits, and then as you try to build around it, you realize that it's not the right piece."

He reached down to his briefcase and pulled out the sketch of Ed's assailant. He laid it on the table in front of the man. "This was the person you described as seeing the night you were attacked," he said. "Do you remember any other details about that night?"

"No, I don't. I told the detective everything I could remember."

Hutchinson pulled out the second sketch and laid it next to the first. "I need to know if you think this might be the same person."

The sketches did have a lot of similarities, but again, it was down to the witness's perception.

"Is this a woman?" asked Ed as he examined Walker's girl.

"Yes, it is."

"You think that my attacker was a woman?" asked Ed. He sounded incredulous and a little bit insulted.

"I'm not saying anything right now, Ed. I'm looking for your opinion, that's all."

Ed grumbled and pulled a pair of glasses out of his coat pocket, perching them on the end of his nose. He picked up both pictures and held them close together.

"There are some similarities. I mean, either one really could be a small guy, too."

"For sure, it could have been a young guy that got to you. But you said that Walker definitely wasn't the guy. And I've looked into him. He had nothing going on in his life. He worked, headed to the bar and then went home to sleep it off. The next morning, he would get up and start all over again.

"But the bartender said that not too long ago, Walker had the attention of a woman. I'd remembered what you said about the size of your attacker and I asked the bartender to talk to our sketch artist. This was the result."

Ed laid the pictures down again and then tucked his glasses back into his pocket. "I can't say for sure. It was dark when I was attacked and I didn't get a real detailed look at the person."

Hutchinson nodded, feeling defeat well inside him. It had been pointless chasing down this little feeling. A waste of his time.

"But," said Ed, filling Hutchinson with hope again, "I would say this girl is more like the attacker than Walker was. It definitely wasn't the guy you brought in. He's just a poor schmuck who was in the wrong place at the wrong time."

That was all he needed to hear. Somehow, this girl was connected to what was going on, he just knew it. Now he had to prove it.

***

2019:

After I'd left Mom's the other night, Nathan had beat me to my trailer. I didn't think I could tell anyone where I'd driven even if I'd been put to the question by the Spanish Inquisition.

I had just needed to get away from all of it. Mom crying, the baby screaming and the claustrophobic feeling I had suddenly developed while sitting at the table.

Thankfully, Nathan had left his son behind when he came to see me. I didn't think I could have dealt with it if he'd brought the plague bag along.

"So, Mom's worried you're going to go kill yourself, or something," he said casually as I got out of my truck.

"Why would I do that?"

"Exactly what I said. You don't care about anyone enough to kill yourself if they died."

"Fuck off, Nathan," I said. I tried to push past him into my trailer. I could hear Thrasher whining inside.

"I don't know why you're acting like this." He had one hand pressed up against my shoulder to stop me from going in. "But I'm upset, too. Mom'll come around once she knows she's got our support."

I didn't say anything. I just pulled his hand off my shoulder and stared at him.

"She does have your support, right?" he asked with a frown.

"Why the fuck would I give her that? She just told me that she wants to leave us, just like Dad did."

"You know, if you were more involved in her life, you might understand her decision a little bit better. You're so selfish, though, that you don't even notice how she's falling apart on her own. Jenny and I do all we can, but you don't even give a shit. I'm not sure why you're so surprised she wouldn't want to stick around for another twenty years. I wouldn't."

"What does she have to be sad about?" I asked. "She hated having us at home, she couldn't make that any more clear."

"No," he said firmly. "She hated having *you* around. You were miserable all the time and constantly screwing up. I can't imagine it was any fun for her."

"Well then, she'll be fine without my support," I said.

"Jess, you're still her kid. She still cares about you. You've never tried to be easy on her. It's like you've been punishing her for Dad leaving." He clenched his fists. "*Newsflash*! She's not the reason he left! It was because he couldn't stand to watch you fuck up your life. He made that very clear."

I felt like someone had jabbed a finger into a wound. The breath whooshed out from me. I was long past this. Why was I feeling so upset about it all? It was nearly thirty fucking years ago that he'd left us behind to fend for ourselves.

And Mom? She had made sure that I never had much for self-esteem. Whenever I had the chance to feel good about myself, she would pull the rug out from under me. Then she would come to me later, crying about how she'd made a mistake and that she was only trying to toughen me up or some shit.

"Nathan," I said through clenched teeth. "Get out of my way."

He left then, throwing his hands up in the air and swearing at me. I waited until he was gone and then I ran inside and threw myself onto the couch, letting Thrasher come in to cuddle me.

I bawled like a small child for what seemed like forever. I hadn't thought I would ever feel that way again. I had vowed not to let anyone make me feel that way.

How dare she choose to leave us behind? Did she hate me as much as Dad did?

I was miserable when I went in to work on Monday morning. I hadn't showered for four days and I didn't bother to change into my work clothes when I left. I threw my hair up in a rubber band and called it good, pulling a ball cap low on my head.

I didn't think Mike could possibly look more depressed than he was after what had happened to Dave. When I told him that I needed to take some time off of work, he turned pale.

This couldn't have come at a worse time at work. With Dave being on WCB, we were already running short-staffed. Mike hadn't been allowed to hire a temporary employee to replace Dave, so the rest of us had been busting our ass.

The only reason I'd gotten the weekend off to see my family was because I was Mike's favourite employee. He didn't want me to burn out or be resentful. He needed me to stick around.

Which was why I felt like shit as I sat in his office. When you'd disappointed people as much as I had, you'd think that I'd grown numb to the feeling I got each time. Instead, it was the opposite with me.

For the most part, I wouldn't set anyone's expectations very high. If they didn't think I would accomplish much, then I couldn't let them down.

At work, though, it had been so easy to run circles around the other guys. They didn't need to work as much as I did. Those guys – kids, really – had families they could fall back on if things got desperate.

I did not. I needed the job and I needed my boss to like me. It wasn't like I had the personality to work any job where I had to deal with the public. This job at the warehouse was like a blessing from Jesus himself.

Mike even stood up for me when the guys were assholes. It was bizarre to feel this reluctance to stress him out.

"How long do you think you'll need off?" he asked.

"Honestly, Mike. I'm not sure. Just, with everything that happened with Dave and stuff. I can't help but feel responsible for that. And then my mom is sick. It's too much for me."

He handed me the paperwork for short-term disability. It didn't fail to register with me that he didn't offer me a WCB report. He definitely didn't want to go there.

It didn't matter, though. All I needed was a reason to see a doctor. The couple of weeks off of work would just be a bonus. Maybe I would even go see my mother and see how she was doing.

It wasn't likely, but not outside the realm of possibility.

She hadn't called me since the dinner. I wasn't sure if I was relieved or hurt by that. I hated wasting my time talking to her, but at the same time, it was nice to have someone interested in my life.

Why had I let that get to me?

The main worry I had was that somehow this was going to get in the way of my plans. It was frustrating that Nathan had come to my house two times in the last few months. Before that, it had been years since he'd dropped by.

Now with Mom being sick, it was very likely that those visits would become more frequent. The only hope I had left was that if Mom did die, he might just leave me alone. We weren't exactly besties.

Maybe there would be some money in it for me, too. Unless she'd spent everything on renos for the trailer.

And now that I thought about it, I realized she would likely leave all of her money to Nathan's kid.

It disgusted me to know that Sebastian would grow up idolizing a grandmother he didn't have to get to know. She would live on in Nathan's memory like a martyr and Sebastian would think that she walked on water when he grew up.

The thought left a terrible taste in my mouth.

As soon as I got to my truck, I called my doctor's office. It was time to put some things into action.

15

Walker didn't fit in at the prison at all. He was currently in the remand centre downtown and Hutchinson had decided to pay the man a visit.

He'd never personally met the guy. There hadn't been any need.

Talking to Walker would be a delicate thing. Hutchinson hoped he still had the touch because time at the desk tended to weaken the mind.

Walker sat there in his orange jumpsuit. His hands were cuffed in front of him and when Hutchinson made the mistake of looking into his eyes, he had to quickly look away. He hoped they had Walker on suicide watch. He hadn't seen such despair in ages.

The silence was almost uncomfortable at first. Both men were waiting for the other to speak.

Interrogation training kicked in for Hutchinson and he managed to keep his silence the longest. It bought him time to think about how he was going to approach the topic and showed Walker that he was in charge.

"Did you just come here to gloat?" asked Walker in a monotone.

Hutchinson waited for a few seconds before answering. "No." Then he leaned forward onto the table.

"I've come here to get a few more details from you."

"Then I want my lawyer," Walker replied.

"That's absolutely your right. But I'm not here to talk about you." A look of confusion crossed Walker's face, but it faded as quickly as it had come. "I want to talk to you about your accomplice."

"My accomplice?" This time the confusion stayed on his face. "How can I have an accomplice when I didn't do anything?"

Hutchinson took a second to think before answering. "We have physical evidence that places you at the scene of the crime. That's pretty hard to refute."

Walker shook his head and then slammed his fists onto the table. "How many times do I have to tell you guys? I don't know how that all got there!"

"You've been spotted with someone else around the same time. In fact, I was told you two were pretty close."

"What? I don't know what you're talking about. I'm not exactly Mr. Popular. I keep to myself. Work, bar, home. It doesn't change."

"That's not what we've been told," said Hutchinson.

"Well, what have you been told?"

"That there was a girl."

Walker burst into laughter at the words. "There's no girl. Hasn't been a girl for years."

"That's not what the bartender tells us."

"Paul? He said I was with a girl?"

Hutchinson could feel the frustration building in him. If Walker was lying, he was a world-class actor. "Yeah."

Walker leaned back in his chair with a sardonic grin on his face. "Look at me. Do I look like the kind of guy who gets the girl?"

"How much do you drink when you're at the bar?"

"A bit." Hutchinson nearly rolled his eyes at the understatement. Clearly, Walker drank enough to put most to shame. If Walker was an alcoholic, it was possible that he had blacked out that night.

That was not something he would want to admit. If he had blackouts often, his defense would be worthless. It also wouldn't explain how he managed to get his vehicle home every night, which he was probably more worried about.

Talking to Walker was a dead end. The man had isolated himself so well that there was nobody except a bartender to give a clue about what he'd been up to. One drunken night with a woman was certainly not a crime. It also didn't necessarily mean anything.

Hutchinson had asked Paul if they still had security footage from that night, but it was as expected. They didn't keep all of the footage, the SD card was only so big and eventually they had to save over the top of it.

"Okay, Mr. Walker," he said. "I guess we're done here for now."

Walker slumped down into his metal chair and the animation that he'd begun to show slid off of his body. He looked like an automaton waiting to be wound up.

Hutchinson lifted his hand to the guard and made his way out.

To say the interview had been disappointing would have been quite the understatement. Now, he felt like he needed a drink.

He wondered if he could have approached things differently. If he'd asked the right questions, he might have received a different reaction. He wished he could go to someone else with the information and get someone else to help him out, but retirement was just around the corner. He would be a fool to toss it all away on a little feeling.

***

1994, twelve years old:

When Jess had first seen Carrie, the scene that remained etched into her mind forever was the locker room. The rest of the movie had whirred by in a blur as she'd tried to process how people could be so horrible to someone.

In the last couple of years, Jess had noticed that the kids at school were treating her differently, too. The thought of going through something like that scene horrified her daily.

As the treatment got worse and worse, she began to have nightmares about it.

She thought she would be just like Carrie. Everyone would have their periods long before her. The boys were already commenting on her flat chest as other girls developed the buds that would soon turn into breasts.

Jess had nothing, even if she tried. Her mom didn't even bother getting her a training bra.

"Why waste the money on it? You should count that as a blessing. These damn things are no fun."

Now that she was required to wear gym strip, though, it was becoming an issue. There were a few private change rooms in the locker room, but for the most part, the girls just changed in front of the lockers.

Every single one of them had a bra. Jess could not bring herself to take off her shirt in front of them for fear of being made fun of.

She prayed for the day she got her period so she could have something in common with the girls giggling in the change room.

When the new girl started in her class, Jess was relieved. The girl was an immigrant and her body was more interesting than Jess's was. And Amara was nicer than the others.

At least she didn't make fun of Jess to her face. If she talked about her, it was safely behind her back where the words couldn't hurt her.

Amara's betrayal of Jess's positive assessment caught Jess off guard. She knew what to expect from the other girls, but when Amara ripped open the curtain to her small change room, she shrieked.

"This is a girl's change room," she said to Jess. Then she pulled Jess's clothes out of the small space. "Just like I thought. No bra. You're in the wrong place."

The girls all gathered behind her, laughing. Jess crossed her arms, doing her best to hide her bare chest.

When one of the girls pulled the curtain closed again, she thought someone had taken pity on her. She was wrong.

The laughter continued as the shower turned on. "Everyone will see your nipples now!" said Amara.

Hot tears streamed down Jess's face. She sat on the bench and hugged her legs to her chest as she listened to the rest of the girls laugh. Every time the showerhead turned off, one of them would run over there and push the button to turn it back on.

It wasn't until she was sure everyone had left that she dared to peek outside of the curtain.

Her clothes were laying in a puddle of water on the floor in the shower room. She crept over there and grabbed her shirt, a white t-shirt. The girls had used ice-cold water. Her hands started to ache as she struggled to wring the water out of her shirt and jeans.

After she had her clothes spread out on the bench, she went back for her gym strip. It, too, had been soaked through. When she'd dried her shorts and shirt as much as she could, she crammed it into her bag. She would have to remember to bring it home or it would go mouldy in there.

She struggled into her jeans and shirt. The cold was so intense, she felt goosebumps break out on her arms. And as promised, her nipples hardened under her shirt, poking hard against the fabric.

Her locker was all the way across the school. She would have to walk down the hall to get her coat to cover up.

Everyone was in class right now, so she felt she should be safe to make a dash to her locker. She poked her head out of the room and looked both ways before she started speed-walking down the hall.

When she finally reached her locker, she had to fight back tears of relief. She pulled it open and yanked her spring jacket out. She pulled it on and zipped it to the top before shoving her gym strip into her locker.

"Excuse me, Jess. Is there a reason you haven't bothered to show up to class?"

She felt her stomach sink. It was Mr. Landers, the teacher of the class she was supposed to be in right now. He had no patience for anyone who was late and didn't tolerate excuses.

He'd told the class many times that in middle school, tardiness was not tolerated. They were expected to act like grown-ups as much as possible.

"I, uh, I needed a shower after gym," she said.

He put his hand on his hips, flipping his tweed jacket back as he did. "In your clothes? You're leaving puddles all over the floor."

She looked down the hall and realized he was right. Her wet socks had made footprints all the way to her locker. There was no way to miss it.

"Some girls threw my clothes into the shower stall…" she said.

That was a mistake. "Yeah, Jess, this isn't the first time you've blamed others for your problems. You need to start taking some onus here. You realize that you've missed your exam?"

That hadn't even crossed her mind. She'd stayed up studying for it, too. She wondered if that was why the girls had picked on her. They hated that she did so well in school. If she cared to put in the effort, she could easily be the top of her class.

She didn't want the attention, though. And now that thought was only reinforced.

"Can I take it tomorrow?" she asked.

"No. People who skip class don't get a second chance at tests. You're going to have to deal with a zero on that one. And detention, I think." He looked at her feet with a glare. "If you can't respect the school or the work the custodians put in, then you can join them for an evening and learn some."

When the bell rang, she received her dismissal from him. But it meant that she had to stand there in a puddle of water as students pushed around her. Some even slipped in the bit of water that she had dripped down the hall.

No one dared to laugh at her in front of Mr. Landers, but she could see the twinkling eyes and the grins as people looked at her.

She stood in front of her locker as long as she could. Eventually, she had to grab her books for her next class and get going. Mr. Landers stayed where he was, making sure she went on her way.

***

2019:

In the end, I decided to go see my mother. She only worked part-time now that she was ill and I invited myself over for lunch.

Almost like she wanted to rub in my previous departure, the menu was ham sandwiches and potato salad. I made no comment as I ate. I didn't know what to say to her. There was nothing she could say that would quiet my feeling of betrayal, and to get what I wanted out of this impromptu date, I had to be civil.

"So how old is Sebastian now?" I asked. It was the only topic I knew she could yak about for hours without much from me.

It hurt more than expected to see her face light up at his name. I didn't recall ever receiving such a look from her. If I had, I must have been a baby myself.

She nattered on as we ate. I learned everything from his age to his latest bowel movements. I also learned more about Jenny than I ever cared to know. Talking about stitches down there and cracked nipples was a little over the top.

It was hard to listen to her talk about someone with so much love. Each word was like a little pin stabbing into my skin. One pin was bearable and hardly noticeable, but having one stabbed into you over and over again was awful.

She must have been able to read the pain in my expression because she eventually trailed off.

"It's too bad that I won't ever get to hold your baby," she said.

If she'd meant for that statement to hurt, she didn't know me as well as she thought. There was no way in hell that I would ever bring a child into this world. *People are horrible and I wouldn't want to put anyone through the shit I've gone through in my life.*

Still, I had to be careful how I spoke to her. A fight was the last thing I needed right now.

"If you'd try the chemo, you might get to one day," I said. Meekness wasn't my strong suit, but I thought I pulled it off pretty well.

"Jess, Nathan and I already had this conversation. I would rather live out the rest of my life knowing it's going to end soon rather than hope for a little more time. Realistically, the survival rate is low, so why would I want to put myself through any additional pain?"

A brief flash of the pain I'd felt before sizzled through my chest, but I quickly tamped it down.

"You're going to miss out on watching Sebastian grow up. And what if they have more kids?"

She gave a dramatic sigh. "Jess, I'm done talking about this. It's depressing."

There wasn't much to say to that, so I let the subject drop. She asked me how work was going and I lied to her. I told her Dave was doing great and that I was enjoying it.

It was none of her business that I had taken some time off.

"I was surprised that you could come for lunch today," she said.

"I have a doctor's appointment, so I took the afternoon off. I figured I would spend some time with you, too."

She reached out and grabbed my hand again. "That's so sweet of you."

I made a big deal about checking my phone for the time. "I'd better get going though. I want to catch the early bus. I don't want to risk being late."

"The bus? You didn't bring your truck?"

"No," I said. "It's been acting up lately, which is really too bad. I have to get up an hour earlier to get into work and that's hard on Thrasher."

"What's wrong with it?" she asked, as though she would have the slightest clue what she was talking about.

"It's making some weird noises. I'm going to bring it in to the mechanic this weekend, I just wanted to wait for payday."

"So you have to take the bus for the rest of the week?" Her mock concern wasn't as endearing as she wanted it to be, but I did my best to play along.

"Yeah, it's no big deal. I just might have to clean up a mess from Thrasher when I get home is all."

"Why don't you take my car? I'm not going anywhere over the next few days. And if I need a ride, I can give Jenny a call."

Bingo!

"No, Mom. I don't want to put you out. Jenny has lots on her plate. And what if there's an emergency?"

"Nonsense!" She pulled her purse out of the hall closet. "Here's the keys. Just make sure to fill it with gas before you bring it back."

"Well…" I said slowly, drawing the moment out. "Are you sure?"

"Of course! And now we can spend some more time visiting since you don't have to catch the bus."

I hadn't thought of that, I did my best to hide the annoyance I was feeling. "I really appreciate it, Mom."

16

The doctor's appointment was really only a formality at this point. I knew that I would be accepted for short-term disability, and so did Mike. Unfortunately, it was an important formality.

The waiting room was packed full of people. I did my best to sit as far from anyone as I could, praying that none of the snot-nosed kids would try to make googly eyes at me. I wasn't in the mood for anything like that.

It had been surprisingly easy to score the car from mom. I hadn't heard from Nathan yet, I was waiting for that one. He wouldn't be happy that she was helping me out. Especially if he found that there was nothing wrong with my truck.

However, I doubted he would run down to check on me again. He hated chasing me around and it was only for a week. It wasn't that big a deal.

I had to do things this week. The weather would be changing soon and there would be no more running along the Marigold Path for the next couple of months.

I couldn't wait that long. I would go crazy, probably end up spending way too much time with my mother, and that wouldn't be healthy, given how well we got along. She'd end up in an early grave and I'd be in jail for homicide.

"Jess," said a voice near the desk. The nurse was waiting to take me to my room, finally. I'd only been sitting here for half an hour.

I followed her down the sterile white hall to one of the ten offices in the back. I hadn't been to the doctor in years. I hated these places, but really, who didn't?

It was another twenty minutes of sitting in the chair inside the office. The only decoration in the room was a weird abstract painting that probably had a hefty price tag attached to it at some point.

When my doctor finally came in with an apology for the wait, I was ready to scream from boredom. I wasn't a reader and there was only so much time a person could spend on their phone before they went crazy.

"So Jess, what can we help you with today?" asked Dr. Herning. I liked this guy, and not just because he reminded me of McSteamy. He never lectured me about coming in more often or that I should be considering mammograms soon.

Not that there was anything to see there.

I pulled the forms out of my pocket and unfolded them for him. "I need to take some stress leave from work."

"I'm sorry to hear that," he said as I handed him the forms. "What's been going on?"

I outlined things for him as quickly as I could. I mentioned Dave's incident but didn't go into too much detail. I focused more on my mom's illness. That kind of stuff was gold and for once, I wasn't making anything up.

He grabbed a pen and started filling the forms out as I spoke.

"Is there anything I can take to help me sleep? I can't seem to turn my mind off."

"Yes, there are a few different options. Can you tell me more about your sleep? What specifically are you struggling with at night? Can you fall asleep easily?"

"I can fall asleep after a while, but then I keep waking up. It's really hard to deal with."

He nodded at my description and then turned to his computer. "Well, I think there is something I can give that will both help you fall asleep and keep you asleep for eight hours. It's important that you stick to the dosage I give you, though. You're a small woman and if you mess with the dosage, you might have some nasty side effects."

He printed a page and handed it over to me but still continued talking. "Also, ask your pharmacist for the pamphlet about the medication. There are some side effects you will notice at first and it's important that you wean yourself off of this one. This drug isn't one that you can take willy nilly.

"I'm giving you enough for four weeks, the same amount of time I'm recommending for your stress leave, too. Obviously, if you feel you're ready to go back to work you can at any time, I just want to make sure you have plenty of time to rest.

"I would like to see you back in three weeks. By then, the side effects should be gone and we should have an idea of whether the medication is working or not. We'll also see how your mental state is and see if you need more time off from work or if you'll be okay."

The diagnosis and prescription couldn't have been more welcome. For the first time in a while, I felt like things were going my way. Mike wouldn't be happy, but he would have to deal. And maybe if things went well, I could come back earlier.

On my way home, I stopped at the drugstore to fill my prescription. I was getting something called Temazepam. Apparently, it was the good stuff, or at least that was what I was told.

It came in gel capsules which was a bit annoying, I would have to figure out some way to get the powder out.

I felt better than I had in weeks when I made my way home. I wasn't even going to go in to see Mike, I decided. I would just snap pictures of the forms and send them his way. The less I had to talk to him, the better. I didn't need a guilt trip right now.

***

2019:

Laura was getting a headache from all of the different scents at Bath and Body Works. They all smelled nice, but it was too much for her. This wasn't a store she would normally find herself in. She preferred unscented lotions and body wash.

Garett had suggested the place because he knew Brandy liked these products. He was wandering around, looking bored to tears. He said he trusted Laura's instincts more than his own, so really he was only there to offer support. She was the one picking out the gift.

She finally settled on a vanilla lotion. She picked out the accompanying body wash and hand lotion to go with it. "Are you sure this is what we want to get her?"

"She loves this kind of stuff," Garett said.

"Okay, but she's turning twenty-one, right? Do we not want to do something a little more extravagant?"

"Like what? Some wine?"

She sighed in frustration. Brandy's birthday was right around the corner and Garett was only now thinking of gifts for his daughter. Laura liked to give plenty of thought to gifts, but she didn't feel like she knew Brandy well enough to get something really personal.

She'd been hoping that Garett would have a better suggestion than body lotion. *What the hell does he do for Christmas? Give her an iTunes gift card and call it good?*

"We could get her a gift card to the Keg and to a movie," Laura suggested. Or do you think she would like to see something at the theatre downtown?"

He gave her a blank stare. Laura set their items in front of the cashier and ignored him for a moment while she paid for everything. She had insisted that she contribute to the gift as well.

"I don't know if she goes to the theatre. But she would probably like the dinner and movie. She and Austin could have a nice night out whenever they both have time."

"All right, we'll swing by Costco on our way back to your place and grab the stuff. Do you have anything to wrap gifts with?"

"Yeah, there's a whole bin of gift bags and tissue paper downstairs. I don't think I'll ever have to buy one again."

She sent a small prayer of thanks to Emily for that one.

"And they're coming over to your house, right? Have you given any thought to her cake?" Laura asked.

He blushed and shook his head. "I usually just grab something from the store. I'm not much of a baker."

"I was thinking we could order something from a bakery. Not a little kid's cake, but maybe something a bit more fancy. Does she like chocolate?"

"Loves it," he said.

When they got into the car, Laura pulled out her phone. "Well, I'm going to order one right now. It's already short notice as is."

Garett had already spoken to Brandy about having her over for her birthday. She was fine with that because it was on a weeknight.

There were no big party plans. That would be happening on the weekend.

"Thanks for helping me with this," he said. "I've never really been great at this kind of thing. I'm not great with anniversaries or anything like that."

She had figured as much. He'd barely recognized her birthday, choosing only to take her to dinner. They hadn't been dating very long, so the gesture was still nice, but she had a feeling the behaviour wasn't out of the norm for him.

"It's no problem. I like doing this kind of thing. It's fun for me," she assured him. "So Brandy and Austin are definitely on board for supper next Tuesday?"

"Yes," said Garett. "She told me that it wouldn't be a proper birthday if she didn't celebrate with us."

Laura was feeling excited about Brandy's birthday. Part of her wanted to book pedicures for the two of them as well, but she decided to rein herself in this year. There was always next year.

17

I had scoped out the Marigold Path down by the river a few times since I'd spoken to Brandy. I made sure to do it at odd times in the hopes that I wouldn't run into her.

I didn't know where she lived, but if she lived near the University, the paths were within walking distance of her place. Which meant I wouldn't have to worry about her leaving behind a vehicle.

The spare room was cleaned out completely, with the exception of a bed and a dresser. I put a small speaker there and a twenty-inch T.V. The bed was also ready to go.

I'd laid a plank of plywood under the mattress and attached some eye hooks to it. Then I also had the ratchet straps laid out underneath the wood so I could hold her down properly.

The closet was stocked with clothes that I thought would fit.

I was nervous about this, but strangely excited. I had meant it when I told the guys at the warehouse that I was not a dyke. But I was tired of being alone. It was too much.

Mom was planning to leave me, too. I was pretty sure she was the only one who was obligated to put up with me. I would be alone and though I'd always thought that was what I wanted, I wasn't so sure anymore.

"What do you think, bud?" I said to Thrasher. He followed me everywhere and seemed especially interested in my project. I hoped that he liked her, too. I wanted us all to be a family.

Now that the room was all set up, I was ready to put everything in the car. It was time.

There was a parking lot that allowed access to the paths that I had scoped out. It was poorly lit and fairly secluded. The paths were along the river bank and the city had left the carefully-cultivated trees to remain to add to the beauty of the area.

I'd come down a few times to check out the paths and from a distance, I had seen Brandy jogging along with her headphones in. The time of her run seemed pretty consistent and she was alone, which was a relief.

I knew that she was dating someone and I was half-afraid that he would be a jogger, too. I wasn't sure if I could take on two people.

I picked the parking spot the farthest from the streetlight. I had put on some old joggers and put my hair back. I had also brought along my phone and headphones. I wanted to look the part.

She was due to be here in about twenty minutes, which gave me time to get into position down the path.

The paved parts of the area were well maintained, making it easy for me to quickly walk down to the spot I'd picked out. It wasn't too far from my car and it was in one of the areas where the path was just dirt.

The path was clearly maintained by the city or some organization. The grass was shorn close to the ground for a width of two meters and there was little in the way of shoots or roots.

However, there were ruts from rain and mud that had hardened unevenly when people had biked down the path. It was in one of those spots that I positioned myself.

A few joggers passed by me, but they didn't think anything of me taking a break. I pretended to stretch, giving myself an excuse to be hanging out there.

The path was cleared for several meters so I would be able to see Brandy coming. When she came around the corner, I recognized her immediately. She wore reflective gear so she could be easily seen in the dim light.

I waited for only a moment before I collapsed on the path in front of her, crying out in pain.

She slowed down and tugged her earbuds out. "Hey, is everything okay?"

"I think I've sprained my ankle in these ruts," I clutched at my left ankle and breathed heavily.

She crouched down beside me. "Can you move your foot?"

"Yeah," I said. "It just hurts. I stepped wrong and felt my ankle give out." Then I did a double-take, looking at Brandy. "Brandy? Wow, imagine meeting again like this. It's me, Cathy."

"Cathy! Yes, I didn't recognize you in the dark." She flashed me a smile. I felt giddy inside at the sight. "Do you think you can walk?"

"Maybe," I said. "I have my car parked not too far from here. Do you think you could help me get to it?"

"For sure." She stood up and held out her hand. "Here, let me help you up and then you can lean on me while we walk."

I stood slowly, making sure to limp every time I had to set my left foot down. She grabbed my arm and wrapped it around her shoulders and held her other arm around my waist.

She giggled a little as we started out. "We probably look so ridiculous!"

I couldn't help but laugh with her. It was as contagious as a yawn.

As we made our way down the path, another jogger came up behind us. He ran up to us, pulling his earbuds out too. "Hey ladies, everything okay?"

Brandy piped up right away. "Yeah, we're fine. My friend just sprained her ankle. I'm bringing her to her car."

That word, *friend*, almost made me smile, then I had to remember that I was supposedly in a great deal of pain.

"Need some help?" he asked.

I didn't know if she saw the panic in my eyes or if she was just smart enough to avoid strangers when she was alone in the dark. "No, thanks, we can handle it."

"I can carry her," he said, but he didn't come any closer.

"It's fine," I told him. "My car's not that much further."

"You sure?"

"Yes," snapped Brandy. I was surprised at her tone. "We appreciate the offer, but we've got this."

He shrugged his shoulders and then turned to resume his exercise.

"I don't have my pepper spray on me," she said quietly to me. "I forgot it at home. Running into randoms down here makes me nervous sometimes."

"Yeah," I said. It hadn't even occurred to me that she would have pepper spray or some other kind of weapon on hand down here. She was clearly on high alert about her safety when she was running. I hoped I had lulled her a bit with my fake injury.

It didn't take long to reach my car. I half-expected her to comment about the fact that I was parked so far from the light, but she didn't say anything.

"Are you going to be able to drive? I can call someone if you need me to," she said.

"No, I'll be okay to drive. I'll call my brother and ask him to meet me at my place." I pulled the keys out of my pocket and unlocked the door. "Shit."

"What?" she asked.

"I forgot about the seat. I'm borrowing my mother's car right now and it's one of those manual seats that you have to pull forward with the lever. I had to push it back to get out from under the steering wheel. I don't know that I can pull it forward again with my ankle like this."

"I can adjust it for you."

"I would appreciate that," I said, leaning back out of the way.

She leaned forward into the car, feeling for the lever under the seat. As she was looking, I pulled out my folding knife, brought out the blade and pressed it up against her back.

She froze where she was.

"Get into the seat," I said firmly.

"What are you doing?"

"Now!" I snapped. She obeyed and climbed into the seat as I held the knife at her side. "Put your hands on the steering wheel."

Once she had her hands on the wheel, I wrapped a zip tie around it and secured one of them to the wheel. "We're going to go for a drive," I told her. "Give me your phone." She reached into her pocket and handed an iPhone to me. I dropped it to the pavement and stomped on it as hard as I could.

I noticed that she was crying and I gently wiped her tears away. "It'll be okay as long as you do what you're told," I said.

I closed the door and made my way around to the other side. She watched me make my way around the car with no difficulty. When I opened the door, I held the knife out again.

"Don't try anything stupid, Brandy. I won't hesitate to stab you. You'll be dead before you pull anything off." She nodded at me but didn't say a word. Her eyes were puffy and red. She looked terrified. Exactly what I was hoping for.

The more afraid she was of me, the better she would listen.

I sat down in the seat and pulled my seatbelt on. "Put on your belt," I said. You couldn't be too careful.

Too many people got caught because of making tiny mistakes. Look at Ted Bundy. His undoing was a simple traffic stop at the wrong time. Our seatbelts were going to be staying on. I didn't want to give the cops any reason to pull us over.

"Why are you doing this?" Her voice was shaky as she spoke. I ignored her and gave her instructions on where to drive. "Seriously, I don't have any money," she said. "Neither does my family."

I pretended that I didn't hear her. We had to head toward Whyte Ave before we made our way to the busier Whitemud from there. I didn't want to drive on the slower roads any more than I had to.

"No tapping the brakes or trying to send any signals. Try any stupid shit and you won't make it."

A short burst of laughter escaped her lips. It was only a staccato beat of sound, then it turned into a sob.

I watched her closely. The last thing we needed was for her to have a full-blown panic attack while driving. She may unintentionally get us pulled over.

I did my best to remain calm and keep my voice at an even keel. Startling her right now would be a fatal mistake for both of us.

Once we were on the Whitemud and heading east, I lowered the knife a bit. "Nothing will happen if you do what you're told. Do the speed limit, but don't speed. I'll tell you when to change lanes. Otherwise, stay in this one."

She didn't ask any more questions. Her eyes had a glassy look to them and I worried that she was going to fall asleep. She followed every instruction, though, so she was still responsive at least.

When we pulled up to my trailer, I looked over at her and put a hand on her knee. "Home sweet home," I said.

She gave another sob and I pulled out the knife. "No funny business, Brandy. If you're good, you won't get into any trouble."

I got out of the car and made my way around to her side. I reached in and unlatched her seatbelt. Then I brought my knife up to the zip tie and cut it off of her.

I stepped back, holding the knife close to her neck. "Come on out," I said.

She was shaking but she listened to me. I glanced around to see if anyone was watching, but honestly, I didn't live in an area of the city where anyone would be spying on their neighbours. The smart people minded their own business and kept to themselves.

I closed the door behind Brandy and stepped up close to her back with the knife. "You're going to open the gate and go up to the front door," I said in a low voice. "Nod if you understand."

She nodded and started to put her hands out to her side. "Stop it!" I snapped. "Act normal."

Her hands dropped back to her sides and she grabbed the latch for the gate. It pushed in and I let it slam shut behind me as we made our way onto the porch.

Thrasher barked behind the door and started snorting and growling. Brandy froze in her tracks.

"That's my pup," I said. "He's a Doberman named Thrasher. He's a good dog as long as you don't piss me off. Go ahead, open the door. He won't attack once he knows that I'm here."

A hesitant hand reached for the latch on the door. I pressed the knife harder to encourage her to hurry up.

Once she opened the door, I called out to Thrasher, letting him know that I was there. He stopped barking immediately, running forward only to sniff at Brandy. She didn't move as he familiarized himself with her scent.

"Go on," I said, shoving her forward.

She cried out as she stumbled forward, but I stayed right behind her, ushering her along down the hall to the spare room.

When I flicked on the lights, she started ugly crying. "Please," she said. "Please don't do this."

I ignored her again and pushed her forward. "Lay down on the bed and put your hands over your head."

She laid down and raised her hands above her head, sobbing hysterically as she did. "Shhh," I said. "You're okay, love. I'm not going to hurt you."

I put another zip tie around her wrists, pulling them together tightly. Then I wove the chain I'd attached to the board through her arms, pulling it down tightly and hooking it back down again.

I did the same with her feet. Then I sat down beside her and rubbed her stomach. "Hey, hey, hey," I whispered. "You're okay." After a while, she seemed to settle down a bit. "I'm not going to hurt you. You're being a good boy."

There was a roll of duct tape on the dresser next to the bottle of medication. I ripped off a piece of tape and covered her mouth. "This is only temporary," I told her. "As soon as I know I can trust you, I will leave you without the tape. You're going to want to stop crying though, it'll get hard to breathe if you don't." I leaned down and gave her a soft kiss on the forehead. "I'll be in to check on you before bed, okay? You can have a bathroom break then."

I hoped she would stop crying soon. I didn't want her to be sad all the time. I just needed her to get used to living with me. It would be good for Thrasher, too. He needed some other people in his life.

I couldn't stop smiling as I settled in to watch some television. For once in my life, things were working out in my favour.

18

She couldn't feel her arms anymore. Her hands had gone tingly hours ago, and since then, all of the blood seemed to have left her arms. She wiggled her fingers, but it had little effect.

Cathy had been right about crying. The more she sobbed, the more mucus she produced and the harder it was to breathe. It had taken great effort, but she managed to calm herself enough to think clearly and take slow, deep breaths.

The door stayed closed and the lights remained off until her captor came in to let her use the bathroom. Thrasher followed her in every time.

Prior to her kidnapping, if anyone had asked her if there was a particular breed of dog she was afraid of, she would have scoffed. In her mind, it wasn't the breed but the owners that caused the problems.

If owners didn't abuse their dogs, there would be far fewer problems in the animal world.

Now that she'd met Thrasher, she wasn't sure about that. The dog was practically rabid with the amount of aggression it showed. Every time she whimpered, she could hear him growling outside of her door.

When Cathy had brought her to the bathroom, he had sat in there with her, teeth bared, watching her do her business. She would never look at a Doberman the same way again. If she could ever handle being around another dog in comfort.

She didn't understand what was happening. She'd been nice to Cathy when they met. Even helped her to her car and helped her to avoid the creepy guy on the path.

The difference in the way she'd been treated since she had been brought to the trailer made her believe that she wasn't dealing with a mentally stable individual. She wondered if Cathy had multiple personalities.

The woman had left her alone after putting her on the bed. And to Brandy's relief, she seemed to be trying to respect her privacy as much as possible. Only Thrasher was allowed in the bathroom with her. Cathy would close the door and wait on the other side.

Maybe the woman wasn't lying when she said that she wouldn't hurt Brandy if she behaved. But she didn't know what it was she was supposed to be doing. If this girl wasn't interested in sex, what did she want? She was confused even more by Cathy calling her a "good boy." Was it a slip of the tongue?

Brandy's dad was not a pauper, but he wasn't rich either. He'd put himself through school after his first marriage and become an accountant. They had never been wealthy, but they were comfortable.

If Cathy was hoping to get any kind of a ransom, she'd chosen the wrong girl.

More than anything, she worried about her dad. At least he had Laura. Still, he hadn't handled the loss of his wife very well and Brandy had taken care of him during that time. If she was gone, it would be another loss in his life.

And Austin – he would think she'd stood him up for dinner. He had planned a special birthday supper for just the two of them. He'd been more than understanding when she'd told him that it was important that she celebrate with her dad and his girlfriend.

Tonight was the compromise she'd made with him.

What would he think if she didn't show up? Would he call her dad right away? Was there someone out there looking for her right now?

All of the thoughts circled through her mind. She wondered if she could convince Cathy to call her family and let them know she was okay. They didn't deserve to worry like that. Not that she deserved to be strapped down to a bed and held captive.

Her stomach rumbled loudly, but Cathy didn't bring her any supper. She hadn't had a single sip of water, either. The thought of dying on this bed was horrifying, but it was something she couldn't avoid thinking about.

In only a few short minutes of kindness, her entire life had been turned upside down. There was no going back to before. She would never be the same again. Even if she had therapy.

She wasn't sure what time it was that she finally fell asleep. It was late, she was sure of it. She could still hear the T.V. going in the living room though. So Cathy had stayed up much longer than she had.

Nightmares plagued her sleep, but she didn't remember them in the morning. The sound of Thrasher snuffling at her door woke her up with a start. There was no confusion about where she was. She remembered instantly and wished she could call out. She had to pee and who knew how long it would be before Cathy came in.

The smell of bacon made her stomach rumble expectantly. She hoped that Cathy would share with her, and then she hated that she was hoping for anything from the woman.

A strong person would refuse to eat or put up with anything Cathy did. But would a strong person still be alive at the end? That was what was important. Her survival, not her pride.

When the door opened, Thrasher came barreling in. He jumped up and put his paws on the edge of the bed to snuffle at her face. She pulled away from him as much as she could, which wasn't much at all.

After a moment, he backed away and Cathy came forward. "Good morning, sleepyhead," she said with a smile.

Brandy didn't know how to respond to her. In the end, she decided that she would play along until she could find her chance.

Cathy carefully gave her a quick peck on the forehead and then peeled the duct tape off her mouth. It was painful, but if she was thinking about silver linings, she might not ever have to wax her top lip again.

As soon as the tape was off, she forced a smile for Cathy. "Something smells delicious!"

"I've made breakfast for us, but I figured you'd probably want to use the bathroom first." Cathy reached down and unhooked the chains from the bed, freeing Brandy's feet and arms. Carefully, Brandy pulled her arms down. The zip tie was still on, Cathy would need to use scissors or a knife to cut that off.

Her arms and legs ached as she bent them and stretched them to get the feeling back. Cathy waited patiently while she did this. When she thought Brandy was ready, she gently removed the ties with a pair of scissors.

The first few steps were awkward and painful, but Cathy helped her along to the washroom where she repeated the process of locking her in with Thrasher.

"Let me know when you're done," was all she said.

Brandy wanted to explore everything, but with Thrasher in the room with her, she was afraid to make any sudden movements. Instead, she stuck to using the toilet and washing her hands. She also snuck a sip of water from the tap; who knew when she would get more water?

When she was done, Cathy brought her back to her room. Her feet were again locked into place, but her hands were left free.

"Wait right here," said Cathy as she left the room. She came back in with a paper plate with bacon and eggs on it, along with a cup of orange juice. "You must be starving."

She sat down on the bed next to Brandy and held out the plate of food with a plastic spoon. The smell of grease was nearly over-powering, but Brandy had never tasted anything so delicious in her entire life.

Cathy saved the juice for last. "I want you to drink this up," she said. "Every last drop, we can't have you going thirsty."

The juice tasted off and Brandy shuddered with the first sip.

"What's wrong?" asked Cathy.

"It tastes weird, has it expired?"

Cathy narrowed her eyes at her. "Do you think I would serve expired juice to my guests? Is that the kind of person you think I am?"

A small but fierce flash of fear travelled through her gut. "No, that's not what I meant. It must just be because of the food, is all." She tipped the glass back and chugged the bitter liquid.

When she finished, she handed the cup to Cathy. "Thank you for breakfast. It was delicious."

Cathy beamed at her. "I've always loved bacon and eggs for breakfast," she said. "So many people want toast or hashbrowns with it, but why? There's enough protein in the rest of the meal to keep you full for hours."

"Yes," said Brandy. "That's so true." She wondered what Cathy meant by that. Was she not going to be fed again for a long time?

"What's your favourite breakfast?" Cathy asked.

"Waffles." Brandy thought of her dad's waffles and felt a pang of homesickness.

"Huh, that's kind of like toast and hashbrowns, isn't it?" asked Cathy with a bit of a frown.

"I know, but it's kind of like chocolate. It's not necessarily good for you but it tastes so good."

"I guess," Cathy said. "Well, I have some errands to run, so I'm going to need you to lay back down, okay?"

Brandy almost voiced a complaint, but then decided that this wasn't the time. Trust had to be built first. Right now, Cathy would expect some kind of ruse. It was best to make her think that she was compliant.

As Brandy laid down, she felt a wave of dizziness wash over her. Cathy said something else to her, but she couldn't quite focus on the words.

She tried to form a question, but before she could make her lips move, more tape was laid over her mouth.

Blearily, she watched Cathy leave the room, and then everything went blank.

***

2019:

Garett paced the room like someone determined to wear a hole into the rug. Laura sat on his couch, trying to think of something to say. For the last hour, all of her possibilities had fallen on deaf ears.

"How long did they say we had to wait?" he asked.

"Right now, she's not considered missing," said Laura. "She's an AWOL twenty-year-old, which is not uncommon."

"That's not something Brandy would do," he whined.

She held back a sigh. "I know. We know that, but they don't. You have to remember that they deal with all kinds of people, Garett. It's not uncommon for kids to just take off in some cases."

"Even Austin knows her better," he said.

"Well, we can be grateful that Austin was so quick to check in on her. If he hadn't, we might not have noticed until her birthday."

"How do we know that he's not responsible?" he demanded.

Again, Laura bit her tongue, the first time she'd wanted to jump to Austin's defence, but this point had been made countless times now. The argument wasn't worth it. All she could do was be as supportive as she could by sitting there with him.

"You should have something to eat," she tried again. She'd brought in some of their favourite Chinese food for dinner, but Garett hadn't touched it. She'd felt guilty, nibbling on food herself, but she was a stress eater and she'd never felt worse.

"I'm not hungry," he told her.

The clock on the stove said it was past midnight. She was supposed to be at work in the morning, but she wasn't sure if she would be going in. Garett definitely wouldn't be. He'd already called in to work and said he wouldn't be in until he found his daughter.

Unlike Garett, Laura hadn't entirely ruled out the possibility that Brandy had just taken off. She didn't think it was likely, but it was possible that with the pressure of school, her dad's new girlfriend and anything else she was going through, that she just wanted some time to herself.

Sure, she wasn't answering her phone, but Laura wouldn't answer hers either if she wanted to be left alone.

"We need to go to bed, Garett," she said. She picked up the cartons of food and brought them into the kitchen.

"I'm-"

She lifted her hand. She wasn't going to let him get away with this anymore. "Garett. We don't know how long this will go on. You will need your strength to get through the next few days if Brandy doesn't surface. Sleep is the best thing for you right now."

He didn't answer at first, he just stood there and stared at her. "You're right." He scrubbed his hands down his face.

She didn't trust his response. He'd given in too easily.

"Why don't you head home for the night?" he suggested. I'll probably just toss and turn and keep you up."

There it was. He was pushing her away already.

"Nope," she said. "I'm staying right here. And I'm going to sleep on the couch. You can have the whole bed to yourself to toss and turn all you like."

"I really don't-"

"And I'm tired and I have to work tomorrow. So it's time for bed."

He seemed taken aback by her assertiveness, but she knew that if she gave in, he wouldn't sleep. He would stay up checking his phone every five minutes and pacing the room.

He sat down on the couch. His shoulders began to shake. She hurried over to sit down next to him. She wrapped her arms around him and held him while he wept.

When he was done, she brought him up to his room and laid him in the bed. She gave him a gentle kiss and tucked him in before turning out the light and leaving, hoping he would get some sleep.

19

For good measure, I had an appointment to get Mom's car detailed before I brought it back to her. I didn't want to leave any evidence there. I paid for the premium service and I specified that I wanted everything shined and vacuumed.

It smelled brand new when I brought it by her trailer. She met me at the door, which was weird. She made her way to the car as I was getting out.

"Oh my, did you get the car cleaned for me?"

I forced a smile and gave her a hug. "I really appreciate you lending me your car for the week. It was a relief to not have to take the bus."

"It was no bother, really. I didn't have anywhere to be anyway. Jenny brought me some groceries, but that was it."

I didn't know why she was giving me the blow-by-blow breakdown of her week, either. We didn't have that kind of relationship.

I wondered if her diagnosis had anything to do with her sudden change in personality. I would have to ask Nathan if he thought she was being weird.

I handed the keys over to Mom. "Why don't you come in for a bit?" she asked.

"I wish I could, but Thrasher has been at home all day. I need to go let him out and feed him."

"I guess," she said, sounding crestfallen. Then she brightened. "Why don't I give you a ride home? I'll come in for a coffee."

"No," I said. My tone took her aback. "My place is a mess, and I've had a long day. I just want to go home and relax."

"How are you going to get home?"

I was planning to take the bus home, in all honesty, but I couldn't say that now. "I have a friend coming to pick me up at the Seven-Eleven," I said.

"A friend?"

"Is that so hard to believe?" I snapped. This conversation needed to be over. Right now.

"Kind of," she said. "You've always been a solitary person, Jess. I don't think you've ever introduced a friend to me. Is it a boyfriend?"

I felt myself blush and it made me even more annoyed. "Mom, it's none of your business. Now I regret even saying something to you about it."

"Well, I'm sorry you feel that way. I guess I'll just go inside and mind my own business, then."

It was much worse to do this face to face when you couldn't just hang up the phone and carry on with your life. It was painfully awkward to stand here and wait for my mom to get the hint. Even when she capitulated, she didn't go inside.

"Okay," I said. "I'll see you, then," I lifted my hand in a half-hearted wave and then started walking down the street.

I didn't look back, but I heard her slam her door when she went inside.

The ride home seemed to take forever. I had been gone all day, covering my tracks from the night before. I'd barely had Brandy home and I already couldn't wait to go home to see her.

While I was waiting for the car to be detailed, I purchased a few things for her. I hoped she would like it.

She was waiting for me when I got home and seemed genuinely excited to see me. It filled my heart with warmth. There was hope for this whole situation.

I had to be careful though, and remember that none of this had been Brandy's idea. It would take time for her to feel the same about the situation as I did.

Still, it was nice to have a human waiting for me when I got home. Even if I did have to go to such great lengths to care for her. It would be worth it in the end.

I took her to the bathroom before I gave her her gifts. I was considering getting some diapers for her. She wasn't used to going all day without using the washroom and I didn't want her to get dehydrated.

When she was done, I put her back in her place on the bed and grabbed the bag from the dresser. "Did you have a good day?" I asked her.

"It was quiet."

I felt kind of stupid for asking her that question. Of course she didn't have a good day. It would be hard to have a good day if you weren't able to do anything.

Still, I was nice enough to give her a pill to help her sleep through the day. I could keep her company tonight now that I was home.

I waited for her to ask about my day. When she didn't, I tried not to let on that it bothered me. "I bought you something today," I said.

I ran to the kitchen and brought back the bag. I set the bag in front of her and waited expectantly.

She pulled it closer to her and then pulled out the contents. "You got me a baseball cap! And some... Tensor bandages?"

"I wanted to have a normal family life and I thought this could help us out."

"What do you mean *normal*?"

"You know," I said. "Husband, wife and a dog. Maybe one day a kid."

She stared at me, open horror on her face. It was too soon. I had been too impatient with this. Still, it hurt that she wasn't even a bit excited. Maybe it would be best if I let her know the rules early on.

"Come on," I said. "We're going to go to the bathroom. I'll show you how to use the Tensor bandage, Brandon."

"Brandon?" she asked.

"Yeah. A normal family doesn't include two wives. I want a normal life. I figured Brandon was closest to Brandy." I stood up and extended a hand to her.

She still didn't move, so I reached down and closed my hand around her upper arm. I pulled her up roughly and pulled her toward the bathroom. "Remember what I told you. If you can't be good, then you will have to deal with the consequences."

"Okay," she said. "Okay! I'm coming!"

I turned her to look at me. "You will *never* speak to me with that tone again. Do you understand?" I realized I was shaking her and I stopped myself. It wouldn't do me any good to actually cause her harm.

"I-I'm sorry," she said. This time, her tone was much more respectful. "What do you want me to do with the Tensor?"

I rested my hand on her cheek and looked her deep in the eyes. "I'll let it go this time, Brandon. But next time there will be consequences. Don't make me do that. I wouldn't enjoy it at all."

"Okay," she said meekly. "I won't be disrespectful anymore."

I handed her the Tensor bandages. "You will take off your bra and bring it to me. I want you to wrap your chest tight. Boys don't have breasts."

"Alright, I can do that. It'll just take me a minute."

"If you don't get it tight enough, I will come in and show you how I want it done. I know you know how to wrap something properly."

I didn't like being stern with her, but if I didn't put her in her place now, she might get some ideas that she shouldn't. I was going to be in control of this relationship. It was going to go the way I wanted it to, which meant that everything had to be perfect.

I didn't want to be viewed as a lesbian. I didn't like girls. I liked men, not that I had tons of experience.

I'd been made fun of my whole life, I would be an idiot to add to it by dating a girl.

When she came out of the bathroom, she didn't have her shirt on, which I appreciated. I could see that she'd made the wrap as tight as she could without cutting off the circulation. I tossed her bra into the living room and brought her back into the room.

"If you're too warm, you can leave your shirt off, I don't mind. Don't most guys only sleep in their ginches?"

She blushed a deep red that went down into her chest. I wondered if there was a way to make her boobs smaller without surgery. Maybe if she ate less?

I waited for her to make up her mind for a moment, but she didn't seem to know what she wanted. "If you're uncomfortable, you can wear pyjamas. I won't judge."

She tugged her shirt over her head quickly and then laid down in the bed, her arms and legs in position. I chained her up real quick and assured her I would be back as soon as supper was ready.

I didn't have much experience with cooking actual food. For the most part, I ate either takeout or I bought something quick to heat up. Tonight felt like it was a celebration so I'd bought some fish to make.

My uncle used to fry it up after dipping it in crushed-up cheesies. It was a nice treat and went great with fried potatoes.

I pulled a couple of beers out of the fridge, too. *Might as well make it officially nice.*

She didn't look as sore when she sat up this time, which was nice to see. She was getting used to the restraints. I had cut her food up for her and brought it in to her on a paper plate with a spoon again. She didn't need to be getting any ideas.

Also, I really didn't want to do the extra dishes. It was bad enough that I'd made such a mess cooking supper for us. Adding more dishes to the mix just seemed ridiculous.

"This is so tasty," she said. "I've never had fish like this before." I wasn't used to receiving compliments so I blushed a little bit.

We finished the rest of the meal in silence. I poured her beer into a Slurpee cup and handed it to her. I sipped mine from the bottle.

"Thank you for supper. That was delicious!"

"I'm glad you liked it." Now, things were awkward. I wasn't sure what to talk about for a minute.

"So you said you had a brother? Is he older?"

I did *not* want to talk about Nathan. "Yeah, just one. He's younger than me."

"I don't have any siblings," she said. "It's just my dad and me now that my mom has passed away."

"Your mom died?" I asked. I realized afterward that I maybe could have phrased the question a little better, but it didn't seem to bother her.

"About five years ago. It was cancer."

This conversation was getting a little too close to home. I wasn't really ready to tell her about my mom or my brother. I wanted her to like me first, not them.

"That's too bad," I said.

We descended into silence again. I'd made the situation uncomfortable somehow. Rather than wanting to fix it, I wanted to run.

I waited for her to finish up her beer and then took her cup with me. "We'll go to the bathroom one more time and then I'll tuck you into bed."

"Can I stay up and watch T.V.?"

The request caught me off guard. I didn't expect her to want to spend time with me. "No," I said.

I was a bit gruffer than I wanted to be, but in my experience, no one was ever nice to me unless they wanted something. And I was sure there was plenty that she wanted from me, right now. She had to earn her privileges.

When I strapped her into bed again I kissed her forehead. I don't know what had possessed me to start kissing her forehead, but the gesture felt right, and I knew I would continue doing it.

"Good night, Cathy," she said just before I put the tape on her mouth.

"Night, Brandon," I said quickly.

I flicked the light off on my way out the door, hoping she wouldn't see my silly grin. I couldn't wait until we could sleep in the same bed.

I closed the door and made my way to the living room. I was probably going to fall asleep watching T.V. again. Thrasher settled down in front of the door, giving a small huff. I wasn't sure if he was watching over her to protect her or me, but I loved him all the more either way.

***

2019:

The bandage on her chest was beginning to chafe. She was going to need to shower eventually and she wasn't looking forward to that. She hoped Cathy would be okay with just letting Thrasher be in the bathroom with her again.

She didn't understand why she needed to bind her breasts, but in the scheme of things, that was preferable to baring them. Cathy didn't seem interested in sex, only in companionship.

Yet when Brandy had tried to get her to open up, she had shut down and refused to talk. Cathy was annoyed that she asked to watch T.V. She should have waited.

The woman reminded her of a skittish horse. She wanted to talk to people, she was interested, but she wasn't ready to commit to it.

It didn't make sense to Brandy. She'd always imagined women to be confident when they reached the age that Cathy was. Admittedly, she had no idea how old she was, but there were many grey strands in her hair.

If she coloured her hair, she would look years younger.

As it was, she seemed downright scary. Especially when she was angry. Brandy was surprised there wasn't a bruise on her arm where Cathy had gripped her earlier in the evening.

When Cathy had said she didn't want to punish Brandy, it had sent a chill down her spine. If she'd had more liquid in her, she thought she would have wet herself.

Who knew what this woman would do to her if she didn't follow the rules? She wasn't exactly a sane human being.

Still, there was a part of Brandy that felt sorry for her. It was clear that this woman hadn't had an easy life. She couldn't imagine what a person would have to go through to be so desperate for a family that they would kidnap someone.

If Cathy had just been normal, they may have even been friends eventually. That would never happen now. Kidnapping had a way of destroying potential friendships.

People like Cathy were unpredictable. They could be nice and reasonable one minute and the next they were angry and hostile. Even violent. Brandy would have to watch her tone and what she said. If she didn't put lots of thought into her words, she would likely push her captor in a direction that she didn't want.

Something had been in the orange juice that morning, she knew it. There was no way to explain her sudden grogginess except to say that she was drugged. It had either been in her food or her juice, and the flavour of the juice suggested it was the culprit.

Since she'd slept all day, she likely wouldn't sleep through the night. The worst was that she would be hungry before long and unable to do anything about it. She was completely at Cathy's mercy.

Thrasher had more freedom than she did.

If she played her cards right, though, she might be able to get Cathy's trust. Her best bet was to just treat her with kindness, as difficult as that might be in her situation.

Hate and anger had never solved any problems. She was hoping that kindness would.

20

2019:

Hutchinson was not happy that he'd gotten no closer to figuring things out for Walker than he had before. Days had gone by and he struggled to sleep. Putting an innocent man away didn't sit well with him.

He didn't seem to really have any other options at the moment. Walker had been no help and after the first conversation, had refused to talk without a lawyer present. That was too risky for Hutchinson. His only hope at this point was that the public defender was damn good at his job.

Walker was all out of other options. Even when Ed had tried to come up with something for Hutchinson, it had been a dead end.

That was why he was somewhat relieved to hear about the missing University student. As awful as it was that someone was missing, the distraction was welcome.

At least they had something to go on with this one. The girl's phone had been found down in the parking lot near the River Valley trails. It was smashed to bits, but it proved that she had actually been there.

And she had family that knew her well enough to help them out.

Brandy Volker was her name. She was a nursing student in her second year and in a serious relationship with another student at the school. The whole city would be behind this girl.

What he didn't need was another sensationalized story on his hands. Two in less than a year was too much for him.

It didn't help that this girl was only a handful of years older than his own daughter.

The night he'd heard about her disappearance, he'd called Lacey and begged her for some time with Crystal. Lacey had obliged him, telling him not to stress her out.

Then she'd asked for all of the details because she worried about their daughter just as much as he did.

The dad was already on their ass with questions, which Hutchinson both understood and hated. It had only been two days and all they'd been able to do was find her phone. Her picture had been released to the media, but again, they were dealing with leads from the public. Most of which were unreliable at best.

People had the best of intentions. Everyone liked to think they were helping out when they called, but most of the calls would lead to dead ends and wasted time.

It was only a matter of time, though, before someone came forward. The River Valley was a popular place for joggers, somebody would have been there that night.

He still had the two sketches in his desk drawer and every now and then he would pull them out and take a look. He wanted to recognize the woman if he saw her. The chances were slim, but still, he couldn't give it up.

He'd taken Crystal that night and made sure he had a talk with her, regardless of what Lacey had said.

"This is pepper spray, I want you to carry this with you at all times. Especially if you have to go somewhere alone."

They'd been at his kitchen table with a whole array of tools laid out before them. He had an emergency rope bracelet, pepper spray, a rape whistle, a knife for cutting seat belts and an assortment of everyday tools that might come in handy in a pinch.

"You want me to carry all of this stuff with me everywhere I go?" she said.

"You carry around a designer duffle bag. What else are you going to fill it with?"

"It's a purse, Dad. Not a duffle bag. And I would look like a psycho if I carried all of this with me all of the time. I can't bring half this stuff to school with me."

She was wrong, it was most certainly a duffle bag. He'd packed for weekend trips in a smaller bag than what she carried around. But that wasn't the point.

"Well, you don't have to bring the pepper spray and belt cutter to school, I guess. But you should keep it in your car and take it out if you have to go anywhere."

She rolled her eyes at him, giving him the look that he knew so many teenagers did. "So, like, if I go to a party, I need to carry this all with me?"

"To a party? Definitely." He knew he was being a bit over the top, but even though he was giving her all of this stuff, it wouldn't be enough to make him feel that she was safe. The only way to do that was to follow her around and that definitely wouldn't fly. "You should also consider taking some martial arts classes or something. Some self-defence wouldn't be a terrible skill to have."

"If I tell you I'll think about it and I dump all of this stuff in my purse right now, will you stop talking to me about it?"

That was not the response he'd been aiming for, but at least she was taking everything with her. At the very least, it would end up on the floor of her car when she had to fish around for her phone.

"Agreed," he said.

She grabbed her purse from the hallway and opened it, sweeping everything inside in one go.

"See?" he said, pointing to it. "It's a duffle bag."

"This is why you don't have a girlfriend, Dad." The words were sarcastic, but he could see the smile playing on her lips. She was still his little girl.

He wondered how Garett Volker was feeling right at that moment and decided to give Crystal a hug. She shied back quickly, giving him a strange look, but she was used to him being a little odd. One of the side effects of his job was a healthy dose of paranoia and a strong desire to overprotect loved ones.

Dropping her off wasn't easy this time. Part of him wanted to follow her into her mother's house and spend the night, keeping all of the bad guys away.

***

2019:

Laura stormed through the office, ignoring the cheery hello from the receptionist. She couldn't believe the audacity of Greg. How *dare* he even think of handing this story over to someone else. If anyone was going to talk about Brandy's case, it was her. There was no one more qualified.

Greg saw her coming and ended the call he was on. Once inside, she slammed the door shut behind her and closed his blinds.

"What do you think you're doing, handing this story over to Aaron?" she demanded.

"It's a conflict of interest," he said.

"Really? Writing about a missing girl would create a conflict of interest? Could you elaborate on that?"

"Because of your relationship with her dad," he replied with a smug smile. "Surely you realize that."

"So you're worried that I'm going to be biased about the victim of a kidnapping? That I'll show through my writing that what happened to her was wrong? I didn't agree with the nightclub burnings but I didn't let that affect my stories."

He stood up and leaned forward on his desk. Laura felt her back go ramrod straight. *How dare he try to intimidate me?* At a good ten years younger than her, he didn't have half the life experience she did.

The only reason he had the job he did was that she had passed it up several times.

"You listen to me, Greg," she said, placing her own fists on the desk. "There will be no one else covering this story. You will not bully me out of it. If you try, you will regret it."

"Are you threatening me, Laura?"

"Watch and find out."

She didn't stop at her desk on the way out. She was going down to the precinct to get all of the information she could for the article. Someone down there would talk to her.

This was the only way she could really help Garett out. All she could do was make sure that the public got the most accurate information possible. There could be no mistakes, the public would need to help with this case.

It had been two days since Garett had been able to report Brandy missing. Her birthday had come and gone with nothing more than tears and worry. Austin had come over that evening and sat with them, but what should have been a celebration was only a strategy session.

Austin was putting up posters all over the campus and the River Valley area. Garett was planning interviews with the media, hoping that if he offered a reward, someone would come forward.

It hurt Laura to see him this way. In the past, she'd done stories for parents with missing children and watching them unravel was almost unbearable. It was even worse watching Garett go through this.

She'd convinced him that he needed to get his rest. Both mornings he'd emerged from his room with red eyes and dark bags underneath. She'd bullied him into making a doctor's appointment so that he could get something to help him sleep.

She had half-considered it for herself. Spending the night on Garett's couch wasn't exactly conducive to a good night's sleep. Nor was listening to him pace above her. She was beginning to wonder if his insistence that he would keep her up was more of a ruse than anything.

He was starting to slip away from her and it was scary. Garett had dealt with some awful losses in his lifetime and he had a pattern that he defaulted to.

Brandy had been the one to keep him out of the deep end last time and Emily the time before that. Laura could only pray that she had the strength and influence to keep him sane this time.

He insisted that Brandy was all right. They just had to find her. The police were sounding more grim each day. With every minute that ticked by, the likelihood of finding Brandy alive was getting smaller and smaller.

The worst was Garett tormenting himself, thinking of all of the things she could be going through. Laura had tried to tell him that he shouldn't think about it and he'd snapped at her. He was right of course, there was no way a parent could do anything else.

Hell, there was little else she could do and she'd barely known the girl for a few months.

Writing the articles was the only way she could even dream of helping him out. Nothing else would do.

And she needed the distraction for herself. Watching Garett fall to pieces wasn't helping her sanity either. While he was the type of person to sit at home and turn in on himself, Laura was the opposite. When problems came her way, she did everything in her power to try to control the situation.

She only hoped that her need to control wouldn't suffocate Garett.

21

I was feeling good enough that I went back to work again. It was all very well to stay at home on disability, but it didn't pay my full wages. Now that I was the sole income earner in the family, I needed to make sure I was bringing in enough money to feed everyone.

Mike was more than happy to have me back. He even went so far as to comment on how much better I looked after taking time off. It was kind of nice to think that someone could see a change in my spirits since I'd brought Brandon into my life.

I was feeling bad leaving him at home alone without being able to use the bathroom. I was worried that he wasn't getting enough to drink in the morning. On my way home, I decided I would pick up some diapers.

And some flannel shirts. I liked the look of those on guys.

Dave still wasn't back at work and the other guys were steering clear of me. Although Mike had told them it wasn't my fault, they were still a little scared, which was fine with me.

At the end of the shift, Mike called me into his office.

"How are you doing?" he asked.

"I'm doing much better."

"And your mom?"

"She's okay for now. In good spirits." I hoped that was something people said.

"Okay," he said. "If there's anything you need, you let me know. Cancer's a real bitch." He clapped my shoulder with the last statement.

I nodded and ducked out of the office as soon as I felt it was appropriate. Why did people need to make things so awkward? I just wanted to be left alone.

Thrasher was waiting in Brandon's room when I got home. I dropped the stuff on the table and went about the after-work ritual.

When I had him back in the room, I brought out the stuff. "I have clothes for you," I said. For some reason, I was feeling a bit shy. I didn't know what kind of clothes he would like.

He pulled the shirts out of the bag and held them out in front of himself. "I like the colours. You have a good eye."

The small feeling of relief inside me was a bit annoying. My feelings were getting twisted and changing. I didn't feel as in control as I had before and that bothered me.

"What are these for?" he asked as he pulled the Depends out of the bag.

"In case you have to go to the bathroom when I'm not home," I said. I grabbed the bag out of his hands. "I haven't been giving you much to drink because I'm worried about you having an accident. If you have these on, I won't have to worry so much."

He had an odd expression on his face for a second and then he brightened. "That's a really good idea, Cathy. You've really put a lot of thought into making me comfortable."

"What's comfortable about peeing in a diaper?" I asked. He was buttering me up and I didn't appreciate it.

He had the good grace to blush at my question. "What I meant was that you don't mean for me to go without while we get to know each other. Not everyone would worry about my basic needs like that."

I was still suspicious, but I decided to let it go. "I'm going to order pizza for supper," I said. "Is there anything you don't like?"

"I'm allergic to olives," he told me.

"Those are gross anyway. Is ham and pineapple good enough? We could have some beer with it again."

"That sounds amazing."

I was letting him sit on the bed without being tied down. He scooched up to the wall and leaned his back up against it, bringing his knees to his chest.

"Will I ever get to meet your family?" he asked suddenly.

"What?" I hadn't thought about that. It would be a long time before I would let that happen. I had to know that I could trust him. Surely he knew that.

"It's just that I was thinking how nice it would be to introduce you to my dad. And his girlfriend, she's really nice."

"I don't want to meet anyone," I said. Brandon didn't need any distractions. He was mine and I didn't want him picking any favourites over me. Our relationship needed to be the priority here.

"Oh, okay. That's too bad," he said.

"Is it?"

He ignored the tone in my voice and carried on. "Yeah, it is. My dad's a really great guy. I think you guys would have lots in common."

"I doubt it," I mumbled.

"It doesn't matter. Obviously, it makes you uncomfortable and I don't want to do that. I want our relationship to progress at a pace that we are both comfortable with."

Why was he being like this? There was no way he actually liked me right now. He hadn't had the chance to get to know me. I motioned for him to lay down again. I couldn't have him wandering around when the pizza guy got here.

He laid down without complaint, even giving me a brief smile before I put the tape over his mouth.

I left the room feeling strange. When the pizza came, I didn't share any with Brandon. I didn't want to be around him right now. He could have some of the pizza for breakfast tomorrow morning.

***

2019:

Brandy had never imagined what it would be like to be kidnapped and trapped in someone's home. That wasn't something that really crossed anyone's mind.

Now that she was in the situation, she didn't really know what to think. Cathy was doing her best to take care of her. She made it clear that Brandy wasn't in charge, but she also didn't want to hurt her.

At first, the thought of the diapers had disgusted Brandy. As she thought about it, though, it seemed like a good solution. She needed more fluids than a cup of orange juice in the morning and a beer at night.

If she was wearing a diaper during the day, she didn't have to try to deny her bladder, which wasn't good for her.

Most of all, she felt that the idea of the diapers meant that Cathy cared about her health and well-being. That meant Cathy probably wasn't going to harm her for no reason.

She hoped her kindness was making Cathy warm up to her. At least it seemed like she was seeing some chinks in her armour. It was hard to tell.

She'd heard somewhere that one of the best things you could do when you were held captive was to humanize yourself. She hoped that if she talked about her dad enough, Cathy would feel bad and want to let her go. Or maybe at least talk to him.

She also fiercely missed Austin, but she didn't dare talk about him. Cathy didn't seem like the type of person who would be exceptionally forgiving of Brandy's feelings.

She and Austin had been together for just under a year when she'd first introduced him to her dad. She wished he was here right now, holding her in his arms.

Her life had never been such a rollercoaster of emotions. She never knew what to expect with Cathy. Tonight she hadn't bothered to feed her supper. Was it a punishment? Or was it just a slip of her mind?

There was no way to tell. She had nothing better to do than think and her mind was going in circles every waking hour.

It started with the thought of how stupid it had been to tell a complete stranger anything personal about herself. *What on Earth possessed me to share my running path with Cathy at the nightclub?*

If she had lied, Cathy would have been none the wiser. Brandy could have given her a false name and Cathy wouldn't have been able to tell any different. If she had been determined, she might have eventually tracked Brandy down, but it wouldn't have been nearly as easy.

And why did she think it was a good idea to jog by herself? Her father had told her many times that she should have a partner when she was running. That or she should have picked a more public space to do it.

She'd blown him off as being overprotective and even told him as much. She wasn't an idiot. But maybe she was.

The man on the path hadn't done anything except offer to help them out. Brandy had turned him away only because he was a strange man that she didn't know. *But the strange woman? Well, she was definitely harmless.*

She would probably have trust issues for the rest of her life because of this. Major therapy would be a must when Brandy got out of this place.

And she would get out. She had to believe that. The best thing she could do was play along and follow the rules.

If she could just get Cathy to open up and to see her as more of a friend than a prisoner. Friends didn't treat each other this way. She could only hope that Cathy knew how to be a friend.

From everything Brandy could see, Cathy didn't have much of a social life.

There were no late-night phone calls. Only Thrasher and the television brought any life to the household.

If Cathy had ever had someone significant in her life before, they had really done a number on her. It was clear the poor woman had been burned many times and Brandy was angry with those people. They had created the monster that was torturing her.

Sure, lots of people had hard lives and never reached the levels that Cathy had, but if people were kinder to one another, maybe these kinds of situations could be avoided.

The fact that she hadn't eaten ensured that she didn't sleep that night. If Cathy didn't start to feed her more, she was going to lose a lot of weight. She needed more than two meals a day to survive. And she needed fruits and vegetables if she was going to get out healthy.

She wondered if that was something she could bring up with Cathy. Her captor looked like she could benefit from some vitamins herself.

She decided to bring it up the next time she talked to her, hoping that Cathy would let her help make supper. And if she could do that, maybe she could get her to pick up something for a salad.

When she finally drifted off into a troubled sleep, she dreamed of fruit smoothies and salads.

***

1997, fifteen years old:

The murder of Reena Virk sparked debate across the country and for the first time in years, Jess felt that there might be hope. If enough people stood up against the type of bullying and violence that this girl had gone through, maybe her life would improve.

She'd never shown much interest in the news before, but this girl's death had struck a chord with Jess. She felt a kinship with this girl who had been beaten and drowned.

Her school held a vigil for Reena at the end of November. Jess had been surprised at her strong desire to attend. She'd never met this girl, but she felt drawn to her. Jess couldn't help but wonder if she would be facing a similar fate if her situation was a little bit different.

"What do you want a newspaper for?" demanded her mom when she first asked for one after hearing about Reena on the news.

"I just want to see what's going on," said Jess.

"We don't get the paper. Why can't you just watch the news instead?"

"I want to keep articles that I'm interested in," Jess said.

"You don't make any sense to me. Why would you want to keep any more junk?"

When she'd finally told her mother she was specifically interested in Reena, her mom had told her that she sounded like a stalker. "The poor girl had a terrible life. Why would you want to read the sensationalized tidbits about her? Let her rest in peace, Jess."

Jess hadn't realized the gravity of her mistake in telling her mother about her interest until the night of the vigil. Once her mom realized that Jess wanted her to drive her to the vigil, she turned her down. "This obsession you have with that poor girl isn't healthy, Jess."

"I know she had a hard life, Mom. I want to remember her, to stand up for others who are going through the same thing."

"Are you comparing yourself to her?" asked her mom. She stood in front of the table with her hands on her hips. "Because you may think that your life is rough, but you've never even been beaten. The absolute worst thing that's happened to you is someone called you a bad name. Do you really think your life is that hard?"

"That's not what I was saying," said Jess. Her mother's words had filled her with guilt and shame. She hadn't ever been beaten up. Her mom was right. This girl had been beaten to death and had cigarettes put out on her body. "I just wanted to pay my respects," she finished lamely.

"Well, pay them here rather than cost me money for gas and newspapers. I don't have the money to be running you all over the city."

Her mom was being unreasonable, as far as she was concerned. The next day, she brought her own change with her. Reena was no longer in the first few pages of the paper, but she was still in there.

Rather than try to hide the whole paper at home, Jess only ripped the articles out and shoved them into her bag.

Reena would not be forgotten. Not while Jess was still around.

22

FATHER OFFERS REWARD FOR INFORMATION ABOUT MISSING DAUGHTER

Edmonton Guardian
Laura Martin

The father of missing university student Brandy Volker has come forward with an offer for a reward for any information in regards to his daughter.

Garett Volker said if someone has pertinent information about the whereabouts of his daughter, he will offer $10,000 if it leads to an arrest or the return of her.

Volker was last seen on the running paths in the River Valley on September 28. Her father reported her missing after she missed dinner with her family.

Volker's disappearance has sparked a debate about the safety of the paths in the River Valley. City Council is set to hear a proposal to add more lighting to the area and to remove some of the foliage to give better sight lines. The university is hosting a vigil for Volker this Friday and has created a Go Fund Me for

her father, who has taken time off of work to
find his daughter.

***

2019:

My mom was calling me nearly every day now. I was starting to
go a little crazy and wished she would just go back to normal.
If I missed more than one call, Nathan called me to see what was
going on and why I wasn't answering my phone.

I wasn't sure how to deal with this sudden influx of communication. Why did it take her dying to want to talk to me? And if she
wanted to talk to me, then why wouldn't she want to prolong her life
to make it happen?

In any case, I had Brandon now and I didn't really need anyone
else, so I avoided the calls whenever I could. If Nathan threatened to
come check up on me, I would call them back, that was it.

Brandon was warming up to me, I was sure of it. The diapers
had been a good idea because he was able to drink more and was
a bit more responsive when I talked to him. He seemed to realize
that I genuinely cared about him and was looking forward to being
together.

He'd made a special request for supper tonight, and I felt
strangely giddy as I stopped by the grocery store to pick up the
things he needed.

We had agreed that I would do all of the chopping and anything
with knives. He had to earn my trust before we got to that point. But
still, it was almost like we were having a date.

I picked up some avocado, lettuce, cucumbers, corn and some
roast chicken. He was going to make me a salad with chicken for

supper. It wasn't something I'd normally make, but he said he missed vegetables.

And truthfully, I wanted him to be healthy. It wouldn't hurt me to eat something healthy either. If we didn't take care of ourselves, how were we going to grow old together?

The chicken smelled delicious and it was hard to resist tearing into it on the way home. I couldn't even remember the last time that I'd had a roast chicken for supper. Usually, my fridge was stocked with food that came in a box.

I dropped the food on the counter when I got home and made my way to Brandon's room. Thrasher was right behind me and burst into the room excitedly when I opened it. He ran over to Brandon and licked his face.

"Thrasher!" I said, pulling him back. That had been unexpected and I wasn't sure how I felt about his demonstration of affection for Brandon. Thrasher was *my* pup, not his.

I unhooked Brandon and showed him to the bathroom, offering him a fresh pair of boxers as he went in.

The clothes that I had bought for him fit him just right. They weren't snug or oversized but they hung loosely on him, hiding the curves that he still had underneath. If someone didn't know better, there would be no doubt that he was a guy.

Except for the hair. I was considering doing something about that. I didn't like men with long hair, especially if they pulled it back into a man bun. They looked so wimpy when they did that.

I wanted someone who made me feel safe. So I just had to figure out how I was going to break it to him that the hair had to go.

He came out of the bathroom with a smile on his face. "Are you ready for an incredible meal?" he asked.

I couldn't stop the smile that spread across my face in return. "I think I have everything you were looking for. I've never picked out avocados before."

We went into the kitchen and Brandon sat at the table. I pulled the stuff out of the bags and showed it to him. "This avocado is perfect. It will mash up really well," he said. Then he pulled the little stem nub out of the end and showed me how to tell if they were ripe or not.

Maybe I would be picking up more of these in the future. Especially if this salad was as good as he was saying it was.

I grabbed a cutting board and knife and started chopping the vegetables as instructed. He pulled apart the chicken, separating the dark meat from the white. "Can Thrasher have the skin?" he asked.

Thrasher was drooling at his feet, staring up at the chicken. I hesitated a moment, then decided that if we were going to be a family, Thrasher needed to care about Brandon, too. I nodded at him and watched him dangle it.

Thrasher jumped and snatched it out of his hands. Brandon jumped back, his eyes wide. "Next time, I'm going to just drop it to the floor for him," he said with a shaky laugh.

"Yeah, he's not very patient," I said as I rubbed Thrasher's head. The pup grumbled quietly, but only laid down at Brandon's feet, hoping for more.

Once Brandon had the chicken separated, he asked for a container for the dark meat. "It'll be great in stews or soups or on sandwiches," he said. I handed him an old takeout container and he used that.

It was a lot of work, but it was worth it in the end. Brandon was right; the salad with the chicken was filling and it was full of flavour.

Far more flavour than I was used to. And it was worth it to see him smile as he ate it.

When I offered him a beer, he requested water. Odd, but I obliged him.

"My mom used to make this salad when I was little. I hated it then, but now it's one of my favourites," said Brandon.

"When your mom got cancer, did she fight it?" I asked. I wanted the question back as soon as I spoke it, but it was too late.

"She did," he said. "But it was too late to do much about it. It was hell to watch her go through the treatments, so in a way, the ending was a bit of a blessing for everyone."

"My mom has cancer, too."

Brandon's eyes widened. He set his fork down and reached across for my hand. "Oh, Cathy, I'm so sorry. It's a terrible disease."

I stared at his hand in mine and was surprised to discover that my eyes were getting watery. I pulled my hand away and continued eating. "Yeah, well, unlike your mom, she isn't even going to try to fight it."

We didn't say anything for a while, just put fork to mouth. The salad didn't taste as great now.

"I think that deciding whether to get the treatments is a very personal choice," said Brandon. He didn't look at me, just kept eating, but I froze. "For some, I think, it's about control. This thing is out of your mother's control. She can fight it, but might not win, and that's not in her control either. But if she doesn't fight it, she's deciding her own fate."

I hadn't thought of it that way. My mom was a control freak, never wanting anyone to make a decision that she didn't play a part in.

It had been hard for her when I moved out. I hadn't asked for her advice, and I hadn't really given notice, I just left. I didn't owe her any explanation, so why would I waste my time? We didn't speak for quite some time after that.

"She's just being selfish," I said. I stabbed at the food on my plate. Brandon looked like he wanted to say something but I interrupted him. "You need to hurry up. I have some errands to run tonight."

He nodded and picked up the pace. When he was finished, I dumped the dishes in the sink and then took him to the bathroom. I locked him up good and tight tonight. Maybe a little bit more forcefully than needed, he'd grunted when I pulled on the chain for his arms.

I was feeling restless and uneasy. I needed to get the hell out of there before Brandon saw me break down in tears. I wasn't going to show him any weakness. He needed to be afraid of me, to respect me. Acting like a baby wouldn't help that.

I locked up the house and hopped into my truck. I wasn't sure exactly where I'd go, but something told me I would end up at my mother's place. It was an alien feeling.

***

2019:

She had made headway, she knew it. How much was unknown, but she had seen tears in Cathy's eyes. Part of her was ecstatic that she'd managed to elicit an emotion out of Cathy. It was one more step toward her freedom, she knew it.

The other part of her was ashamed that she was only pretending to care about Cathy. When Brandy had learned about Cathy's mom, had felt a strong sense of empathy for her captor, not a feeling she was expecting. Nobody should have to watch their loved ones go through that, even if they were horrible people.

Still, if she didn't look after number one, no one else would. Cathy might have been pretending she was looking after Brandy, but she wasn't. She was looking after her own needs by using Brandy.

And they were weird, twisted needs.

She hadn't been allowed to remove the Tensor bandage around her chest. Even when she told Cathy that it was chafing and that she needed to wash, she'd been told to leave it there. All Cathy would allow was a wash with a facecloth. She wasn't allowed to get in the shower yet.

She was beginning to feel pretty disgusting. Especially her hair. It was long, lank and greasy now. Cathy had allowed her to brush it, but even then, she made comments about how vain Brandy was about her hair. Instead, she'd taken to twisting it in a knot and tucking it underneath the ball cap that Cathy had her wearing.

The fact that Cathy was bound and determined that she was a guy was one of the scarier things for Brandy. Right now, Cathy seemed happy just to have a platonic relationship with her. What happened when she wanted something more?

Cathy was already slipping her sleeping pills every morning. How long before she started adding testosterone supplements to her food? Or before she decided the best way to deal with Brandy's boobs was just to cut them off?

There was no way out of this mess except through it and Brandy was hoping to make the ride as smooth as possible.

If she could get Cathy to want her help every evening with supper, she could make more progress. She wanted everything to move along faster. It had only been about a week, she thought, since she'd been kidnapped, but it felt like it had been months.

Brandy's main concern was her father. She hoped that Laura was taking good care of him. She thought about Austin, too, but she felt like her memory of him was fading. She wasn't sure if that was because she hadn't known him as long or because he wasn't as important as her dad. Either way, she found it worrisome.

Most of the time, though, she thought about what she was going to do to get away from Cathy.

So far, she had a whole lot of nothing. She was making progress with Cathy, little bits at a time. But for every one step forward, there were two back.

This evening, Cathy had seemed unusually rough when she tied Brandy down to the bed again. Since she was tied up nearly all of the time, Brandy's arms were starting to get used to being tied down. Tonight they ached again, as though Cathy had made things tighter.

She went over everything they had done that evening with a fine-tooth comb, but she couldn't see what she'd done to set the woman off. Another factor to add to the scary side.

Cathy's moods were unpredictable and Brandy worried that one day she would break through the thin ice she'd been walking on and drown.

It was a long time before Cathy came home again that night. When she did, she didn't even come check on Brandy. Instead, she turned the television on and sat watching a show for the remainder of the evening.

All Brandy could do was pray that she would be forgiven in the morning.

23

2019:

It had almost been like my mother was waiting for me when I showed up at her place unannounced. She was sitting at the table with a fresh pot of tea, reading the newspaper.

She offered me a cup, and even though I didn't like tea, I took a cup. I added a generous dollop of honey to make it palatable.

"Have you seen this?" she asked, shoving the paper toward me.

"No, I haven't looked at a paper in months." I pulled the Guardian over and noticed the headline, *Father Offers Reward for Information About Missing Daughter*. I pushed it back across the table, not bothering to read the article.

I had no doubt it was about Brandon, but I didn't want to hear a story about his dad boohooing because he was gone. He'd had years to spend with Brandon, now it was my turn to have some bonding time.

Also, it made me strangely uncomfortable to think about Brandon's family. He was always telling me little anecdotes about them, trying to make me like them, and I really didn't want to like them. No more than I wanted Brandon to meet my family.

We could be our own little secret. I'd always thought that was more romantic, anyway.

"You're not going to read it?" she asked.

"I don't have any information to give him, so why do I care?"

"It's just with that girl in B.C., Renna or something, you were pretty upset about her. I thought you might be following this, too."

"I've seen posters, that's about it. How're you feeling?" The subject needed to change in a big bad way.

"I've been better," she told me, still holding tight to the paper. Her tea was sitting next to her, forgotten.

"I guessed that much," I said, trying to keep my sarcasm to a minimum. "Did the doctor give you any pain killers?"

"No, not yet. It's not been that bad, just a little discomfort… So, you haven't been following this story at all?" she asked.

Why the hell would she not drop it? What the hell did she care if some guy lost his daughter? It happened all the time.

"No, Mom, and I'm not interested. I don't need to add someone else's problems to my plate. I think I've got enough."

"Hm," she said, then she picked up the paper and tossed it in the recycle bin in the addition. "That's a good point. Maybe I don't need to be reading that crap, either."

Finally. Good God. I was starting to regret picking her place as my destination. I should have hit up a bar somewhere or something.

"So how are things at work?" she asked. "Is that one guy doing better?"

Dave still wasn't back at work and I doubted he would be anytime soon. I'd learned from Mike that on top of having his face smashed in, he'd also had broken bones in his legs. I kind of hoped he would never walk properly again. He deserved it.

"I don't know. They don't tell us much. It's confidential and stuff."

"I guess," she said. She twiddled her thumbs for a second and then remembered her tea. "How have you been?"

"I'm good." It was true. For once, I didn't have to lie to her about how I was feeling. It was an odd feeling.

"You seem good. Different. You seem a bit different."

"What do you mean?" I asked. Mike had said the same thing and I couldn't understand how I was acting any different than I had before.

"Well, for one, you came to see me without me having to beg you," she said. That was a point for her. It had been a long time since I'd willingly set foot in this place. "And for another, there's a bit of a…glow?… Around you. It's hard to describe."

"I'm not pregnant if that's what you're getting at," I stated.

She burst into laughter and shook her head. "I'm not counting on seeing any of your babies, Jess. No, it's something else. Can't put my finger on it though."

We fell into a long silence then. I was looking at the dregs of my tea and considering making an excuse to be on my way, when she finally spoke again.

"I've been thinking about your dad a lot lately."

"Okay…" I said. I didn't trust any other words to come out. I had nothing nice to say on the subject.

"You know, we never did get married." She poured herself another cup out of her copper pot. Then she held it up to me. Reluctantly, I pushed my cup forward. I couldn't leave now.

"I didn't know that."

"Engaged, but never married," she told me quietly. "We gave you kids my last name." I wasn't sure where this was going. It had been years since this subject came up and longer yet since she was the one to bring it up.

"Why not?" I asked. I was genuinely curious.

She shrugged her shoulders and said, "Kids, that's why. It turns out they're more expensive than most would guess."

"So you didn't get married because of me and Nathan?"

"That's one way of looking at it. But no, it was because we didn't have the money. Not to spend on the fancy day that I wanted, anyway."

I had never imagined my mother as the person who wanted a flashy wedding. She'd always seemed so level-headed and down to Earth. "Waste not, want not," was one of her favourite sayings. It drove me nuts as a kid.

"Why didn't you guys elope or something?"

"We just didn't."

"Why are you telling me this now?" I asked. This conversation was not one I ever expected to have with my mom. It didn't make sense to me that she was suddenly feeling the need to actually talk to me about something meaningful. I wondered if it was because she was dying.

"Jess, I haven't ever really talked to anyone about your dad leaving me. I…" Her eyes watered and she covered her hand with her mouth for a second. "I was so hurt that he didn't want to be with me. With us."

"That was his loss, Mom," I said. "Besides, you went to a therapist, remember? I remember writing that letter." I couldn't believe I felt the need to reassure her. I'd never been granted the same courtesy from her.

There was a slight hesitation before she answered me. "I meant friends and family, Jess." She sniffed once, and just like that, my mom was back. "You guys were better off without him."

"Are you upset because of that article? Because that girl's dad wants to be with her?" I asked.

Mom gave me a startled look and for a moment I thought she was going to cry again. But then she shook her head. "No. I'm sure that man isn't the saint he's made out to be, either. It's easy to look good when something bad happens to you. Doesn't mean he always did the right thing for his family."

"You should take a break from the news. It seems like it's filling your head with all kinds of crap."

"You're probably right. Thanks for stopping by tonight. It was good to see you," she said.

"Yeah. No problem." It was a dismissal, just more polite than I was used to. "I'm going to head out. You should get some sleep or something."

On the way out, I gave her a hug. I hadn't done that since I was a child. I didn't like how sensitive, how weak, I was becoming. The worst part was that I didn't know if it was because of Brandon or because my mom was dying.

Either way, if I wasn't careful, I would wind up getting hurt, and I'd had enough of that for one lifetime already.

***

2019:

Garett was still pulling away from her. He didn't call anymore and Laura didn't think he'd even notice if she didn't swing by every day to check on him.

At first, she'd intended to stay by his side every step of the way. She'd insisted he go up to the bed and get a good night's rest and she'd slept on the couch. Eventually, though, she couldn't sleep as she listened to him pace above her.

The couch started to be uncomfortable. She asked him if he was okay with her sleeping with him again and he'd said he was.

The result, however, was that she slept on the bed and he paced in the living room so he didn't wake her. It defeated her entire plan, so she'd gone back to the couch.

The more tired they both got, the more she walked on eggshells. One night, one she would regret forever, she went upstairs and yelled at Garett to get into bed and take one of the pills his doctor had prescribed.

"You expect me to sleep when my daughter is out there? What if I take those pills and they find something? Then what? I'll sleep through it?" Even when they had fought before, she'd never heard his tone be so hostile.

"They don't knock you out forever, Garett. And I would come wake you. How do you expect to be there for her if you can't stand on your feet?"

He didn't respond to Laura, just gently pushed her back out of the room and slammed the door in her face. She didn't hear him pace as much that night, but it didn't mean that he had necessarily slept. His face was pale and his eyes were puffy when he came down for coffee the next morning.

"I'm sorry about last night," he said. "I shouldn't have pushed you out of the room."

"I shouldn't have raised my voice like that." She walked over to him and tried to give him a hug, but he stepped back and shrugged her off.

"I need coffee and an update."

She stepped back and let him past her into the kitchen. At first, she brushed it off as the time of day. Maybe he wasn't ready for anything until he was more awake; some people couldn't handle anything in the morning without their coffee first.

That afternoon, she brought him up a sandwich and a glass of water. He was sitting on the bed, staring out the window. She wasn't sure if he had fallen asleep for a moment or if he was just zoned out.

She laid the sandwich on his night table and then sat beside him on the bed, leaning her head on his shoulder. He jerked away from her like she was a hot poker. Then he resumed his pacing.

"I've made you a sandwich," she told him. "You should probably eat something." She stood and crossed her arms as he paced. He made no move toward the food, not even acknowledging that she had spoken.

"So now you're going to starve yourself, too? Do you plan to die before they can find Brandy?"

"What would you know? You don't even have children," he snapped at her.

Laura felt her face flush. "Pardon me?"

He stopped in his tracks and glared at her. "You've been pestering me this entire time, telling me how I should react to losing a child. You don't know how it feels. This isn't the first time I've lost a child and I got through it then, too."

She felt rooted to the floor. He'd never spoken about any other children before. All she knew about was Brandy. Had he and Emily had more than one child? Brandy hadn't mentioned anything, either.

"What do you mean, this isn't the first time?"

He rubbed his hands over his eyes and then over his head before sitting on the bed. "Before Emily, I had two other children. I lost them. I never got to watch them grow, to graduate school, to realize their dreams. I dealt with it then and I will deal with it now."

"Why didn't you tell me that before?"

"Some things are quite frankly none of your business, Laura. The fact that those children are gone has nothing to do with you."

"Does Brandy know?"

"Of course she does. They were her siblings."

The fact that he hadn't trusted her with the information struck her hard. She had thought they had no secrets between them. She'd bared everything to him, even her most shameful moments. Why would he hold back something so important?

"Was that when Emily found you?" Laura asked.

"What?" He had started pacing again.

"When you lost your other children, was that when Emily found you and helped you out of your dark time?"

"Does that really matter?"

"It does, because from what Brandy was saying, you weren't in a good place. If you're in a similar place now, then I should be worried."

He turned and pointed his finger at her, his face contorted in rage. "You do *not* get to tell me how to deal with this."

She stepped back from his finger as though it had struck her. He hadn't, but the effect was still the same.

"I'm not telling you how to deal with this," she said with a chill in her tone. "I'm trying to help. You'd be able to see that if you had some sleep or ate something."

"*Get out!*" he screamed. Spittle sprayed from his lips as he flung his hand toward the door, screaming, "Get out of my house!"

She didn't recognize the monster standing before her. Grief and anger transformed people. She knew that, but she hadn't expected to see something like this.

She made her way downstairs and grabbed her toiletries from the bathroom before tossing them in her suitcase and zipping everything shut. She had clothes in the washing machine, but she decided she could live without them.

On her way out, she slammed the door and hoped he felt terrible for the way he had treated her.

24

It was getting harder to go to work. While Brandon wasn't allowed to come out and visit me often, yet, I still felt comfort, knowing he was there.

I seemed to cry a lot lately, and more than anything, I just wanted to cry with him. But I couldn't do that. I couldn't crack and let him see my bare soul. He would leave, just like everyone else had. Leave or hurt me.

Our relationship had to be special. It would take time and it would take patience. I had to make sure that I stuck it out.

I brought him more clothes and a treat yesterday. I figured it had been a while since he had something sweet, so I stopped by a local bakery and grabbed us some doughnuts. He had been in heaven eating his. I felt great sharing that with him. He even giggled when he slopped some onto the bed.

I had never heard him laugh like that before, I realized, and once I heard it, I never wanted it to stop. His laugh wasn't malicious. There wasn't some secret, mean joke that was hilarious to him. He was laughing at himself. I didn't want him to ever stop.

It was another weakness I had to overcome. I mentally added it to my list, right next to not crying in front of him. If I broke down in front of him, he couldn't possibly respect me.

Work used to be a bit of a refuge for me. I could get out of my house and move around and do things. Now, I wanted nothing more than to be at home.

Mike noticed my reluctance to stay late. In the past, working a little bit of overtime wasn't a big deal for me. I would never leave an order incomplete when I left. I always got them done and ready for pick-up before I finished for the day.

With Brandon, I felt like my home life was more important than work.

"Jess," he said one day as I was doffing my work boots right at five. "What's the rush?"

I was kneeled on the floor in front of my locker, undoing the laces. These things had been expensive and I wanted them to last me a long time. I looked up at him and shrugged. "I've got stuff to do," I said.

"It's just that I've noticed you've been leaving right at five a lot lately. Usually, you're okay to put in the overtime."

"I'm still getting my hours in, right?"

"Well, yeah." He was looking uncomfortable right now.

"So what's the issue? I get paid per order and if I don't finish it by the end of the day, that's on me."

"I just always counted on you, is all. You're my superstar," he said.

"This superstar wants a life outside of work. I still work circles around the other guys and you know it. I'm just not putting in the extra time."

"Okay, it's just not like you." He had nothing to go on and he knew it. I didn't even feel kind of bad taking off at five every day. I barely stopped for lunch and I was never late. He had nothing to complain about. His main concern was probably that he couldn't look as good with his superiors if I didn't go that extra mile.

Still, I wondered if my willingness to stay for overtime was the reason I still had a job. I wasn't exactly a likeable person most of the time. That was why I felt like I had to go above and beyond.

"Tell you what, Mike," I said to him. "I'll work late a couple days a week, but I want a raise."

He raised an eyebrow and gave me a strange look, but then he nodded. "No guarantees, but I'll see what I can do. Are you going to start tonight?"

I didn't want to start tonight, but I figured I probably should. I slipped my feet back into my boots and tied them up. He definitely seemed happier now that I was going to stay and finish my order. It wouldn't take really long, but still, I needed to stop at the grocery store on my way home.

It turned out that Brandon was pretty good at cooking. Well, really, I did the cooking. He gave me the recipes and the grocery list. I enjoyed having him out in the kitchen with me to do that.

There were all kinds of delicious foods that I had been missing out on all my adult life. I didn't know why I hadn't done more for myself, but Brandon was definitely bringing some new things out in me.

After I finished my order, I stopped by Mike's office to let him know I was leaving. He was waiting on me with his coat on. "You have somewhere to be tonight?" I said.

He had the good grace to blush at least. I moved my gaze from him before I rolled my eyes. I didn't want to push things too far, but I was anxious to get out of here, too.

I was easily half an hour at the grocery store, trying to find everything for Brandon. He wanted some kind of stirfry tonight that had things like hoisin sauce in it. I walked up and down several aisles before I gave in and asked one of the store clerks where to find it.

I rushed home after that, feeling guilty that I was over an hour late getting home. I knew Thrasher would be fine, but Brandon wasn't used to spending that much time alone.

I was in one hell of a hurry when I turned onto my street. When I saw Nathan's SUV, I nearly had a stroke with rage. What the hell was he doing here?

He was just getting out of his vehicle when I pulled in. I couldn't remember if the curtains were closed in Brandon's room or not. I may have left them open a bit so he could get sunlight. My hands were sweaty by the time I got out of the truck.

"Hey, Jess."

"What are you doing here?" I demanded.

"It's good to see you, too," he said with a forced smile on his face.

"Seriously, Nathan. You didn't even text me."

"No, I didn't," he said while crossing his arms. "I came by just to talk to you. I was in the area."

"About what?"

"Are you going to invite me in?" he asked. After a moment, he could see that I was going to do no such thing. "Wow, okay. I came by to apologize for the way I behaved at Mom's dinner. Jenny pointed out that I was an ass to you, and with Mom being the way she is, I just, I don't want things to be bad between us anymore. You know?"

I didn't know what to say to that. Where was all of this mushy shit coming from? First my Mom and now my brother. Could things get more weird?

"Uh, thanks for saying that," I said. I had nothing to apologize for, so I offered nothing up. He seemed to be expecting something from me, though. "Have you seen Mom lately? She seems kind of weird."

That was not what he wanted to hear, I could tell by the disappointed look on his face, but I'd done nothing wrong. "Yeah, I saw her the other day. She seemed fine to me. She's obsessed with that case about the missing girl, for whatever reason. I made her turn the T.V. off."

The thought gave me a chill. What would he think if he knew that missing person was tied up in my house right now? Would he call the cops? Or would he understand?

"Yeah, she wanted me to read some story in the Guardian the other day, too. I told her to stop taking in so much news. She doesn't need to be down in the dumps any more than she is."

"I don't know that she can help it. She's always been a bit of a news addict and something about this has struck a chord with her. Maybe she's imagining what it would be like to lose her child."

I reached into my truck and pulled out my groceries. The sooner this conversation was over, the better. "I doubt that. She seems eager to leave us behind."

"That's what you think?" he asked. "That she's leaving us like Dad did?"

"I'm just calling a spade a spade."

"Or," he said with a menacing tone in his voice, "she's had a shitty life and she's not that excited to continue with it. The love of her life left her to raise two children on her own. Her brother disowned her and her daughter can't stand to be around her. I do everything for her, Jess, *everything*, but it's not my attention she wants."

I didn't understand what he was talking about. My mother had never seemed interested in me or how my life was going. Every time I had tried talking to her about a problem, she'd been annoyed and told me off. I couldn't remember a single time that I hadn't had to beg or act out for some affection from her.

"You're the favourite, Nathan. It's never been me. I don't know why you think otherwise." I raised the groceries up to show him. "Anyway, I have to go make some dinner. Thrasher has probably already pissed all over my floor."

"You know what," he said, throwing his hands in the air, "forget it, Jess. One day, you are going to look back on this conversation and realize what you missed out on. Your brother wanted to make peace with you and you couldn't be bothered. Have fun dying alone and unwanted."

He slammed the door to his SUV and threw gravel with the tires as he backed out of my driveway. He was pissed at me and all I could think was that my mom would soon be calling me to find out what had happened.

I had opened the door and put down the groceries before I noticed the smell. It was rank and it didn't smell like Thrasher. I made my way down the hall. He sat outside of Brandon's room. The smell was coming from there.

I called Thrasher over to the back door and let him outside before I went in to see Brandon. I felt horrible for leaving him this long. I couldn't do this again.

There were tears running down his face. I rushed over to pull back the duct tape. "I'm so sorry," he said as soon as he could. "I tried to hold it." His face contorted and he started sobbing.

I put my hand on his cheek and stroked his eyebrow, trying to calm him down. "It's okay. Don't worry. I was late getting home and accidents happen." I leaned down and kissed his forehead. "Come on," I said as I reached up and undid his chains. "Let's get you cleaned up."

He was still crying but he didn't seem as distressed as he had before. I led him into the bathroom and then grabbed a couple of towels for him. "Why don't you have a quick shower. Leave the door open, though."

"Can I take the tensor bandage off?" I hesitated and then nodded. He could put it on again as soon as he was done.

While he jumped into the shower, I pulled the sheets off of his bed and threw them in the washing machine. He was going to have to be out with me for a while if the sheets were going through a full cycle. It annoyed me that I hadn't thought to get a spare set of sheets for that bed.

When Thrasher came in, he headed down to the bathroom and kept Brandon company. I pulled out the groceries and started making our dinner. I was getting the hang of things now, so I was confident doing this on my own.

It wasn't long before Brandon emerged from the bathroom with his hair wrapped up in a towel and bandage strapped tight around his chest. He wore only the jeans, not having bothered to put on his shirt.

My breath caught as I looked at him. "You're so beautiful," I said and then blushed when I realized I'd said it out loud.

He smiled at me. "Thanks, Cathy. You're not terrible looking yourself." Was that a compliment?

"I don't need you to lie to me," I said gruffly. I motioned for him to sit down at the table and continued chopping the broccoli.

"I'm not lying." I didn't know how to respond to that, so I didn't. "You don't believe me?"

"I don't. I think you're trying to butter me up and I don't appreciate it." I wanted him to drop the subject.

"Well, Cathy, I don't lie to people. And I think that you are beautiful, but you try to downplay it."

I took in a deep breath and turned to face him. I was ready to tell him to shut up, but something about the look on his face stopped me. "What do you mean, I downplay it?"

"Well, when we met at the club, you didn't have any makeup on and the clothes you were wearing were a loose fit, not exactly a flattering look for you."

"There's nothing flattering about my body. There's no curves, only straight lines and angles."

"Who do you think the big fashion designers get to model their clothes? It's not girls like me." I frowned at his pronoun mix up and he seemed to pick up on it. "I mean, guys like me. I couldn't fit most of their stuff with my hips. You, though, you could pull it off with style."

He sounded almost envious of my body, and I didn't understand it. I was a twig. I had no boobs and no butt. No man could grab a handful of me because there wasn't anything to grab.

I'd never really looked at fashion magazines growing up. There was the odd one that I flipped through, but I knew that I didn't stand a chance at looking like any of those girls. My mom couldn't afford the clothes and I didn't know how to apply makeup. Plus, I hated all of those girls. They were the mean ones.

"I bet the girls were super jealous of you in school," he said.

"No, they were horrible to me."

"Yeah, because they were jealous. If they didn't stomp on your feelings, you would have been a potential threat. That doesn't make it right, but junior high and high school have a survival-of-the-fittest culture."

I turned back to the cutting board and finished what I was doing. I couldn't believe what I was hearing and I was battling the instinct inside of me that told me he was lying. I wanted to believe every word he was saying, but I didn't want to open myself to that kind of hope.

"So, what would I do if I wanted to show off my beauty instead of downplay it?" I asked.

Brandon was eager to share. As soon as I had opened the gates, the advice started flooding in. It was a bit overwhelming. I had never worried about eyeliner, lip gloss or contouring. I didn't even know what most of that meant.

"If you buy the stuff, I will show you how to do it." He gave a little squeal. "This could be so much fun!"

The enthusiasm was unexpected and I found myself caught up in the undercurrent of his excitement. I couldn't stop smiling as we spoke, and I even heard myself giggle.

After supper, I let him stay up and watch one episode of Criminal Minds with me before I put him to bed.

As we watched the show, I felt dread building up in me. Agreeing to all of this was a mistake. It was all a trick to sucker me in. The other shoe would drop, and I wasn't sure how I would deal with that.

25

She hadn't expected to feel grateful to Cathy for any reason. Cathy was the reason she was in the position she was in. Cathy was the reason that she was forced to shit in a diaper because she couldn't get to the bathroom.

She wondered if part of the reason she felt more sympathy for Cathy was because of their conversation that night before. It was hard to truly hate someone when you knew that they were sick because of someone else's actions.

Brandy hadn't had that problem in school. She had always been well liked, even though she wasn't the most popular in the school. But she had seen the treatment some students had received and she was now ashamed that she hadn't stood up for them. Was her lack of action going to create someone else like Cathy?

She tried to think back on all of those she'd watched without saying a word. Now that she had time to think, she decided she would make a list of those she could have helped but had chosen not to. If she ever got out of here, she was going to track them all down and personally apologize.

The way Cathy had handled the situation with the bed had comforted Brandy. Cathy didn't fly off the handle like she had expected. Instead, she'd acted like her mother had when she was small. No shower had ever felt better, and she was surprised she was allowed to release her breasts.

As she showered, she'd looked around the room, trying to think of anything that could help her escape. There was a tiny window, but even if opened, there was no way she could fit through there. The only way out of the bathroom was through the trailer.

There was no razor in the shower, only cheap shampoo and conditioner and a bar of soap. There wasn't even moisturizer on the vanity.

If she was more clever like people on T.V. shows, she would come up with something, but she felt hopeless. When Thrasher trotted in and made himself comfortable beside the tub, she gave up any intentions of escape. He would rip her throat out first if he thought she was a threat.

In many ways, Thrasher was more effective in keeping her in the trailer than Cathy's chains and drugs. It seemed like the dog was psychic. Cathy barely had to look at him and he knew what to do.

If she had tried to open the window in the room, the dog would have been on to her in no time. Even if Cathy didn't hear her moving around, Thrasher would lose his marbles.

There was no way she could ever get him to be as comfortable around her as he was with Cathy, but she hoped he was warming up to her. When he'd licked her face, she'd had to fight down a smug feeling of victory.

She had to remind herself that it didn't mean anything other than that Thrasher recognized her. Maybe he even thought of her as a tasty treat.

She'd tried to think of different ways to kill him or distract him, but Cathy had things covered. Her sleeping pills were mixed in with her morning drink, and Cathy watched her as she drank the entire glass.

At first, she'd considered vomiting the juice up. The tape and her inability to turn her head prevented that. She would just drown in her own vomit. So avoiding the pills was out.

As far as being tied down, there wasn't a lot she could do there. Cathy ensured there was no give in the chains. There was no way for Brandy to push her hands down into the mattress and free up a link or two. It was the same with her feet, too.

If she tried to scooch off of the bed, she would just end up with the mattress and board on top of her while she laid there helpless, waiting for Thrasher.

She had long since decided that her best bet for getting Thrasher on her side was to try to be extra kind to him when they were alone in the bathroom. At first, she talked to him and made funny noises, the kind that made the dog cock his head to one side. Once he seemed to thaw toward her a little bit more, she even reached out to touch him. He'd been reluctant at first, but now she was able to reach over and pet him. She hadn't yet worked up the nerve to try to play with him, she had the feeling that he was going to be rough.

Time had slipped by and she had no way of knowing how much had gone. It felt like forever, especially when she was laying there at night. All she could do was weasel her way into Cathy's good graces and hope the woman would relax some of her restraints.

The idea for a makeover had been brilliant. It wasn't something that Brandy had seen coming, but once she spoke about it, she could see a twinkle in Cathy's eye. It was terrible that Cathy didn't believe she was pretty.

She wasn't conventional, that was for sure, but if she put some effort into herself, she would look amazing. The key to sexiness,

Brandy always found, was confidence. Cathy hadn't had confidence at the club. She'd had beer and that was it.

Around Brandy, she was in control, so of course she felt confident. But whenever Brandy brought up something personal, she could see the insecurities float to the surface. That was where Brandy needed to make her move.

Getting in someone's good graces meant making them feel good about themselves. She had started with trying to get Cathy to eat better. She thought if she had more of a variety in her diet, she would likely be less grumpy. People who didn't eat properly often had issues with their mood.

Their routine of building supper together was starting to become a bit more relaxed. Brandy had never been stupid enough to try to help Cathy with anything besides instructions. If she did anything more than that, she would be destroying all of the work she'd put in.

But she was paying attention. Each day, Cathy was getting more and more careless with what she left lying around. She would walk a few feet away from the knife now, rather than carry it with her. Brandy had noticed that Cathy kept her back turned to her more often, too.

If Thrasher hadn't been laying at her feet every time, she would have made her move by now. She was going to have to get the dog out of the picture or have him warm up to her. She wasn't sure which would be best.

Cathy's consent to buying makeup and a razor had shocked Brandy. She had expected to be shot down immediately. It surprised her that she was so excited to show Cathy how to dress up.

Clearly, her mother hadn't shown her any of these skills and Cathy had never bothered to learn them on her own. Brandy knew she would be amazed at how the world changed for her if she only put in a little effort.

Maybe it would change enough that Cathy wouldn't need her in her life anymore. If Brandy could help her to find some inner confidence, maybe she would set Brandy free.

***

_2019:_

Walking into the makeup aisle was like walking into a sex shop for the first time. There were all of these products around me and I didn't know what any of them did. I was embarrassed to ask for help, too.

There were pretty girls looking at things around me and I felt a strong urge to run. But Brandon had thankfully given me a list. If I just stuck to the items on the list, I should probably be okay.

Only, there were four different brands for foundation and each has twenty different shades. Those come in liquid and powder.

Then there was the lipstick, the mascara, eyeliner, blush, contouring sponges and something called primer. I had no idea what that last one was and I was desperately reading all of the tags to try to find a description that would enlighten me.

"Can I help you with something?" asked a woman with a blue smock. I prayed for the ground to just open up and swallow me whole. What the hell was I doing here?

"I'm just picking some stuff up for a friend," I said. I shoved the list in her direction.

"Okay." She read over the stuff. "Are there any particular brands she likes?"

"Uh, I don't know. She wasn't very specific."

The woman was a saviour. Not only did she find everything on my list, but she talked me through the pros and cons of everything to help me make a decision. I left the store with confidence in the products I was bringing home to Brandon.

I'd even found a nice razor that had some kind of gel strips on it to keep your legs moisturized or whatever.

Truth be told, I had never shaved before. It was never a priority for me. Anything I could do to avoid the unwanted attention of some asshole or some bitch who wanted to give me grief, the better. I always did my best to just fade into the background.

Putting on makeup and making yourself look nice was the exact opposite of that. It was walking out into the world with a sign that said "Look at me!"

When I'd talked to Brandon about it all, I'd been excited. It was an alien feeling to look forward to making myself look pretty. I felt like a fraud and worried I would look like a clown. But just because Brandon showed me how to do it didn't mean that I had to wear it every day.

Besides, part of me was doing this because he had been so excited about it. There had been a transformation about him when he started talking about the possibilities. I had reined him in as much as I could. I wasn't buying new clothes or getting my hair done, I would start with something less permanent.

All of this left me feeling strangely unbalanced. Brandon was doing all of these things for me, and all I was doing was playing along. I decided that I would do something for him, too, and made one more stop before I hit the register on the way out.

Brandon seemed genuinely excited to see me. As I unchained him, I considered for the first time maybe easing up on some of the restrictions. If he was feeling like this, maybe he would stick around.

I knew there was another shoe coming down from the sky, though. And once it dropped, it would shatter this illusion of trust between us. That little feeling in the back of my mind had saved me from hurt more times than I cared to admit. I didn't want to think that way about Brandon, but survivor's instincts were there for a reason.

We had agreed on pizza and beer for supper. Brandon had also requested a rom-com for a movie, but first, we had to get dolled up.

"Let's see!" he said.

I pulled out all of the makeup and lined it up on the table. He sorted through everything and studied the label before setting it down. There were also some sponges, Q-tips and other things that the lady said were used to apply the makeup.

"Did you get the razors? I think we should start there because we'll likely get wet."

I hesitated for a moment and pulled them out of the bag. "I've never shaved before, so I hope I got the right stuff."

"What?" he said, clearly shocked. "Even for a bathing suit or shorts?"

"I haven't worn anything like that since I was little. My mom never showed me and I never asked." Another screw-up on my mom's part to add to the list. It was a long one.

"Okay, well these razors are perfect. Do you want me to show you how to do it?"

I was a bit nervous about this part. Razors could be deadly, but I'd looked at the ones in this pack. You'd have to take everything apart for it to be majorly dangerous. And if I had Thrasher with me, I didn't think it would get that far.

I was going to have to trust him to not hurt me.

"Is it hard to do?" I asked.

"No, it's really not. For the most part, the biggest concern is getting a little nick or accidentally shaving off a mosquito bite. That hurts," he said with a laugh. "It'll take some practice, but if it's something you want to continue to do, you'll get the hang of it in no time."

"Okay, I'll try it. Should I order the pizza first?"

"Nope. We'll shave your legs and then you can order pizza. That way when the delivery guy comes, you can be wearing makeup for him."

"Why do I care about him?"

"Bad choice of words," he said. "When you see him, you'll know that you look good and you'll feel more confident. While he'll get to enjoy looking at a pretty girl, you'll get to enjoy that you made him look. Know what I mean?"

I'd heard people talk about feminine wiles, and I decided makeup probably fit under that label. Never once had I thought that I had the power to make anyone look though.

When I'd been seducing Lyle, part of me thought it was pure luck and that I'd found myself a desperate man. And maybe I had, but something about me had commanded his attention and I realized now that it was purely the fact that I was female.

I wondered how differently I would be treated if I did wear makeup on a regular basis. Or if I styled my hair before I went out. I'd never considered that part of the reason I was treated so terribly growing up was my lack of basic care for my body. I'd thought my lack of give-a-damn was armour to prevent pain, but instead, it was an iron maiden. Nothing could get in to hurt me, but it wasn't doing anything to stop the pain within.

"All right," I said. "Let's do this."

Brandon was so gentle and caring with me as he took me through the steps to doing it. I held the razor in my hand over my leg that was lathered in conditioner of all things. To my utter humiliation, I was frozen.

In my mind, this was a terribly painful process. Weren't you peeling off a layer of skin as you pulled the razor up your leg? Would it be sharp enough to cut the hairs or would it pull some of them out?

Brandon saw my hesitation and suggested he shave his own leg first. "Here, I'll show you." He rolled up his pants and then covered his own legs in conditioner. "We use conditioner because it moisturizes your skin. If you don't use anything to buffer between your skin and the blade while you're shaving, you'll get razor rash. Some people use soap or buy the special shaving cream, but conditioner works just fine. You might find soap dries your skin out too much."

He placed the razor on his leg. "I don't have to put any pressure down. I just set it on my leg and pull up. It's easy to see what you've done because you can see where the conditioner is missing."

He finished both of his legs up in a short time. I was amazed at the confidence with which he wielded the thing. There was no flinching as he went over his Achille's tendon or under his knee. Just a smooth long line in the conditioner.

"Does it hurt?" I asked.

"No. The only problem you might have is some ingrown hairs, only because you've never done it before. The best way to avoid that is to shave *with* your hair. You won't get as close a shave, but it's worth it."

"How do you do that?" I asked. What the hell did that mean? Shave with the hair.

"Instead of pulling the razor up the leg," he demonstrated on his right leg, dragging the razor from his ankle to his knee. "You pull it down the leg." He flipped the razor around his hand and then pulled the blade from his knee to his ankle. "It's a bit awkward, for sure, but I think it's the best way to avoid all the bumps and rashes."

It looked more than awkward when he did it that way. It looked damn near impossible. I wasn't sure I could even bend that way.

"Do you want me to show you?" He was hesitant to ask that, I could see it in his eyes. He knew just as well as I that we were pushing past something. We were taking the next step in our relationship, one that relied on trust.

I looked over at Thrasher lying quietly on the floor and then quickly nodded. "Yes, please. I don't want to have any ingrown hairs."

He gave me a gentle smile and lifted my ankle and rested it on his knee. Slowly, he drew the razor down from my knee to my ankle. "Tell me if you're uncomfortable. I'll stop any time," he said.

With each stroke down my leg, he would follow with his other hand, checking for hairs that he'd missed.

I didn't realize how much I could blush. My face felt heated and there were these strange butterflies in my stomach. His gentle touch made me crave more from him.

He finished the first leg and started on the next one. I closed my eyes as he rubbed on the conditioner and he dug his fingers in a little bit, massaging the muscle. I felt the razor slowly move down my leg, followed by the tips of his fingers.

This was easily the most intimate, erotic moment of my life to date. I could see the ledge and I was inching toward it. If I wasn't careful, I was going to fall over the side, deeply into the abyss of love, hoping that there was a net or water at the bottom and not stone.

"And that's all there is to it," he said. He turned the tap on to rinse off the razor and then handed it back to me, handle first. "Quick, put your pants on. Freshly-shaved legs in your pants feel amazing."

I laughed at him and did as he suggested. He was right, I thought I could feel every fibre in the denim as I pulled it on. It felt like I was pulling it on over silk.

I looked over at Brandon. He was smiling at me. Not a fake smile, but a genuine one. He was delighted that I felt good. I felt another blush come on and looked away from him.

"I'm going to go order the pizza," I mumbled.

26

Something had happened, but she couldn't put her finger on it. Cathy had opened up to her somehow without saying anything. Brandy was surprised that she had been allowed to even touch the razor. She had fully been expecting Cathy to do all of the shaving.

When Cathy had closed her eyes as Brandy put on the conditioner, there had been a moment of utter beauty in the room. It was like they had forgotten who they were. Brandy didn't feel like a captive at that moment, more like a friend. Maybe even a little more than that.

It had been a dangerous feeling, but one that she couldn't control. She'd never seen Cathy so relaxed. Even Thrasher had seemed less on edge, as though he could sense her joy.

More and more, Brandy was realizing that despite Cathy's faults, she was just a human. She didn't know how to behave, didn't pick up on social cues as easily as others, but she still had the same feelings. Being kind and helpful to her made Brandy feel closer to her somehow.

Now that it was time for the makeup, she felt a bit nervous. The stuff that Cathy had picked out would work. The foundation might be off a bit, but otherwise, it would be fine.

But if she wasn't careful and Cathy didn't approve of what she did for her, it might not go as well. She didn't want to be punished for trying to help someone.

Cathy was unstable enough to see her act of kindness as one of malice and wouldn't hesitate to act as she saw fit. The last thing Brandy wanted was to go hungry or be left in a diaper for several days. She had to be careful.

After ordering the pizza, Cathy and Brandy sat themselves down at the table. Brandy told her to bring her brightest lights, which ended up being the kitchen light and the lamp from the end table. Still, it was better than nothing.

"So, you have brown eyes. That means you can get away with nearly any kind of eyeshadow, so pick the one you want."

Cathy stared down at the two palettes she'd picked out. Slowly, she reached out and pointed to the gold/bronze palette.

"Perfect," said Brandy. "Usually, we wash our face first, but tonight it's only a temporary thing so we'll skip that. First, we put on the primer. This is like the conditioner on your legs. It's a barrier between your skin and the makeup. It will allow the foundation to go on more evenly, prevent your skin from drying out, and make it easier to remove at night.

"You don't need much." She put a little dab on her finger as an example. "Then we spread it out like this." Slowly she traced the t-zone on Cathy and then rubbed the primer on in tiny circles on her cheeks and forehead.

Leaning so close made her self-conscious about her breath. Maybe Cathy would smell it and take the hint? There wasn't much she could do about it.

"Now we put on the foundation. You can use your finger or a sponge. Some even come in sticks like lipstick." She traced the colour onto Cathy's face and used a sponge to blend it in. "The foundation is your base. It's like painting the canvas white. Now you can do whatever you want with your face. Some people completely transform themselves. Personally, I prefer just emphasizing what I have. I don't want to be someone else, you know?"

Cathy nodded with a concentrated look. Brandy thought she'd be taking notes if she could.

"Here we have a highlighter, which is a white powder that will draw attention to certain areas of your face. We'll put that on after we put the darker concealer on. With this, I will darken the shadows on your face, like on your cheeks, helping to highlight the cheekbones." She put two strokes of the concealer on either side of Cathy's face and then leaned back to make sure it was even.

"We just blend it in with the foundation a little. Then we're going to put on the highlighter. That's going to go on the tip of your nose, your forehead and your cheekbones." She held up another powder next. "This is the setting powder. It will help to keep all the foundation in place."

The next step was the eyeshadow. She layered the shadow on Cathy's eyes, giving her a mature but sexy look. Not too naughty, but not exactly innocent either.

When she was done, she pulled out the eyeliner. It was an ink liner, which meant she had to be precise. It also meant that Cathy had to trust her and not move at all. Once again, in the same evening, she was pushing the envelope. She could only hope that Cathy would allow her.

"Okay. This is likely going to tickle, and it's always a tricky part. Please don't move. This kind of liner can be hard to fix. I'm going to close one eye at a time and draw the line along your lashes."

Cathy didn't even hesitate this time. She closed both eyes immediately, and Brandy felt a rush of giddiness. She was getting through!

She couldn't play her hand just yet, though. Things had to
progress slowly.

With a delicacy she didn't know she possessed, she traced the
line of eyeliner on Cathy's upper eyelids. She'd decided on the fash-
ionable cat's eye look. "Okay, now open your eyes and look up. I've
got to do the bottom lid."

Cathy did as she was told with no complaint.

"Next is the mascara. This one requires a particular face. For
whatever reason, it works best for stretching out your eyelids and
putting this stuff on. Are you ready?" She lowered her jaw in an
exaggerated "oh" face.

Cathy scoffed at her. "You want me to make that face? That's
ridiculous."

"It really is," said Brandy. "But it works, I promise." The last two
words slipped out of her mouth before she even thought about them.
Cathy seemed to take them to heart, staring into Brandy's eyes for a
moment before nodding.

Then she stretched her face into the "oh" and opened her eyes
wide. It was Brandy's turn to laugh, though she stifled it as quickly
as she could. She expected a rebuke, but Cathy kept the face and
moved her finger through the air in a circle. Brandy had to move on.

The finishing touch was Cathy's lipstick. The colour was more
neutral, which suited Cathy very well. She had been worried she
would come back with cherry red or blood red. The pink brought
the whole look together, giving Cathy the look of a businesswoman.

"And we're done," Brandy said softly, taking in the whole look.
"Go see!"

For a moment, Cathy didn't move, then she slowly made her way down to the bathroom to look in the mirror. Brandy heard a soft gasp and she couldn't help but smile.

She busied herself with cleaning up and putting everything away. She wanted Cathy to have a private moment to appreciate her beauty.

When she came out, Brandy could see tears gathering in her eyes. "Don't cry!" she said. "Your makeup might run. Look up at the ceiling with your eyes wide open. It'll help."

Cathy did as she was told and took a deep, shuddering breath. Brandy waved her hands in front of Cathy's eyes for no reason other than that was what she would do for herself.

When Cathy finally had it under control, she looked back down at Brandy. "Thank you," she said. "I-I've- thank you."

"Any time," said Brandy with a smile. The expression on Cathy's face almost made everything seem worth it.

The doorbell rang and Cathy froze. "Go on," said Brandy. "I've got to go to the washroom, I'll take Thrasher with me."

Cathy smiled and nearly skipped over to the door. Brandy chewed her lips on the way to the bathroom. For some strange reason, she was fighting her own tears.

She listened as Cathy flirted with the pizza guy. It was a bit awkward, for sure, but he was definitely into it. Now, all she could hope was that her kindness would be returned. Maybe Cathy would let her go and… and then Brandy would have charges pressed against her. There was no way she could be her friend knowing how dangerous she could be.

When she came out of the bathroom, Cathy had plates set out on the table. Not paper ones, the real ones. Brandy smiled and said, "Oh my God. That smells delicious!"

"It's the best place in the city. A bit expensive, maybe, but worth it."

Brandy sat down and dug right into her pizza. She was starving and partially afraid Cathy would change her mind at some point and take it away. After a moment, she noticed that Cathy was only picking at her pizza.

"Is everything okay?" asked Brandy.

"Yeah, I've just been thinking," said Cathy. Brandy felt her heart flutter but schooled her face, hoping to hide any emotion the words gave her.

"About what?"

"Nobody's ever been as nice to me as you have tonight. I know you're having a hard time adjusting to things, so I bought something that might help out. You can think of it as a gift."

Not the answer Brandy was hoping for, but it didn't sound negative. It sounded like their relationship was becoming more of a give-and-take thing, rather than a captor-and-captive situation.

"That's very thoughtful of you, Cathy..." Brandy considered going on and then thought better of it. Too much and Cathy would think she was making fun of her and Brandy didn't want to ruin the mood.

They finished their pizza in congenial silence. Brandy ate three pieces and thought her stomach would burst, but at least she would be full through the night. There were some nights as she lay awake that her stomach would growl so much, it nearly ached. Especially if she'd somehow managed to piss Cathy off and miss her supper.

Afterward, Brandy grabbed the plates and started washing up right away. There was no harm in giving an impression of domesticity. That was what Cathy was looking for after all.

When Brandy was putting the plates away, Cathy snuck up behind her. She wrapped her arms around Brandy and gave her a swift hug.

"Close your eyes, okay? I want this to be a surprise."

She decided she didn't like surprises anymore. Especially from people like Cathy. She wanted predictable and boring. "Okay," she said and forced a giggle out.

Cathy turned her around, "I'm just going to bring you over to the chair so you can sit down, okay? I'll tell you when you can open your eyes."

Brandy sat down in the chair and waited, but Cathy didn't say anything. She heard a plastic bag rattling and something was set on the table, but no further instructions.

Then she felt Cathy pick up a lock of her hair and she felt her body turn to ice. "What are you doing?" she asked. She didn't care that she sounded tense and alarmed.

"Keep your eyes closed," said Cathy.

Adrenaline coursed through Brandy and she felt her body start to shiver. She had to bite her lip to prevent her teeth from chattering.

Then she heard the slick, metallic sound of a pair of scissors shutting. Something fluttered past her face on the way to the ground. Cathy had another lock of hair in her hand and the sound repeated.

She couldn't stop the tears that streamed down her face any more than she could the shaking. She could taste blood in her mouth, but she was afraid to sob.

Cathy didn't seem to notice her distress. She continued along Brandy's long blonde hair, cutting off chunk after chunk and letting it fall to the floor.

"Brandon, you're going to look so much better after this. I can't wait to hear what you think."

Brandy could feel her nose begin to run. She tried to sniffle discreetly, but Cathy stopped. "Are you crying?" she asked. She didn't sound concerned about Brandy's feelings, only confused.

Brandy had only a second to decide what to say. There was no point in denying the tears so she nodded. "I'm- I'm just so overwhelmed that you thought to do this for me," she said.

"Are you upset?" asked Cathy, a slight hint of menace colouring the tone.

"N-No! This is just- This is just so emotional for me. I never expected you to do me this kindness." The lie burned in her mouth, but with Cathy standing behind her with a pair of sharp scissors, there was no other choice.

"You just wait, there's more!" said Cathy in an excited tone. She started snipping away again.

"Can I open my eyes now?" asked Brandy.

"No, I'm not done," said Cathy. Brandy heard something unzip and then the unmistakable sound of a razor. "Okay, lean forward, I want to try to get this even for you. I don't want it looking silly."

As her hair was sheared from her head, she wondered if she would pass out. Little prickles of hair were falling into her shirt and onto her face. She didn't brush them away, even when they tickled her nose. She wanted to pick up all of her hair and hold it tight.

It was an infinity of seconds as Cathy moved through her hair. The buzzing noise clogged her ears, blocking out anything else. Her body still shook and her snot ran freely, mixing with the hair on her face.

When Cathy was done, she turned the buzzer off and then started brushing the hair off of Brandy's shoulders.

"Keep them closed! I'm going to bring you to the bathroom so you can see yourself,"

She helped Brandy stand. Brandy's legs shook so much, she wasn't sure if she could make it to the bathroom without collapsing. She knew she held her face in a grimace and she was squeezing her eyes shut with every bit of might she had.

When they reached the bathroom, she heard a smile in Cathy's voice, "Okay, open them."

Slowly, she opened her eyes to stare at the reflection before her. All two-and-a-half feet of her hair was gone. All that was left was stubble on her head.

"You like it?" asked Cathy. She rubbed her hands over Brandy's head. "It feels kind of neat. It'll be easier to keep your hat on now."

With a strength Brandy had never known existed inside of her, she forced a smile onto her face. "It's amazing, Cathy. Thank you so, so much." She reached up and touched her head. If Cathy had cut any closer she would have been bald.

"You're welcome. Tonight was really nice," said Cathy. "Come on, let's go watch a movie and snuggle."

The tears had stopped; not because her grief was done, but because she'd entered the stage where there was only numbness. Her mind could no longer handle the situation and was choosing not to feel anything.

When Cathy pulled her toward the living room again, she didn't fight it. She followed her like a robot. If she didn't obey Cathy, she probably wouldn't live.

***

2019:

I had expected a different reaction from Brandon when I showed him his buzz cut. I'd thought he would think it was cool, not be so emotional. He was weird the rest of the evening, too. It was almost like he wasn't there watching the movie with me.

If I laughed, he did, too, but it sounded almost mechanical. The tears had stopped eventually and I couldn't decide if they were from joy or sadness.

I'd experienced a moment of joy earlier that had brought me to tears. Brandon had transformed me from an ugly, middle-aged woman into someone who actually looked attractive. I'd barely been able to recognize myself in the mirror.

At first, it had felt like clown makeup, but I forced myself to leave it on. He had looked so happy while he was doing it. I felt like we finished the evening with a stronger bond.

He definitely hadn't been expecting me to cut his hair, that much I could tell. But I knew he would grow to like it; he looked more manly with a buzz cut than with long hair. More attractive to me.

I kind of wished I had someone else to share this moment with me. Taking before and after pictures would be a mistake. If someone got my phone and looked through the photos, I would be in trouble.

Instead, all I could do was stare at him and try to create a mental image that I could hold onto.

When I put him to bed that night, he asked if I could leave the duct tape off. My gut instinct was to say no. But he was pleading with his eyes and I finally capitulated.

"But I'm leaving Thrasher in here tonight, and if you make a peep, he'll be on you." That seemed to hit home and he nodded with wide eyes.

I leaned down and kissed him on the forehead. "Goodnight, Brandon. I'll see you in the morning."

"Goodnight," he said.

I smiled at him as I flicked off the light and shut the door. I didn't want Thrasher coming out.

After I washed my face, I went to bed feeling rejuvenated. I had an energy in me that I'd never experienced before. I couldn't wait for tomorrow.

27

S he was worried about Garett now more than ever. He'd stopped taking her calls and his door was locked whenever she came by. A couple of times she'd called the police and asked if someone could stop by to check on him.

It was like he was waiting to die rather than trying to actively find Brandy. Since Laura couldn't talk to Garett, she was reading every headline she could find about it. She'd written a couple of pieces to keep it in the paper, but with every passing day, people were forgetting about Brandy.

Even the police seemed to have less and less enthusiasm for the case. The last time she'd called for an update, they'd told her that they couldn't share anything with her because she wasn't a member of the family.

Instead, she'd resorted to texting Austin every now and again, but he also wasn't sharing much. She wondered if he was already moving on.

Every night, she'd taken to walking the paths that Brandy used to run in the hopes of seeing something. She kept her flashlight out at all times and didn't wear any earbuds. Pepper spray and a rape whistle were tucked into a small backpack that she kept with her. There were also bright orange missing persons posters that she handed out sometimes.

About the only thing she had noticed was that there were regulars who came to the path. How come no one had seen anything?

Sure, the lighting wasn't as great as it could be, but unless everyone was really self-involved, they would have seen a struggle. Unless it wasn't a struggle and Brandy had gone along willingly.

Was it possible that Brandy had run away? Even as she thought it, she dismissed it. Brandy wasn't that type of person. If she had issues with someone, she would bring it up and deal with it. Her family was too important to her to just leave behind.

But maybe she knew her kidnapper. If she did, that would explain why no one had seen any arguments or struggles on the path.

Undoubtedly, the police had already considered all of these things. She was sure they'd gone through all of Brandy's known connections and checked with all of them.

It was all so frustrating. Sometimes she considered just walking away and forgetting about all of them. Obviously, Garett didn't want her support or even her presence, so why did she bother?

There was a small wooden bench around the next corner and Laura decided to take a seat for a minute. She needed to decide what she was doing and why she was letting her entire life be dedicated to someone who didn't want her around.

She heard footsteps coming and instinctively reached for her backpack. Nobody would catch her off guard.

As she pulled the pepper spray out of her backpack, the posters spilled out onto the ground.

"Shit," she grunted and knelt down to pick them up.

A few seconds later, she saw a man jog up and stop to help. He pulled his earbuds out and knelt down beside her.

"Thank you," she said.

"Anytime." He handed her papers he'd grabbed and then frowned down at the page. "Hey, I've seen this girl." He pulled the page up to get a better look at it. "She used to run down here."

"You know her?" asked Laura. A ray of hope opened in her chest. "When did you see her last?"

"A while ago. She was helping a friend who had hurt herself or something."

"Did she say anything? Any names?"

"She told me to go away. I get it. It's not always safe to trust strangers on paths like these. Especially men. I left her alone."

"She's been missing for a couple of weeks. The last time anyone saw her was down on these paths."

"Really? Wow," he said. He handed her the poster.

"It's been all over the news. Haven't you seen her picture there?"

"I don't watch the news, really. Or read papers." He shrugged his shoulders uncomfortably. "Nobody does anymore. Besides, I only run here occasionally, when I'm staying with my parents."

That made sense. The people who knew Brandy would get most of their information from social media. If there wasn't a campaign there then her peers wouldn't know anything about it.

"Listen, the police haven't had any leads, would you be willing to talk to them? Tell them a little bit about what you saw?"

He looked like he regretted saying anything now. "I don't know."

"She might still be alive somewhere. She has a father and a boyfriend who are worried sick."

He was still hesitant and she understood. Most people would think they would be wasting the cops' time. Either that or they were getting mixed up in something that would take more commitment than they wanted.

"You could save her life. Please," she said.

"Okay, fine. Who do I talk to?"

Laura pulled out her wallet and handed the guy the detective's card.

"You can give him a call tonight and set up an appointment if you'd like." He nodded at her and grabbed the card, but she didn't let go. "This is really important. Please don't forget." Then she released the card.

"Tell you what," he said, pulling his phone out of his pocket. "I'll call right now and make an appointment for tomorrow. Can I have one of those posters?"

***

2019:

When Jenny had told him the news that she was pregnant with their second child, Nathan had had to put on a smile like it was the happiest day of his life. In reality, it had been like she'd punched him in the gut.

Sebastian was only about six months old, it was too early for this. He was barely figuring life out as a father.

When he'd gone to see Jess, it had been to talk to her about the baby. Now that his family was going from three to four, it occurred to him that the rest of his family had fallen apart long ago. When he thought of his kids in that situation, it was heartbreaking.

Jenny's family was quite close. In the beginning, it had made him uncomfortable knowing that her parents could swing by any day and that her sister might just come grab Sebastian as she felt like it.

Her brother was always hanging around. Jenny said it was because he really liked Nathan and he'd disagreed. Then he started paying attention to what Jeremy was saying to him and he realized that he valued Nathan's opinion.

Suddenly forced into the position of a role model, Nathan had panicked. He and Jenny had had a huge argument that night and he'd slept on the couch.

His life had never prepared him for a proper family.

Now he looked forward to the breaks that Melissa gave them and encouraged Jeremy to come over for a couple of beers. Her parents were always so kind and loving in a way he hadn't experienced from his own mother.

He'd grown up in the shadow of Jess. She was forever doing something that required all of his mother's attention. It had made for a lonely childhood of listening to them fight.

When his dad had left, he hadn't really understood what had happened. He'd blamed Jess when he was younger. He couldn't remember much about what he'd heard before his dad left, but he knew Jess's name had come up.

Now that he was older, he realized it was likely much more complicated than that.

He'd never seen his dad again after that. Jess said it was because his dad didn't want to see them anymore, but he'd never had any confirmation from either of his parents. Eventually, he decided that if his dad wasn't going to reach out, then neither was he. *What kind of parent doesn't want to be around their child?*

Then they'd had Sebastian and he'd realized that a parent could have a deep love for their child and still not want to be around them. He would die for Sebastian, but he also prayed for Melissa to keep him overnight so that he and Jenny could get some sleep.

As he watched his son grow, he had wondered if everything had been as cut-and-dried with his dad. When he'd asked his mom about it, she'd shut down and refused to talk about it.

That gave him even more reason to second-guess his childhood reality.

He'd been to visit his mom several times and the final straw for him had been when she refused to talk to him, but instead made him sit through the news footage about a young girl that was missing. Every time he tried to change the subject, she would bring it back.

There were several newspapers on the table, all opened to the story. He couldn't understand her obsession with it, but he could see it was taking a toll on her. She was behaving differently. She was more affectionate and motherly than usual.

Still, she hadn't given him any real answers to his questions.

After meeting with Jess and being rejected by her, he decided he wouldn't put any more effort into either of them. He still cared about his mom, so he answered her calls, but he didn't go out of his way to see her anymore.

He didn't need either of them to make his little family great. Jenny's family was caring enough. At least that was what he hoped. You didn't get to choose your family and you only got one of them, so he was out of other options.

***

2019:

Hutchinson was now looking at three different sketches of women that looked eerily similar. One had attacked Ed, forcing him into retirement. One had shown interest in Lyle Walker, which was an unlikely coincidence.

The third girl had been seen with the missing university student, Brandy Volker. A young man had come in and said he'd seen Volker with this girl on what was probably the last night before she disappeared. The girl had been injured and he hadn't gotten a great look at her. He'd been distracted by Volker's hostile attitude toward him.

For a moment, his mind drifted to Crystal, and he hoped she was as smart as Volker. Or maybe wiser. Because maybe it wasn't a man that had kidnapped her. Maybe it was a woman, disguised as a helpless injured person.

If all of these women were the same, Edmonton was dealing with an extremely dangerous and unstable mind. And the profiles everyone had come up with were only good for wiping an ass.

He didn't have a lot to go off of right now other than his instincts. Somehow he needed to connect the dots and find some credible evidence. Or at least a likely scenario.

It would be ideal to put this picture out in the papers or on the news, but that was something he would have to run by his superiors first. And they might not be as gung-ho about it as he was.

Volker's case was getting frostier by the day and other cases were taking priority. Cases where the vic' was likely still alive.

He stacked up all of the papers and tucked them into a folder in his desk. He picked up his phone and dialled an internal number.

"Hey, Janine," he said when a woman picked up. "I was wondering if the Inspector had time to chat with me this afternoon. I have something that I don't think should wait."

In the meantime, he decided he wanted a drink. It was time to hit up Whirls and Spurs again, but this time, he would bring along copies of all of the sketches. He hoped that if he could show them to Paul, he might get something from him. Or, Hutchinson hoped, he'd remembered a little something extra.

Either way, he had a short period to get something together to present to the Inspector. He picked up his phone and called the receptionist, asking her for help with making some photocopies of the sketches as well as copies of the transcripts.

By the time he had everything together, he called Janine again. "I'm on my way down.If you could fit me in, that would be great."

Miller didn't appear to be remotely excited about Hutchinson's appearance. He looked like he'd just gnawed on a lemon. His pinched face suggested that whatever Hutchinson had to say had better be good.

"Sir," he said before he sat down. "There's an issue here that I think that needs considering."

He laid out all three of the sketches on the desk. Miller glanced down at them, then back up at Hutchinson, and wordlessly indicated that he should carry on.

"What we have are three sketches of suspects from three individuals. One is from Ed Keller, the security guard who was assaulted during one of the Rooftop Arsonist fires. The second is from a bartender of Whirls and Spurs, where Lyle Walker was a frequent guest. This woman was spending time with Walker shortly before he was arrested and he has no recollection of her.

"The third is a description we received from a man who was probably last to see Brandy Volker before she disappeared. He said she was helping a woman who had sprained her ankle get to her vehicle."

Miller raised an eyebrow in response.

"All three people also gave the same physical description; short and small body."

"Get to the point, Hutchinson."

"I know we have physical evidence that places Walker at the scene of the last arson, but I can't shake the feeling that it's no coincidence that the woman he was spending time with a couple of days earlier looks a lot like the assailant who attacked Ed."

"And what does all of this have to do with Volker?" Miller asked.

"As soon as Walker was arrested, the arsons stopped. Shortly thereafter, Volker is kidnapped by a woman who looks eerily similar."

"I can see that. What do you want, Hutchinson?" Miller leaned back in his chair now and laced his fingers across his stomach.

"I want to run these pictures to see if we can get any response from the public. Worst-case scenario, we get nothing, best-case scenario, we learn who captured Volker."

"And Walker will get to…walk." Miller closed his eyes and frowned for a moment. "This could potentially be a huge waste of resources and money, Hutchinson. We'll have to look at every single tip we get and we both know that will be quite a few."

"I understand that, Sir, but I feel it's worth the risk. At the very least, we will be able to tell Volker's family that we did everything we could."

Miller looked at the family picture on his desk and heaved a sigh. "Fine," he said and Hutchinson felt a wave of relief inside, "But, if this doesn't pan out, I don't want to hear another word about Walker again. You hear me? Not one word."

Hutchinson was quick to agree to Miller's demand. He rushed out of the office, wondering if he had time to catch the papers before they went to print.

***

2019:

I had decided to make Brandon an omelette today. I made sure to add as many vegetables as I could because I knew he actually liked them.

I'd hardly slept last night, thinking about how amazing it had been. I'd never felt so connected to anyone before and I had a hard time shutting my mind off. Thus, I was up at five in the morning, cooking.

As I poured the orange juice, I struggled with deciding whether to give him the sleeping pill or not. After last night, I was sure we were moving past that. But there was still a small voice in the back of my mind, quieter now than it had ever been, that wanted me to stay vigilant. Besides, he needed his sleep as well.

Carefully, I pulled open the gel capsule and dumped the contents into the juice. I was running low and would have to go in for another appointment soon. There were no refills, he'd just told me to come see him if I was still struggling to sleep.

I pulled out one of the real plates for Brandon's omelette, along with a metal fork. I wanted to show him that things had changed last night.

I caught myself humming under my breath as I walked toward his room. When I opened it, he greeted me with a smile. Thrasher jumped up on me right away, but I pushed him down and set the plate down on the dresser.

"Good morning," I said.

"Morning," Brandon replied.

I immediately loosened the chains for him and helped him sit up. "I've made you an omelette, with mushrooms, peppers and onions."

"That sounds wonderful," he said. He yawned and I noticed that his eyes were baggy. He obviously hadn't slept at all last night, which was too bad. I always hoped he got some sleep during the night.

I brought the omelette over to him. "I'll be right back," I said, grabbing the fork. I wasn't a complete idiot.

Thrasher followed me out into the hall where I let him out the back door. As I was closing the door, I heard something smash.

I ran toward Brandon's room and found him sitting on the bed with his plate shattered on the floor at his feet. "What happened?"

He was crying again. "I'm so sorry, Cathy. My hands are just a bit shaky and I accidentally dropped the plate."

"Hey, shh, shh, it's okay," I said to him. Then I knelt down and picked up all of the biggest chunks of glass. "I'm just going to toss this out and then I'll be back with the vacuum to get the rest."

I stacked the broken pieces into my hand and then made my way to the kitchen. I opened the trash can and then I paused. Some kind of radar was going off in the back of my mind and I needed to see if it was right.

I set the pieces down to give myself a minute and let Thrasher in. He scampered off to see Brandon right away, while I went back to the kitchen.

Very carefully, I laid the pieces of the plate down on the table like a puzzle. I pushed all of the pieces together to see if the puzzle was whole. A long, thin, triangle-shaped piece was missing from the outer edge of the plate.

I pulled it apart and tried things differently. After several tries, I had to put it back to the way I had originally started with. And I could only come to one conclusion.

Brandon had a piece of the plate hidden in the room.

Fury instantly lit inside of me. Rather than let it loose, I picked up the pieces of the plate and threw them in the trash. Then I grabbed a knife out of my block and made my way down to the room.

Brandon hadn't moved under Thrasher's watchful eye. He eyed the dog warily and only scrambled back to the wall when he saw I held a knife.

"Where is it?" I asked, keeping my voice cool and collected. "Don't make me ask twice."

It took a moment for him to come to a decision. Then slowly he reached under his pillow and pulled out the missing shard from the plate.

"Throw it onto the floor," I said.With a shaking hand, Brandon threw the shard onto the floor. He was crying again. It was really starting to get unmanly. "Lay down." He assumed the position.

I called Thrasher up onto the bed. "He's been a bad boy, Thrasher," I told him. "He's going to have to go without breakfast and without a diaper change. You keep an eye on him for me, okay?"

Then I walked up to Brandon and laid the blade at his throat. He sobbed hysterically now. "Why did you have to do that? We were getting along. Why would you want to hurt me?"

"I di-didn't," he said through sobs.

"Don't lie to me. I hate it when people lie to me." I pushed the knife a little harder, not enough to draw blood, but enough to leave a mark on his skin. "We are going to have a conversation when I get home from work."

I tucked the knife into my back pocket and went about the routine of tying him up. I chained him down tight this time. I heard him gasp in pain, but I didn't care.

Once he was secure, I grabbed the glass of orange juice off of the dresser.

"Open up," I said. He opened his mouth and I poured the juice in his mouth bit by bit. I didn't care if it spilled on him. If he struggled to swallow or breathe, that was his own fault. "I would suggest you stop crying. It will make it awfully hard to breathe once I put the duct tape on you."

"P-p-please," he sobbed. I didn't listen, I ripped the tape off of the roll and smushed it on his mouth.

"Thrasher is going to keep you company today. Don't try anything stupid."

I left without looking back and closed the door behind me.

28

Brandy drifted in and out of sleep throughout the day. When the duct tape had first covered her mouth, she had panicked. The result was her passing out due to lack of oxygen.

When she woke up, she had a screaming headache but her breathing came more regularly. Thrasher kept up his post, laying on her legs and not moving.

This morning when Cathy had tied her down, she had thought her arms were going to be dislocated. There was no feeling in them only a few minutes after the door had closed.

Last night, Brandy had thought she'd made headway with Cathy. They had become friends, or at least that was what she thought. She had forgotten that Cathy was a nutcase. There was no predicting her behaviour.

Losing her hair had nearly driven her mad. She'd spent the night wide awake on the edge of total despair. If Cathy had been hoping to break her, she'd just about succeeded.

Then she'd come in this morning, acting like nothing had changed. It seemed like Cathy thought she'd genuinely done Brandy a favour by cutting off her hair. She couldn't understand why Cathy was so fixated on making her look like a guy.

Now that her hair was gone, she wondered how far Cathy would go. If her captor ever decided to get intimate with her, would she want her to make changes to her body?

That thought had tormented her throughout the night. Every time she had thought she'd distracted herself by thinking about her dad or Austin, the thought came sneaking back in.

The other thought that had bothered her was that if Cathy could get her hands on hormone pills, she might start administering them to Brandy without her knowledge. She didn't know exactly how hormone therapy worked when people wanted to transition from one sex to the other, and it was the unknown that frightened her. Cathy could make potentially permanent changes to her body without her permission.

The headache never faded throughout the day. She could only fall asleep for a few minutes at a time. If she was developing a tolerance to the sleeping pills, she would have to try to use it to her benefit.

Though, her bright idea this morning had turned into a bust with unknown consequences.

She had been an idiot; she'd reacted instead of thinking about what she was going to do. If she'd been smart, she would have held out. Cathy had clearly been starting to trust her and now she'd ruined it.

When the knock came at the trailer door, Brandy had no idea what time it was. She'd finally been drifting off to sleep. Thrasher startled her awake when he barked.

The knocking was persistent, though. Hope flooded her and she tried to make as much noise as she could. For all of her efforts, though, Thrasher was much louder than she was. Eventually, the knocking ended.

Several minutes later, Thrasher calmed down, making only the occasional huff or growl.

Then the front door opened.

"Jess, honey! Are you home?"

Brandy's eyes shot open. *Who the hell is Jess?* She didn't make out another word, though. Thrasher threw himself at the door, making it shake in the jamb. His deep bark hurt her ears. When he began to scratch at the door, she was certain he was going to break it down.

Whoever had come in made their way down to the room. Brandy screamed as loud as she could behind the duct tape, but she didn't have a hope of being heard over the dog's fury.

Then she heard the footsteps recede and the person must have eventually left. She only knew because Thrasher calmed down again. He didn't leave the door, though. Every sound that he heard made his head twitch. He was clearly unhappy that someone had come in and he couldn't fight them off.

In her mind, she was screaming at herself. If she hadn't been stupid enough to pull the stunt that morning, she probably wouldn't have had her mouth taped shut. She could have escaped today.

***

2019:

I was late for work, which only added to my misery today. It had been a mistake to trust Brandon. I'd let the weakness take over me and in the end, there was only one person to blame; me.

Mike was giving me a bit of a stink eye when I made my way past his office toward the lunchroom. I pretended not to see him. I would definitely be working late tonight, not much to be done about that.

Maybe it would do Brandon some good to stay home and be hungry and gross for a bit. It might teach him a lesson.

I shoved all of my stuff in my locker and laced up my boots as quickly as I could and raced out to the order board. It was warm again in the warehouse. It was unseasonably warm outside and the damn furnace was kicking in now during the night, rather than the air conditioning.

There were only long, complicated orders left. The guys had all grabbed the easy ones, I was sure of it. I muttered under my breath as I grabbed the first one off of the board. We were supposed to only take the one we were working on, not hoard them like a middle-aged spinster.

Avoiding Mike was a bit tricky for me that morning. I knew he would want to talk to me about why I was late and I wasn't in the mood to make up some bullshit excuse. We would both recognize it for what it was, so the game was pointless. Yet he would insist we play it.

Every time he rounded a corner, I made sure to push my cart down to the next aisle. He wanted our run-in to be natural. He probably didn't want me to know how much he actually watched the clock, especially given how much extra I did around here.

Finally, just before lunch break, he went over the intercom and paged me to come see him. With a sigh of defeat, I made my way over to his office.

"Hey, Jess, how's it going?" he asked as though I'd just showed up of my own accord.

"It's fine," I said. I crossed my arms and leaned on the jamb in the doorway. I hadn't had breakfast, either, and I was hungry.

"I called you in here because I noticed you were running behind this morning. I just wanted to make sure everything was good."

"Yep. I just overslept."

"Because normally, we prefer employees to text us if they are going to be late."

"I didn't text you?" I asked. I scrunched up my face, trying to look thoughtful. "I'm sorry, I meant to let you know."

"That's fine. I just wanted to remind you is all," he said with a nod. "You'll make up the time this afternoon?"

"Sure will." He gave me a nod and I walked away before he could see the scowl on my face. I'd never been late before, but the other guys often were. I doubted they got the same questions when they walked in.

I decided to go out for lunch rather than sit in here and stew. Even if I cut my lunch hour short, Mike would still expect me to work late this evening. I didn't feel like it.

There was a Subway not too far from the warehouse and I decided to head there for lunch. I ordered my usual – ham and cheese on white – and grabbed my drink before I sat down. Someone had left a paper on the table so I unfolded it, thinking I would look it over.

I froze as soon as I saw the image on the front page. There were three sketches of a woman alongside a news story about how the police wanted this person for questioning.

All three of the pictures were slightly different. One had a nose that was too narrow, on another the eyes were off. But in the end, they all looked like me.

I felt heat suffuse my face. I flipped the paper over and looked around the restaurant.

To my relief, the world seemed to carry on. Nobody was paying attention to me in the corner.

It still felt like I had a neon sign over my head, screaming at everyone to look at me.

My insides were churning and my legs shaking as I attempted to stand from the table. I nearly fell over and grabbed the table to steady myself, knocking over my drink. It hit the floor with a splash.

I froze and looked around me. Everyone was suddenly staring. "Everything okay?" asked the cashier.

I didn't answer. I grabbed my sandwich and darted out the door. I jumped into my truck and sank down in my seat while I caught my breath.

Where did they get those sketches from? Nobody ever remembered me, why were they suddenly starting now?

Then a worse thought struck home: *my mother reads the paper.*

I pulled out my phone and saw that I'd missed a few calls from her. I'd put it on silent the night before to give Brandon and I some privacy. There was also a call from Nathan.

I turned on the voicemail and listened.

"Hey, Jess. It's Mom, just calling to check up on you. It's been a few days since we've talked."

"Hey, Jess, I stopped by. I wasn't sure if you were home or not, Thrasher wasn't at the door, so I used your spare key. I hope you don't mind. I dropped off some of those date squares."

"Hey, Jess, would you please answer your goddamn phone? Mom is freaking out trying to get a hold of you and I'm at work. I can't be dealing with this shit right now."

If I called them now, it would be a mistake. I was too rattled and they would hear it. I needed time to think, to come up with a plan. If my mother had gone to my trailer, that meant she'd put it together herself. There was no other reason for her to let herself into my house.

I wished that I had changed the locks back when I'd planned to. After I told her where to find the spare key when I'd first moved out, she'd come to check on me a few times. I told her off good and well, though; since then, she hadn't stopped by unannounced and it had slipped my mind. It was a stupid mistake. There was no room for errors here.

She obviously hadn't told Nathan what she suspected or he would have been looking for me as soon as she said something. Instead, she was only pestering him with calls, which maybe meant she would be on my side if it came down to it.

But she would never leave me alone.

I wasn't going back to work now. In fact, I wasn't even confident about going home. If my mother had called the police, they would already be there and Brandon would be gone.

I sat there for a while, mechanically eating my sandwich, hoping a brilliant plan would come to me; it didn't. I was going to have to fly by the seat of my pants on this one.

29

Laura was debating whether she should use a cup for her wine with supper, or if she should just drink directly from the bottle. Greg, the little weasel, had given the story she should have had to her coworker Aaron.

On its own, that was bad enough. She had seniority and should have been given the option to take the front-page story or not.

Worse, though, was that it had to do with Brandy.

The front page of the Guardian was covered in three pictures with one headline: Police Looking For This Woman.

None of the sketches were exactly the same, but they were all similar and from three different sources. Naturally, that meant there would be some deviation in the pictures themselves. When she turned to page two for the story, she found out that this woman was the one last seen with Brandy. She was also wanted for questioning about the Rooftop Arsonist.

The last part didn't make any sense as far as she was concerned. They already had that guy in jail awaiting trial. Why would the police seek more information?

She had tried to call Garett, but he had ignored her. One ring and straight to voicemail, which, of course, was full.

Now she was sitting down to a frozen pizza and a bottle of red wine. She would regret it tomorrow, she knew, but it would be oh-so-satisfying right now.

She decided against the glass and cut the pizza in two. Netflix had released some new episodes, so she would binge television, food and alcohol all at the same time. If that didn't treat her emotional despair, nothing would.

Everything was swept off the coffee table and she set the pizza there on a cloth. The corkscrew and the cork were also on the table. She held up the bottle and took her first swig.

It was awful and she had to build herself up to the next glug.

She'd just managed to lift it to her mouth when the phone rang.

Annoyed, she set the bottle down and made her way to the kitchen. If Greg thought he could send her an assignment now, he was sadly mistaken. Her phone should have been on silent for this evening, but she'd forgotten that.

The caller ID showed that it was Garett calling her. She stared at it, stunned, before answering.

"Hello?" she said.

"Laura, I need you," he said. "I need somebody, please."

"I'm on my way." She hung up the phone and grabbed her purse, not giving two shits that she was in her comfy pants and an old ratty sweatshirt.

When she pulled up to Garett's house, there was an SUV already in his driveway. She'd never seen it before and wondered if there were relatives visiting.

She almost went straight in, but then she remembered how strained their relationship had been recently. Instead, she pushed the doorbell and waited.

Garett opened the door almost immediately. He was in a faded blue housecoat and slippers. His hair was a matted mess and his face had a waxy pallor to it. But when he smiled at her, he'd never been more handsome.

She ran into his arms and he folded them around her in a tight hug. "I'm so sorry, Laura. I've been a monster, I know."

"It's all right," she told him. "You've been through too much."

"No. I've been an ass. I have an appointment to see a therapist tomorrow morning."

"Is that why you called me here?" The news that he was getting some help was unbelievable. She had thought for sure they were over and that he was lost forever.

"No," he said, and the smile slipped from his face. "No, I called you over here because there is someone I need to introduce you to."

***

2019:

Brandy had just managed to fall asleep when the door to the trailer burst open with a bang. Her body jolted and then she cried out in pain. Thrasher's response drowned her out again.

The dog smashed his body into the door repeatedly. His barking and growling reached a pitch she hadn't heard before and she felt sorry for whoever was on the other side of that door. She prayed it was someone to rescue her.

Maybe the lady from earlier in the day had heard her after all. Didn't the police usually bust in doors if they had a warrant or something? Probably not, she decided, but still she hoped.

Footsteps marched down the hall and then she heard Cathy's voice. "Hey, boy, it's me."

Thrasher immediately calmed down and began wagging his tail. Cathy opened the door to let him out. She didn't even look at Brandy.

Outside of her room, it sounded like chaos. Thrasher was outside barking and Cathy was running up and down the hallway. She could hear drawers and doors being whipped open and closed. Whatever was going on, Cathy was in a hurry.

Then Cathy stepped into Brandy's room again. She had a glass of orange juice in her hand and a determined look on her face. In her other hand, she held a knife.

She set the glass down on the dresser. "I'm going to take the chains off and you're going to sit up, Brandon. Then you are going to drink this entire glass of orange juice, do you understand? If you try anything stupid, I will slit your throat. Do you understand?"

Brandy nodded as much as she was able to. Cathy pushed the knife under her nose and gave her a stern look. She twisted her head away and closed her eyes, certain these were her final moments.

Then she felt Cathy cut the zip tie on her hand and pull her arms free of the chain. "Sit up."

Brandy couldn't feel her arms and urgent instructions from her brain didn't make them start moving right away. Before she could force her body to respond to Cathy's demands, Cathy was grabbing her by the collar and pulling her into a sitting position. "I said sit up."

Once she was sitting, Cathy released her and grabbed the orange juice. Brandy's arms flopped to her sides. Sharp pain shot from her shoulders down to her fingertips as the blood started to flow once again. She tried to wiggle her fingers and was rewarded with a painful twitch.

Pins and needles cascaded down her arms, forcing her to stifle a groan. If she didn't focus on sitting up, she would fall over. Her arms weren't going to stop her.

Cathy grabbed her collar again and ripped the duct tape from her mouth. "Drink up, quickly. Don't waste a drop."

Before Brandy could get a mouthful of air, Cathy started pouring the juice into her mouth. It was even more bitter than the stuff she drank in the morning. She could feel grit in her mouth and she shuddered.

If Cathy didn't have such a good grip on her, Brandy would have pushed away and closed her mouth, but the cup was jammed between her lips and she was being held firm. "Don't fuck around," said Cathy, as though she could read her thoughts.

She didn't choke on the juice, at least. Cathy had never given her more than she could handle, which worried Brandy. She had no idea what was in the drink and for all she knew, it could be arsenic or cyanide.

When she was done, Cathy released her shirt and stood back. She didn't tie Brandy up and she didn't put the duct tape on her again. She just waited.

After a moment, Brandy decided to ask her a question. "Who's Jess?"

Cathy gave her a sharp look, then walked out of the room. The knife was on the dresser and Brandy urged her limbs to function again. She was able to move her arms, but it was a slow, painful process and she didn't trust them just yet.

After only a moment, though, she realized that part of the problem was grogginess. Whatever Cathy had put in the orange juice was making her even more sleepy. The room blurred around her and she fell back onto the bed as she drifted off into a dreamless sleep.

***

2019:

I had given him three of the pills in his orange juice instead of the usual one. Part of me was worried that it would be too much for him. He had a small frame and he wasn't all that muscular. But I had to take the risk.

Once I was sure he was out, I brought an old duffle bag into the room. It was one of the ones we'd used when I was little to visit Uncle Daryl's cabin. If I curled him up, I could fit Brandon into the bag and carry him out to the truck.

My phone buzzed in my back pocket and I pulled it out to take a look at it. It was Mike. He was probably pissed. Maybe he was even calling to fire me. It didn't matter, I wouldn't be going back.

On my way home, I'd stopped at the bank and made a large withdrawal of cash. I hadn't wanted things to play out this way and hadn't imagined a scenario where it would. My arrogance had cost me.

Now, I was packing for an extended vacation somewhere else. Eventually, I would have to come up with a solid plan, one that could bring in steady money, at least. But at the moment, Brandon and I just needed to get away.

I wasn't sure where that was going to be when I was at the bank. In fact, even when I was casing out my trailer to make sure there were no cops, I still didn't know where we would be going. Money was an issue, as was the fact that Brandon and I had been in one too many newspapers.

The odds were not in my favour.

When I got home and saw the date squares, it had come to me. When my dad and I would go fishing with my uncle, my mom would always pack the squares. My dad and I loved them.

My uncle had chosen sides when my parents had split, and it wasn't my mother's that he landed on. I hadn't seen him in years, but Mom talked about him every now and then.

He was retired now with a home down in Arizona with some young wife. They were like snowbirds, coming back to Canada for the summer and living in the States for the winter. That meant his cabin was currently empty.

Snow was coming, and he was always gone by the end of September.

I was sure there was a bit more development in the area now, but it was still pretty isolated. And nobody would think to look there.

It was the perfect place to stay until I had a proper plan in mind.

Getting Brandon into the duffle bag wasn't easy. He was a dead weight and probably weighed as much as I did. At least I didn't have to worry about zipping up his hair.

Lugging him out to the truck reminded me of hauling my rucksack to the truck when we went out to the cabin. It brought a smile to my face, even though I was still freaking out. We'd figure things out there, I just had this feeling.

Once I had him secured in the cab, I ran into the house and started hauling out a few other bags. I'd packed up all the food we had into a box and hauled it out to the truck as well.

I debated whether I should take Thrasher with me. The cabin didn't have a fenced yard and there were all kinds of predators out there. Worse, if Thrasher got away, someone might figure things out.

I watched him in the backyard for a second, though, and realized I couldn't leave him behind. He was part of our family. Besides, I might need his help keeping Brandon under control.

His bed and food went out to the truck, too. After a brief moment to check on Brandon's breathing and pulse, I went back to the trailer and locked the door.

Saying goodbye to that place wasn't hard. The only special memory I had there was with Brandon, and I was taking him with me. Other than that, it hadn't been a spectacular life. It had only been a place to sleep.

The route was exactly as I remembered it. The view had changed. There were more acreages out by the lake. It hadn't grown much, but it was enough to make me feel odd. Like I wasn't coming home, but that I was visiting somewhere for the first time.

I stopped periodically along the way to check on Brandon. He was still breathing, but I wasn't sure how long he would be sleeping for. The trip itself wasn't very long. Only about an hour and a half, but it was a relief to get out of the city.

Once I was out there, I couldn't figure out why I hadn't come out sooner. I hadn't spoken to Uncle Daryl in years, but now that I was out here, I thought that I should have. But there was no room for regrets now. I had to forge my way forward.

The driveway was well maintained, all gravel to the house. It was good to know I wouldn't be leaving behind any tracks. I was thankful it hadn't snowed yet. I didn't want to alert the neighbours that somebody was home. I wasn't sure what I was going to do when it did snow.

Around the bend, the cabin looked exactly like I remembered. It was a small log cabin with a deck. When I was younger, the colour had been the natural wood colour, now it was painted a greyish blue. It was ugly, if you asked me, but it would do just fine for now.

I pulled up to the house and got out. Thrasher tried to follow me, but I told him to stay. I was going to have to tie him up or something so he wouldn't run loose. I unzipped the duffle bag, checked on Brandon and then decided to leave it undone.

He still had duct tape on his mouth, so he wasn't going to make enough noise for anyone to hear, anyway.

As expected, the doors were all locked. I checked where the spare key used to be, but it wasn't there anymore.

I walked around to the back, hoping I would find a key somewhere there. Instead, I found a dog run that hadn't been there before. That was a relief for me. There was a dog house in it and everything. Thrasher was going to love it.

There weren't any plants out anymore, but there was the odd planter. I checked under all of them and along the sills and door jambs. No luck there either.

I was going to have to break into the place.

My tools were in the back of my truck. I took the entire box and the crowbar with me. If these windows slid up and down, this wouldn't be difficult. Windows that moved to the side would be okay as well. If they swung out, though, I would probably have to break one.

I was in luck; the windows in the back bedroom moved to the side. I pulled out my flathead screwdriver and hammer and got to work, prying the window open.

It didn't take me long. It was more difficult crawling inside the window. The cabin was old and the window size hadn't been changed when they'd been upgraded. I was small enough, though, so I was able to make my way in.

Unfortunately, it was a tub on the other side of the window, so I didn't have a soft landing. But I was able to climb through carefully and not fall face-first.

Once I was in, I made my way to the front door and unlocked it. I swung the door open and took a deep breath.

This was going to work.

30

When Brandy first woke, she was sure she was dreaming. Her little room in the trailer was gone, as were the tight shackles that made it impossible to move. Instead, there were rough-hewn logs overhead and she had some movement in her legs and arms. There was also no duct tape.

She had clearly been moved to another location.

The hope that had blossomed just the other night wilted inside her. One time she'd heard Oprah say that allowing your captor to get you to the second location reduced your chances of being found significantly. She wondered how bad her odds were with being moved to a third location.

It wasn't long before Cathy came in to check on her. The woman seemed lighter, somehow. "Good morning, Brandon."

"Morning," she replied.

"I've brought you some breakfast, you're probably pretty hungry. But since your little incident, you're only getting paper plates from here on out. And you can eat with your hands as far as I'm concerned."

There wasn't much to say to that, so Brandy just nodded and tried to look ashamed. The scent of scrambled eggs and bacon made its way to her nose and her stomach growled.

Cathy put the plate on a nightstand beside the bed and then undid Brandy's chains. She sat down in a wing-backed armchair across the room to watch her eat.

Brandy had a long haul ahead of her to regain trust and she figured she'd better get started. "This place is cute," she said.

Cathy sighed with annoyance. "Brandon, stop speaking like a girl. It's unattractive and irritating."

It appeared that Cathy had regressed even further into her delusions. Now she was going to have to change the way she spoke, too.

She cleared her throat and aimed for a deeper voice. "I'm just saying I like it."

"That's better," said Cathy.

"Where's Thrasher?" Brandy asked.

"He's outside in the dog run."

That confirmed things to Brandy. They were now out in a rural area rather than in the city. It would be even harder for her to be discovered out here. She was going to die as Brandon. She fought back tears.

"What's wrong?" asked Cathy.

"I'm just thinking of how I screwed up the other morning."

"You did screw up. You're lucky that I'm not a psycho. I could have killed you for that."

"But you didn't."

"No," said Cathy. "I still think there's a chance for us. You just need to be trained."

"Trained?" said Brandy, completely forgetting to lower her voice.

Cathy narrowed her eyes at her. "Yes, Brandon, trained." She snatched the plate out of Brandy's hands, even though she hadn't finished eating. "For example, we're going to start here. If you can stop talking like a girl, you get to eat. If you speak like a girl, you don't get to eat."

She watched as Cathy left the room, carrying the plate with her. She wondered how long it would take before Cathy broke her completely.

"Who's Jess?" she yelled in her regular voice.

She heard Cathy's footsteps come back to her room. "I don't know what you're talking about," she said.

"When that person came in, they asked for Jess. Was that the previous owner of that trailer? Did you kill someone?"

Cathy gave her a flat stare and then chained her back up. She didn't respond to any of Brandy's questions. Instead, she left the room, closing the door behind her. She offered no orange juice to help Brandy sleep, which surely meant that she was going to lay here for hours, staring at the ceiling.

***

2019:

Laura sat in the living room, looking from the young man on the couch to Garett in the armchair. She could see the similarities between the two. Nathan's hair was blond, though, and he had a more prominent jaw than Garett. There was also something different about his eyes, but she couldn't put her finger on it.

"I thought you said you lost your other children?" she asked. The whole thing had been confusing to her.

"I did," said Garett. "I was told they wanted nothing to do with me and the court ruled in my ex's favour. I haven't seen Nathan since 1993."

"You never tried to reach out to them? Even when Brandy was born?"

He shook his head sadly and she could see the shame etched on his face. "I was a coward, Laura. I couldn't look at them and realize they didn't want me. I had left the family, I thought that I was getting my just desserts."

"We were told you wanted nothing to do with us," said Nathan. "You were a no-show so many times that we stopped believing you cared about us at all."

Garett gave him a sharp look. "What do you mean I was a no-show?"

"Well, there were plenty of weekends where we were scheduled to go with you, but you never showed up or you cancelled at the last minute. Jess took it really hard."

"She's your older sister, right?" asked Laura. They both nodded, but Garett didn't respond to her.

"How is Jess?" asked Garett.

"Jess is…Jess. She's aggressively independent and I don't know that she ever got over you leaving."

"I wasn't allowed to see you two. I was denied any access. Your mother had sole custody."

Nathan hesitated before he spoke again. "That's not what Mom said."

Garett opened his mouth to deliver an angry response, but Laura shook her head at him. So he closed it and took a deep breath. "Well, I'm sorry, Nathan. There must have been some miscommunication along the line."

Nathan looked away and Laura could just see the tip of his nose turning red. She wondered how much he had resented the man he was sitting in front of. She could only imagine the bravery it would have taken for a son to confront the father he thought had rejected him.

"Does your mom know that you're speaking to your dad?" asked Laura.

"No," he said quickly. "And she can't know. She wouldn't understand. And she's sick, so she doesn't need the extra stress."

"Sick?" asked Garett.

"She has cancer. It's Stage Three, but she's not going to do any chemo or radiation," said Nathan. "Like Jess said, she's going to leave us, too."

Garett moved over to the couch and sat next to Nathan. "I never left you two. My heart was always with you. I thought of you every single day."

"Really? Because it doesn't look that way. Instead, you started over again with a new family." Nathan's voice was beginning to rise.

"If my wife hadn't come along, I would have died of grief. I couldn't function when I found out I wasn't even going to be able to see you two. I closed in on myself, lost my job and many friendships because of it.

"I left your mother because I couldn't stand her jealousy anymore. Anytime I gave attention to you kids, she would have her back up. If she wasn't the center of my world, she couldn't handle it. I didn't want you two to grow up competing with your own mother for attention.

"I wish now that I had found you guys and you had the opportunity to meet Brandy."

"I don't have a problem with meeting her. It might be nice for Sebastian to have an aunt that's interested in him."

Garett's face crumpled for a moment and then he took in a deep breath. "Brandy is missing right now. We have the police looking for her."

Nathan gave his father a shocked look. "Wow. Go figure, just when I come forward, she's gone. I can't imagine what I'd do if I lost Sebastian, that must be hard for you."

Garett only nodded, unable to look at Nathan.

"What happened?" he asked.

"We don't know, Nathan. She was supposed to meet her boyfriend for dinner and didn't show up. Then when she didn't show up for her birthday, we knew something was wrong. It's been all over the news," he said.

"I think I heard something about it. Mom's obsessed with the story. The girl didn't have our last name though, so I never made the connection."

"You and Jess have your mother's last name," said Garett sullenly.

A moment of silence passed between the two and Laura decided to break up the awkward moment.

"What made you come looking for your dad now?" asked Laura.

Nathan twiddled his thumbs for a moment before looking up at Garett. "I have a son now. And another child on the way. I want to be a good dad for my kids and I have no role model for that."

Tears started running down Garett's face. He wouldn't look away from Nathan. "I don't think you need a role model," he said gruffly. "You're already showing that you are willing to do anything to do what's best for your kids."

Then Nathan started to cry. Garett reached over and wrapped his arms around his son, holding him close while they both cried over memories that had been taken away.

The only thing that could have made this moment better was having Brandy and Jess present. She prayed that Garett would get to spend time with all of his children together.

***

2019:

Hutchinson flipped through the file on his desk one more time. He was hungry and knew he should really head home, but he'd been hoping for more of a response from the public than he was receiving.

Following the publication of all of the sketches, he hadn't had one credible witness come forward to indicate that they may have recognized the woman. There had been several calls, of course, but none even remotely close to the mark.

The Inspector had only agreed to this course of action reluctantly. Hutchinson was sure the Inspector was only being courteous to him. Everyone on the force respected the gut feeling of a hunch, but that didn't mean they always agreed with it.

The condition to run the pictures had been that he would drop his concerns about the Rooftop Arsonist and not speak about it again. He had agreed, reluctantly, because he was certain that this move would pan out.

Now he wasn't so sure. The sketches had been released two days ago and they still had nothing.

In front of him was a list of leads and tips they'd received since the release. Many of the leads had already been ruled out due to inaccuracies in the statement or a quick look at the person in question.

There were some that would take several days to follow up on, and he had some small amount of hope for those, but they weren't promising at all.

One came from a guy in a hospital, claiming that he worked with someone who looked like that. That she was the reason he was in the hospital in the first place.

When they'd looked into it, they'd learned it was a workplace incident involving a forklift. The guy had been hanging out where he wasn't supposed to be and gotten hurt for his stupidity. OH&S was still investigating the incident and were reluctant to release any information to the police because they hadn't reached their own conclusions yet.

He had one officer breathing down the neck of OH&S and putting the pressure on. They just needed to confirm if the other person involved could be this woman. That was all they needed, just a tiny bit of information.

It was a nightmare that didn't seem like it would end. He shut the file and decided to head home for the evening. He would skip Whirls and Spurs tonight; it would only be a reminder of work and what was on the line if his plan didn't work out.

31

Nathan had tried calling Jess several times and she hadn't called him back. He was now annoyed and a bit concerned. The deliberate non-answer from Jess was expected. She never wanted to answer her phone. However, she always got back to him, if only to get him to stop calling.

He'd left four messages and hadn't heard a thing in return.

She deserved to know that he'd found their father. In fact, he hoped that reuniting with their dad might heal her and help her in some way. He'd even told her about their dad in the last message and how everything had been a big misunderstanding. That should have elicited a call from her at the very least.

Jenny was still unaware that he was trying to piece his family back together. He felt terrible keeping it from her, but he also knew he wouldn't be able to bear it if he brought it to her attention and it all fell through.

Since he couldn't speak to his wife about things and his sister was avoiding his calls, it left him with only one option. He was going to have to see his mother.

Her car was parked in the driveway as usual. He doubted she'd driven it at all since he last saw her. Neighbours brought her groceries and any prescriptions like she was unable to look after herself. Though, to be fair, he wasn't sure what they'd all been told.

He knocked on the door and waited patiently for her to open it. The T.V. sounded like it was at full volume, so he rang the doorbell as well.

She answered in her bathrobe and some jogging pants. The sight alarmed him. He'd never seen her answer the door in such a state. He wondered if it was a show for the neighbours, or if she genuinely wasn't well.

"Hi, Mom," he said, leaning in for a hug. "How're you doing?"

"Not good. I'm worried about your sister."

He contained the sigh that wanted to escape and worked hard to not roll his eyes. Of course his sister was the only thing they were going to talk about.

"Have you heard from her lately?" he asked.

"No, and that's why I'm worried." She sat down in front of the T.V. She'd been watching the twenty-four-hour news channel. He reached for the remote and turned it off. "What are you doing?" she demanded.

"It's hard to talk over the T.V.," he said. "Why are you worried about Jess?"

"She hasn't been answering my calls and I stopped by her place the other day and something didn't feel right. Thrasher was locked in one of the bedrooms, which is odd, don't you think?"

"She works during the day, Mom. That's why she wasn't at home. And if Thrasher was locked in a bedroom, maybe it was because she didn't want him to shit all over her house? That dog does whatever he wants, I think."

"She says he's a good dog."

Of course Jess said he was a good dog. She had rescued Thrasher and taken him in like a child. Everyone loved their children regardless of their personalities or mental illnesses. Thrasher was a hazard to society, but Jess didn't see it.

"Fair enough," he said, "but that doesn't mean that anything weird was going on. What gave you that feeling?"

"It smelled different, too. Like she'd been cooking real food or something."

"Would you feel better if I went and checked on the place tonight?" he asked.

"It would." Ahe reached over to her stack of magazines on the coffee table. She pulled a newspaper out from the bottom and handed it to Nathan. "This bothers me, too."

On the front of the paper were three different sketches of a woman. At first, Nathan didn't think anything of it and nearly tossed it back onto the coffee table. And then something about the eyes in the final picture caught his attention.

"Does that woman look familiar to you?" asked his mother.

"You don't think-"

"I don't know what to think," she said, cutting him off. She sniffled and rubbed her hand under her nose. "She's been acting strange lately, and I have a bad feeling about this."

The article was about the Rooftop Arsonist and the suspected kidnapper of Brandy Volker. He tried to picture Jess doing those things, but he couldn't. He hadn't known her to be bold enough to pull anything like this off. If anything, she preferred to cower and hide from the world.

"Have you talked to Dad about this?" he asked.

She gave him a sharp look and frowned. "Why would I talk to him?"

"Because you think his daughter might be in trouble?"

She folded her arms and leaned back, looking out the window rather than at him. "He won't care. He's not interested in his kids."

Neither one of his parents were sharing the same story and it was confusing him. He clenched his fists for a moment and then forced himself to relax. "Why do you say that?"

"He told me so himself."

"That's strange," said Nathan in a sarcastic tone, "because I just visited him and he told me that he always wanted to be in our lives."

His mother stood up and backed away from him, hands to her heart. "You went to see your father? After all he's done to us?"

"I went to see my dad because I missed him and wanted him in my life," said Nathan. "And the stories don't line up."

"Of course not, he's nothing but a lying cheat!"

"Whatever the case, it's up to me to decide if I want him in my life or not. Not you. And I think he deserves to know about Jess. If you don't say something to him, I will."

He couldn't stand watching her cry, so he took his turn looking out the window. Years of hurt and anger were building up inside of him and he didn't know how to express himself without hurting her feelings. She didn't need the extra stress right now. Then again, he might never get to ask her any questions if things went her way.

"What do you want me to say? I think your eldest daughter has something to do with your youngest daughter's disappearance?"

He looked back at her in surprise. "What?"

She picked up the paper and threw it at his feet. "The missing girl, she's your half-sister. And after reading this article, I'm pretty sure your full sister had something to do with her disappearance."

Slowly he bent down to pick up the newspaper. His mother had been obsessed with the stories and he hadn't even glanced at them.

In fact, he'd avoided them even more once he knew that she couldn't get enough of it. Now he understood the obsession.

He sat down on the couch and read over the article. The woman in the sketches was last seen with Volker just before she went missing. Her father, Garett Volker, had a reward out for any information leading to the arrest of the kidnapper.

And those pictures could easily be Jess.

He pulled out his phone and called her again. Still no answer and he knew she wasn't ignoring him. There were four rings before it went to voicemail.

"You haven't heard from her since this paper came out?" he asked.

"No." She seemed to wilt. "I haven't heard a thing."

He searched through the drawer on the end table until he found a pen. Then he wrote a number on the top of the paper. "This is Dad's number. Mom, listen to me." She was kneeling on the floor with tears streaming down her face. "You have to call him right away. I know you don't want to talk to him, but he needs to know what is going on."

He knelt down beside her and helped her over to the couch. "Everything's going to get sorted out, okay? We don't even know for sure if this is Jess."

He held her phone out to her and she finally took it. He placed the newspaper beside her on the couch. "I'm going over to Jess's place. I'll let you know what I find."

***

2019:

Out here by the lake, I felt a million times lighter. It was as if all of the problems I'd had until this point didn't exist. Out of sight, out of mind.

There were no papers for me to look at, no television to watch. I spent my time looking after Brandon and taking Thrasher for walks. I made all three meals myself every day. After a couple of days, I even started experimenting with some of the recipes and I realized for the first time that I was a good cook.

Brandon was on his best behaviour now. I wasn't giving him the sleeping pills anymore because I wasn't gone all day. He'd suffered through some withdrawals the first couple of days and lost a bit of weight, but he seemed okay now.

I had decided to bury the hatchet tonight. It was time for me to forgive and forget his infraction from the other day. That was what couples had to do. Otherwise, they didn't make it for the long haul.

He was sitting down in an armchair in the main area, doing a wordsearch with a crayon I'd found for him. I was making us grilled cheese sandwiches for lunch.

"I was thinking we'd have a date tonight," I said. He looked up at me with a concerned expression. "Nothing fancy," I added quickly. "Just a nice night out, looking at the stars."

"That sounds nice."

I loved that he was using his proper voice now. He still slipped up, but I was patient with him. As soon as I had to remind him, he apologized and started over.

"Yeah, I'm thinking I'll pack us a bit of a picnic. We'll leave Thrasher behind, of course, it's too dangerous out there for him."

"Where are you thinking?" he asked.

"There was a place out here that my Dad used to take me to. It's got a clear view of the sky, especially this time of year when there aren't any leaves on the trees."

"You used to come here with your dad?" he asked.

I realized that I hadn't told him very much about this place. Once I handed him his sandwich, I sat down and started telling him about my childhood.

"When I was little, we used to come out here to visit my uncle," I said. I told her about the fishing and the s'mores. How my dad used to make me guess the bands that used to come on the radio.

As I was telling her, I realized that the only good memories from my childhood were in the cabin. The rest was just a long struggle to survive.

I missed him so much, right then, I felt like there was a black hole inside my chest, sucking away at me. We had been so close, the two of us. Why did he leave?

"My dad did that, too," he told me with a laugh. "Every time a band came on, I had to pass this quiz. After I showed him that I knew a few songs, he would let me change the station to something I liked."

"At least you had your dad for the rest of your life," I said. My tears were falling onto my plate. I rubbed my cheeks, hoping that he hadn't noticed.

"That's true. And he was a damn good one. He was always there for me when something went wrong. Whenever I needed support, he was beside me, helping me along. When my mom died…" He trailed off and I saw his eyes glistening. "When my mom died, I thought I would lose him, too. He loves so deeply and he didn't know what to do when she was gone."

I started to feel uncomfortable with the conversation. I didn't want to hear about Brandon's dad and how awesome he was. He was rubbing salt in the wound, as far as I was concerned.

There was also a tiny bit of guilt making its way into me. By taking Brandon with me, I had made sure he would never get to see his dad again. I only hoped that our shared experience would make us closer.

I changed the subject, asking what he wanted me to bring for dinner. He said it didn't matter to him. It was spending time with me that was important. I knew he was sucking up to me, but still, it was nice to hear.

***

2019:

She still didn't know who Jess was and she was beginning to think she would never find out. The name was important, she knew it, but she also knew there was nothing she could do with it. There wasn't a phone at the cabin and she had no idea where she was. She hadn't even been awake for the ride, it could have been hours long. Or maybe if she got out to the end of the driveway, she would find herself on the edge of the city. She would likely never know.

The idea of spending a romantic night with Cathy wasn't exactly comforting. Yet she was still conflicted about how she felt about the woman.

Cathy needed help, that much was certain. She was sick. But if that were taken care of, she might not be a bad person.

Brandy couldn't even imagine a world where her dad abandoned her. The pain that Cathy must have experienced would be enough to break any child. And although Cathy didn't say anything, Brandy had the sense that the rest of her life didn't have any high points to it.

On the night of the makeover, Cathy had told Brandy that she'd never been treated so kindly. Which was abnormal. Most girls did that kind of thing with their friends or their mothers. Cathy had missed out on it all.

In fact, she didn't even talk about any boyfriends. Was it possible that she'd never felt the love of another person since her dad left?

If that was the case, then Brandy felt sorry for her more than anything.

Still, she wasn't interested in spending the rest of her life pretending to be a guy for some messed-up chick. First, it was her boobs, then her hair and now her voice. What was next? Would Cathy force her to wear a dildo in some crazed sexual fantasy?

She shuddered at the thought. There was no way she would let it get that far.

Tonight was an opportunity that she couldn't pass up.

Cathy was allowing her to use the bathroom freely now. Of course, she still had to leave the door open, but at least she didn't have to wear a diaper.

She needed to get a message to someone. Something that anyone could pick up on. She pulled Cathy's brush from the cabinet and tugged a couple of hairs from the brush.

Then, before she could talk herself out of it, she reached into her armpits and plucked out a couple of hairs; since she hadn't been able to shave, they'd grown long, and wrapped it in tissue paper along with Cathy's. The hair samples were shoved into her pocket before Cathy could see that she was done peeing. Then on second thought, she pulled the tissue out and scribbled something down with the red crayon she'd kept before pocketing it again.

On the way out, they stopped by Thrasher's run and Cathy told him she would be back. While she was talking to him, Brandy grabbed a tuft of his hair off of the fence and shoved it into her pocket as well.

Her plan wasn't well thought out, but it was all that she had.

Cathy insisted on holding her hand the entire time. And although there was the appearance of freedom, Brandy knew that Cathy had a knife with her at the very least. Maybe even a gun now that they were out in the bush. She had to be careful.

"Here we are," said Cathy once they reached the bank of a lake. "I used to come here with Dad and watch the sunrise in the mornings. Sometimes we fished, too. But it's also great for star watching."

She pulled a blanket out of a backpack and laid it out in the sand. Then she pulled out a sliced apple, some cheese and a couple of tuna sandwiches. There was no beer. Brandy wasn't allowed to be near glass objects anymore.

Cathy sat down and patted the blanket beside her. "Come on, I'm starving."

Brandy sat down and Cathy handed her a Ziploc baggy of apples. Brandy ate them quickly. When Cathy wasn't looking, she shoved the bag into her pocket. Then she helped herself to the cheese.

"Is this gouda?" she asked.

"I don't know," said Cathy. "It was on sale at the grocery store."

By the time they finished their food, Brandy was getting cold. She could see her breath and there was a pretty heavy breeze blowing through. Cathy pulled Brandy close and wrapped her arms around her. "We're going to be so happy here, Brandon."

A feeling of panic rose up in her, but she tamped it down. "It's a beautiful view," she said. Cathy nodded and pulled her to the ground.

"Let's watch the stars."

Brandy lay close to Cathy, seeking as much heat as she could. "My friend and I used to play a game," she said. She'd almost said boyfriend, but she didn't want to ruin Cathy's fantasy. "We would stare at the stars and pick out a constellation. Then the other person would have to guess which one it was."

"I'll go first," said Cathy. Brandy closed her eyes, waiting for Cathy to find her stars. When Cathy was ready, she opened them and started guessing.

"Ursa Major?" she asked.

"Nope," said Cathy.

"Ursa Minor?"

"No."

"Orion?"

"Yes," said Cathy with a grin. "Your turn. I have to close my eyes, right?" Brandy nodded and waited for the usual threat of compliance from Cathy, but it didn't come.

She looked up to the heavens and mentally prayed while looking. She and Cathy took turns naming constellations for at least half an hour.

"I have to go to the bathroom," she said. Cathy looked over at her with a frown.

"I'm not going far, you'll be able to see me, I promise," said Brandy.

She walked over to a thicket and pulled her pants down, squatting with her back to Cathy. She pulled the tissue and hairs out of her pocket along with the baggy. While she was peeing, she threw everything into the bag and dropped it beside the thicket. She prayed someone would come by at some point. It couldn't just be Cathy that loved this place.

When she was done, she made her way back over to Cathy and laid down with her again. They played the game until Cathy was yawning.

"It's time to head back," Cathy said. "Grab the garbage, we don't want to be leaving litter in a place like this." Brandy grabbed a couple of the bags and handed them to Cathy and then started folding up the blanket.

"Hold up," Cathy said. "We're short a bag." She stood up and started looking around. "It's got to be around here somewhere."

Brandy's palms were sweaty as she finished rolling up the blanket. Cathy was walking through the area in a grid-like pattern. "Are you sure we're missing one?" she asked.

"I am, there should be six here, but I've only got five. The wind must have blown one away."

"Maybe we can come back and look in the morning?" Brandy suggested.

"There it is!" said Cathy triumphantly. Brandy looked in the direction she was pointing and saw a baggy floating a few feet from the shore.

A gust of wind blew past Cathy, blowing her hair up and around her. Brandy looked around her, wondering which direction she should run in. But her response wasn't fast enough. Cathy was back by her side.

"Did you find it?" she asked with a shaky voice, completely forgetting that she was supposed to speak like a man.

"No, it was just a piece of garbage. Oh well, hopefully someone finds it," she said.

Brandy closed her eyes and let out a breath. As Cathy grabbed her hand with a firm grip, she sent another prayer out into the world. *Please let someone find it.*

32

When Garett hung up the phone, all of the colour had drained from his face. Laura rushed over to him, afraid he was going to faint.

"What is it? Did they… Did they find her?" she asked.

"No," he said. "I don't know." He took a deep breath and rubbed his hand through his hair. "That wasn't the police. It was Lorraine, my ex-fiancée. Jess and Nathan's mother."

"Oh," said Laura. She hadn't been expecting that. "What did she have to say?"

"That she thinks Jess is in trouble," he said.

"What kind of trouble?" A sense of dread hung above Laura and she was waiting for it to enfold her.

"She thinks…" He paused and licked his lips. "She thinks that Jess is involved in Brandy's disappearance."

"What!?"

"The newspaper. Lorraine said those sketches looked just like Jess."

Laura grabbed the paper from the kitchen and brought it out for Garett to look at. "This is Jess?"

"I don't know," he said. "I haven't seen her since she was a little girl, Laura. Why would she do this?"

Laura stared down at the paper in disbelief. This monster was Brandy's sister? This person was involved with the Rooftop Arsonist, too. It didn't make any sense.

"Does Nathan know?" she asked. "Or the police?"

"Do I call the police?"

"Yes, Garett. Jess is an adult and she's made her own decisions. Brandy could be hurt."

"Or maybe they ran off together. Maybe Jess told her all about me and she decided she wanted nothing to do with me."

She picked up the phone and handed it to him. "Either way, the police need to know. You should give the detective a call."

He held the phone in a shaking hand. Then it slipped from his fingers as he started sobbing. Her heart broke to see him this way. She knelt down beside him and laid her head on his lap, holding him and waiting for him to be ready.

***

2019:

The door to the trailer was locked. Nathan knocked a few times, but nobody answered. Thrasher didn't even bark, which was strange.

Cursing Jess and her inability to clean up her yard, he picked his way around the trailer and looked through the windows. Everything was dark, all of the lights were out. Where would she be this time of night? She didn't have a life.

He made his way back to her front door and knocked again. When there was no answer, he decided to call her. He heard a phone ring inside the trailer.

He looked inside the kitchen window and dialled her number again. A phone lit up on the table, showing a chaotic scene of open, empty cupboards.

She was gone.

***

2019:

The Ziploc baggy felt like a lead weight inside my pocket as I walked Brandon back to the cabin. Something was inside it, but I couldn't see what it was in the dark.

I felt like I had been stabbed in the back, even though I wasn't yet certain. I should have gone with him when he had to use the bathroom. I should have made him face me. Why did I keep screwing up with this over and over again?

Was I that weak that a cute smile was all it took to make me lose my mind?

Back in the cabin, I put Brandon to bed, pretending that everything was normal. I let Thrasher into the house and put him in with Brandon. The trust we'd developed was gone.

Inside my room, I pulled out the baggy in the lamplight. There was a tissue inside with the world HELP written on it in red crayon. After the initial wave of rage had subsided, I opened the bag up and pulled the tissue out. Several hairs were mixed inside, including my own hair and Thrasher's. Brandon had obviously pulled out some pubes or armpit hairs, too, because there was nothing on his head.

Carefully, I tucked the hairs back inside the tissue and then back inside the baggy. I opened the nightstand drawer and put it in there.

I turned off the lamp and laid on the bed on top of the covers. I tucked my hands behind my head so I could think.

After a moment, I realized I was crying. Tears were tickling my cheeks as they made their way down. Once I noticed it, I couldn't ignore it. I quickly flipped over and shoved the pillow over my face so Brandon couldn't hear me sobbing.

It had been years since I was that hysterical. In fact, I didn't think I'd cried that hard since my dad had left.

All I could think was that nobody wanted me around. Everyone I ever cared for wanted to leave me. First my dad, then my mom and now Brandon. What was wrong with me?

After I had cried all the tears I had, I laid awake in bed, thinking. I went through every memory of my life that I could to see what I could have done wrong. How had I made myself so unlovable?

And then it hit me at about three in the morning. It wasn't that I was unlovable. I had been naïve and gullible. I had let people know that I cared about them and they had used it to their advantage and then thrown me aside.

I couldn't sleep for the remainder of the night. At six, I got up and went into the bathroom to see how bad I looked after crying all night. My eyes and lips were puffy, so I turned on a cold shower and hopped in.

I stayed in there for as long as I could bear it. Then I got out and decided to make Brandon breakfast. We would be having a conversation today. I would be making it clear to him just how badly he'd fucked up by trying to betray me.

33

Brandy woke to the smell of coffee, pancakes and eggs. It was a magnificent scent and her stomach rumbled. She'd hardly slept during the night, worried sick about how close she'd come to being discovered by Cathy.

She'd thought she'd heard Cathy in the night, but couldn't be sure. With both of the heavy doors closed and Thrasher snoring, it was a wonder she even heard Cathy get in the shower this morning.

She shifted to a more comfortable position on the bed and was rewarded by a lick from Thrasher. His presence was oddly comforting, as though he was protecting her now as much as Cathy. He'd curled up next to her sometime during the night. The bed was much roomier and far softer than the one in the trailer.

Cathy came in with a breakfast tray and a smile on her face. "Good morning!" she said in a sing-song voice.

Brandy gave an easy smile in return. This looked promising. "Morning, Cathy."

"I've made some breakfast. I'm just going to set it here while I put Thrasher in the run, and then I'll be back and we can eat together."

She was gone a few minutes and then she came in with her own plate and coffee. Cathy pulled the nightstand over to the armchair and set her food on it. Then she handed Brandy her paper plate and styrofoam cup.

The coffee was only tepid, but it was better than nothing. Cathy obviously wasn't at the point to trust her with hot liquids.

She took a deep gulp and then stopped as the strange flavour hit her mouth. She pulled back, ready to spit it out, but the look on Cathy's face told her not to. "Is there something wrong with the coffee?" she asked, taking a sip of her own steaming cup. Brandy shook her head and forced herself to swallow the liquid. "Good, then drink up," said Cathy. After a brief pause, she said, "All of it."

Brandy hesitated, lifting the cup to her mouth. This time she smelled it before she took a sip and she could tell that there was something off about it. Cathy had probably put more drugs in it. She hoped it was only sleeping pills.

Once she managed to finish the coffee, she dug into the food. There were no utensils as usual, so she ripped off pieces of the pancake and shoved them in her mouth. There was no syrup on it, but she wasn't going to complain.

A moment later, she felt a hair in her mouth. Carefully, so as not to offend Cathy, she pushed the hair out of her mouth and looked at it. At first, she thought that one of Thrasher's hairs had made it into her food, but then after a closer inspection, she realized what it was.

"Look familiar?" asked Cathy.

It looked like one of the hairs she had put in the baggy. An ice-cold feeling slid down her back and her hands started to shake.

"Eat. Up." said Cathy. "Hairs and all. If you puke it up, I will make you lick it off the floor."

The coffee had been laced with poison, she was sure of it. She was going to die choking on this nasty food as the poison overtook her.

Slowly, she ate her food, bite by bite. It seemed that Cathy had managed to incorporate all of the hairs into the meal. She gagged with each bite, sometimes swallowing some vomit that rose from her stomach. She found a tuft of Thrasher's hair in the eggs and the pancake contained several of Cathy's hairs along with her armpit hairs. Cathy watched her with a satisfied look the entire time she gagged and choked her way through.

When she finally swallowed the last bite – and held it down, that was the important part – she looked up at Cathy. From her pocket, Cathy withdrew the tissue paper she'd used for her message. She tossed the paper onto Brandy's bed.

"You think you're clever? This proves that you're not. This proves how stupid you are." Brandy crawled back from Cathy, leaning her back up against the wall. "You clearly don't understand who is in charge here, who makes the rules. You have bitten the hand that feeds you."

Her terror was so bad that she couldn't even cry. All she did was shake and stare at Cathy. She felt a warmth in her pants and realized she had wet herself.

"I was prepared to spend my life with you, Brandon. I opened myself up to you, and this is the way you treat me?" There was no heat in her tone, only ice. "Once I'm done with you, you're going to beg to obey me."

She grabbed the duct tape off of the nightstand and pulled off a chunk, pushing it so hard on Brandy's mouth that she left a bruise. She kissed the duct tape over Brandy's lips when she was done.

"By the way, I pissed in your coffee."

Bile rose in Brandy's throat and she fought the urge to puke. With the duct tape on, she would surely drown. Cathy stood and laughed over her as she watched her struggle, then she hocked up a loogie and spit on Brandy's face.

"Have a good day," she said as she closed the door behind her.

***

2019:

Nathan sat at the kitchen table with his dad, Laura, his mom and Detective Starling, the man who had been assigned Brandy's case. Another officer stood in the corner of his dad's kitchen with his arms crossed as he overlooked the situation.

"We've had a chance to talk to your sister's employer, and it seems that she also hasn't been showing up for her shifts. He says she's been gone for several days now and he's writing up the termination papers for her."

His mother wouldn't stop sobbing, and the sound of her snuffling was starting to get under his skin. She was making everything about her.

"We're also sending a crew down to look at her trailer. Do any of you know any place she might have gone?" They all shook their heads. Except for his mother, who blew her nose instead. "Does she have any friends she might be visiting?"

"Jess has never had any friends," said Nathan.

He heard a soft moan from his dad, but he didn't care. If the man had stuck around, this might never have been an issue.

"A boyfriend?"

"No," said Nathan. "Never, as far as I know."

"Where would she normally spend her time?" Starling asked.

"At her trailer. She really didn't go anywhere except for work that I knew of. She's a loner."

The detective flipped his notebook shut and looked around. "So you're telling me that all of you, her family, don't know anything about her that might give us a clue as to where she would go."

The statement brought another round of sobs from his mother and Nathan closed his eyes. "No, what I'm telling you is that she didn't have any special places. She didn't like anything. She was always fucking miserable."

"She used to like fishing," said his dad quietly at the end of the table.

The detective looked over at him. "What was that?"

"When she was little," said Garett. "We used to fish."

"So you think that your eldest daughter took your youngest out fishing. Just for old time's sake?" asked the detective. Garett shrugged, it looked like the sharp comment stung. "Listen, I'm sorry. That was uncalled for. I just had my hopes up that we were finally getting somewhere with this case. Now it feels like we're just chasing our tails."

He stood up and nodded to everyone. "Hopefully, the boys can find something at the trailer." He looked at his watch. "They should be there right now. We'll call you as soon as we know something."

Once the detective and his buddy left, the others sat in silence for a while. It wasn't the most comfortable reunion.

Finally, Laura spoke up, "We all should get some food in us and then get some rest. It's going to be busy over the next few days."

"Are you the lady that's been writing the articles?" asked Nathan's mother.

Laura gave her a cautious look and then nodded. "I am. I'm a reporter for the Edmonton Guardian."

"Well, that must be nice for you, Garett. Having an in at the paper."

"Lorraine, don't st-"

"So, is everyone okay with pizza?" asked Laura over him. Nathan nodded and then left the table before hearing what anyone else had to say.

"I'm good with whatever," he said.

He pulled out his phone and made his way out the back door to the patio. He hadn't spoken to Jenny about anything. She was in a delicate stage of pregnancy and he didn't want her to stress over anything.

"Hello?" she said. He could tell right away that she was upset.

"Hey, babe. I just wanted to let you know that I'm going to be a bit longer before I come home. I hope that's okay."

"Where are you? I know you're not at work, Glen called earlier."

Shit. Now it looked like he was cheating on her. "No, I'm not. I didn't want to bother you about it, but I'm dealing with some family drama right now. Mom's a mess and Jess is… missing."

"What is your sister up to now?" she asked.

"I don't know anything for sure yet, but I'm just here with Mom, trying to keep her calm and figure out what the next steps are. I'll be home later tonight, I promise."

He hung up the phone and collapsed onto one of the patio chairs. What a nightmare this had all turned into. Emotions rippled through him, making him feel like he had to cry one minute and laugh the next.

Only a day ago, he'd learned that he had a younger sister. In the same breath, he learned that she was missing and he might have missed his chance to meet her. Now it looked like his older sister had kidnapped her and she was missing, too.

He'd never felt so alone in his entire life.

"Nathan?" said Laura from the door. "We've just got a call. You're going to want to hear this."

With a groan, he stood up and made his way back inside to sit down with his family once again.

"... Thank you for everything." His dad hung up the phone and then set it carefully into the center of the table.

"They've been to the trailer," he said. Everyone leaned forward, waiting to hear what he said, but he choked up before he could spit out the next words. "Th-they found chains in one room. Someone had been tied down to a bed. There were used diapers in the garbage, along with locks of long, blonde hair."

He broke down after that, sobbing hysterically. Nathan looked over at his mother, but she was in a world of her own. She stared off into space, tears trickling down her cheeks. He would be surprised if she'd heard a single word.

Laura comforted Garett, offering him a tissue. The doorbell rang and Nathan jumped to get it. Any excuse to leave the table would work. He didn't care if he ended up paying for the pizza. He just had to get away from them all.

***

2019:

Brandon had tried making several apologies to me over the course of the day. I recognized them for what they were and ignored him. I hadn't decided yet if I was going to keep him around for the rest of my life.

I had to come up with a plan to get us out of here safely and if I had to watch him every step of the way to make sure that he was behaving, it was only going to be that much more difficult. I hadn't decided if it was even worth it to me.

It was clear that he didn't want to be around me. *Maybe I should just let him go. I could just leave him behind here when I leave. He would starve to death before the homeowners return.*

In the meantime, though, I was keeping him alive. I wasn't letting him use the bathroom anymore. I couldn't even trust him in there. He was bound to his bed all day every day. When the diapers ran out, that would be too bad for him.

I poured myself a coffee and put some pancakes and bacon onto my plate. Then I grabbed his bowl and made my way down to the room.

He was wide awake and shaking in the corner of the bed. I had tightened his shackles enough that he couldn't reach the duct tape on his mouth, but he could still move around a bit. I placed his bowl on the bed and then pulled the tape off.

He cowered in the corner, turning his face away from me. I reached down and grabbed his chin, squeezing it firmly and forcing him to look at me.

"I'm going to watch you eat your breakfast, Brandon. I don't want you going hungry."

I backed off then and handed him the bowl. I grinned at the look of revulsion that covered his face. The canned dog food would have all the nutrients he needed and I wasn't going to waste any more good food on him.

"Bon appetit!" I said as I sipped my coffee.

"Please," he said in his girly voice.

"Are we going to play that game, Brandon? You whine at me in the girly voice and I take away your food?"

Tears streamed down his face and he shook his head. He was hungry, I knew that much. I hadn't given him any supper last night. I was too furious with him. I'd let him stew in his own waste until I changed the sheets shortly before I went to bed.

He picked up a chunk and put it to his lips with shaking fingers.

"Make sure you chew it properly, we don't want you to choke," I said. He nodded and I watched him chew with a smile of pleasure on my face.

After all of the chunks were gone, I asked him to lick the bowl clean. Once he had cleaned the bowl, I stood and handed him a milk bone from my pocket. "You've been such a good boy, you deserve a treat."

I handed him the bone and watched him until he put it into his mouth. He crunched down and chewed it slowly. I could see the disgust in his eyes as he watched me.

It would be fun breaking him.

I taped his mouth shut and then patted his head. "Lay down, I'm going to tighten your chains up. I don't want you getting any funny ideas while Thrasher and I go for our hike."

I tied him down, forcing his arms and legs to sink into the mattress as I tightened the chains. "If you had been good, you would have been able to come with us. Instead, you get to sit in your room and think about what you've done."

I leaned down and gave him a peck on the mouth. His nostrils flared but he didn't look away from me.

Out in the kitchen, I had a backpack filled with a day's worth of food. I was planning to spend the entire day down by the lake, exploring and relaxing. At the moment, I couldn't bear to be in the same house as Brandon. It was too much.

I needed this break from him.

34

Laura had been more than happy to see Lorraine leave the night before. Garett, bless his heart, had offered for her to stay the night. She refused with an air of offence at the thought, looking at him like he'd grown a second head. Then she'd been on her way, neglecting to offer to pay for part of the pizza.

Nathan had tossed a twenty down on the table before he left. He also seemed strained, but then, it had not been an easy night.

Garett didn't have much to say. The sudden expansion of his family was overwhelming. The situation with his daughters left him feeling torn and guilty. He had wanted to condemn the person who'd kidnapped Brandy. Once he found out it was Jess, he just wanted to hug her and tell her he was sorry.

There was no winning for him right now. It might be impossible for him to ever imagine a win coming out of the situation.

The next day, he'd only sat in his chair, leaving only to use the washroom. Laura brought him food occasionally and then removed it when he didn't touch it. She was beyond trying to force him to do anything anymore. Coping with the stress he was going through would be nearly impossible. All she could do was support him and be there if he needed it.

He did lay down that night to sleep beside her. She snuggled in closely and fell asleep instantly, exhaustion winning out over the need to keep him company. He didn't sleep as well, she knew. Several times, she woke to find him staring at the ceiling.

"We had so much fun fishing," he said, waking Laura sometime after midnight. "We used to go out and spend the whole weekend at Daryl's cabin. If I could get away from work, we'd go for a week. Lorraine and Nathan hated it, so it would just be us two."

"Who's Daryl?" she asked groggily.

"Lorraine's brother. That's how I met Lorraine, actually, it was through Daryl."

"You've never mentioned him before."

"Well, after I left Lorraine, I stopped talking to him. I didn't want to force a wedge between the two of them. They never did have the greatest relationship to begin with."

"Well, it sounds like there was a wedge anyway," said Laura. "Nathan said he hasn't seen him since he was a child."

"Yeah, that's really too bad. Daryl's a good guy."

"Why don't you give him a call tomorrow?" asked Laura. She thought it might be good for him to have someone to talk to about happy memories.

"Lorraine said he's down south somewhere. He does the snowbird thing."

"Oh," she said. So much for that idea.

Garett sat up in bed, startling Laura. "His cabin is empty right now."

"If he's in the States, then yeah, it probably is."

He flipped back the covers and stood up to begin pacing. "Would she?" he muttered.

"Garett?" She turned on the light. "What is it? What are you thinking?"

He looked at her with a triumphant smile on his face. "I think I know where Jess would go. She loved the cabin." He ran over to his dresser and started pulling clothing out. One foot went into his black dress pants and he danced around, trying to get them on as quickly as he could. "I'm going to go out there."

"Is that safe? If Jess has been doing everything the police suspect she is, she's a dangerous person."

"She's my daughter. I'll be fine." He pulled a black long-john sweater over his head. He looked ridiculous, but she didn't comment. Laura was just happy to see him dressed.

She got out of bed and followed him as he made his way down the stairs. "Shouldn't we call the police?"

"Yes!" he said. "Give them a call, tell them to meet me out there." Then he was out the door and running down the driveway.

She ran over to the door and leaned out. "Where is it?"

"Lorraine can tell you!"

***

2019:

With Thrasher by my side, I walked for hours. We never wandered too close to public areas. I didn't want to be seen, but when I came across a girl and her dad fishing, I couldn't help but watch for a while.

Thrasher was obedient and stayed quiet by my side the whole time. It was like he sensed that I was going through something. I knew that I was, but I couldn't understand it.

Watching the two left me with an aching feeling. A hole where my heart should be. For a while, I didn't think about Brandon at all. I only ran through the memories of times I'd spent with my dad out there at the lake.

When they finally packed up a couple of hours later, Thrasher and I moved on. I threw a few sticks into the lake for him, but it was clear that the water was too cold for him. He didn't seem excited to chase after anything in the lake.

I laid out a picnic for the two of us in the evening. I had brought along some bacon for him. It was cooked, but I knew he would appreciate it. I had made myself a couple of fried egg sandwiches.

When we were done, I laid down to stare at the stars. I tried to bring back the feeling I'd had with Brandon that night. It had felt so… normal. We were doing something that a normal couple would do. He had snuggled into me to keep warm.

The night was nearly as special as the night of the makeover.

But try as I might, I couldn't separate that evening from the sense of betrayal I'd felt when I realized what Brandon had been up to. I had been so kind to him, why did he treat me that way?

It was too much after a few moments and I ended up closing my eyes and ignoring the stars. Just the scent of the lake and the leaves was enough to make me happy. After a few moments, I drifted off to sleep.

When I opened my eyes, I could see that several hours had passed. The moon was making its descent to the horizon now. As I sat up, Thrasher stood and stretched beside me.

I carefully packed up our supplies and shoved them into the bag, counting every piece of garbage. It was something my dad had instilled in me as a child. When you're out in nature, you leave everything as you found it. *Don't leave the signs of humanity everywhere if you can help it.*

Then we began our trek home. It was a good half-hour's walk back to the cabin in the daylight. At night, when it was harder to see, it took longer. Thrasher would often run ahead of me and then double back when he realized I had slowed down to get better footing.

Eventually, worried that he would come across a bear or a coyote, I put a leash on him. He didn't care for it and it made things a bit more tedious, but I felt better.

I was just bending down to take Thrasher's leash off once we could see the cabin, when a light flicked on inside of the house. I crouched down beside my dog and froze.

Had Brandon gotten loose somehow? I quickly decided that he hadn't. If he had, he wouldn't be stupid enough to turn on a light. He would have taken off down the driveway, hoping to find help on the main road.

Either that or he would be waiting somewhere inside to ambush me.

No, the light inside the house meant there was someone else in the cabin.

Thrasher sensed my sudden tension and started a low growl beside me. I looked down at him. "Quiet," I said in my commanding voice. He looked up at me and whimpered, but he didn't make any more noise.

It was a good twenty feet to the dog run across open ground. I decided against the risk and tied Thrasher to a nearby tree. "Stay," I said to him. Then I gave him a quick pat on the head.

He whined quietly while I walked away, but made no other noise. He was a good dog.

I made my way around the yard through the edge of the bush. I kept the cabin in sight the whole time. When I had circled around to the front, where the treeline was closest to the cabin, I saw a white sedan parked beside my truck.

It was only a matter of time until the police arrived at this point. Whoever was inside would discover Brandy sooner rather than later.

Then the light went off and I heard the front door open. After a moment. it closed, but no one came down from the porch.

I counted to two hundred before I moved forward. I had my hunting knife pulled out of my backpack and held tightly in my hand. I crept forward, crouched as low down to the ground as I could manage.

There was no one at the door. The light inside flicked on again. It was the kitchen light.

I darted over to the sedan and stabbed my hunting knife into all four tires. This person wasn't going to be moving anywhere. I doubted it was my uncle, he wouldn't have turned the light off and left, he would have all the lights in the cabin on at this point.

The cabin was small. If I wasn't careful, I would be seen. I closed my eyes and tried to remember where the breaker box was. I was pretty sure it was in the kitchen. If I could get in and turn off the lights, I could sneak up on the person. They wouldn't know the cabin as well as I did.

I crept up to the porch, pausing every couple of steps to listen. I didn't hear anything. I pulled the door open quietly, praying there were no squeaking hinges, and then made my way inside, not bothering to close it behind me.

I was right about the breaker box. It was on the wall near the entrance. Peeking around the corner, I saw the shadow of a man in the hallway, just outside of Brandon's room. I stood and flipped all of the breakers before ducking back down again.

As the lights went out, I grinned. Now it was time to get to work.

***

2019:

Hutchinson slammed his hand on his steering wheel as he made his way out of the city. He had the lights flashing and was driving the highest speed he could. Why the hell had Garett gone out there without calling the police first?

According to Starling, he had over a half-hour's headstart on them by the time they were able to track down Garett's ex, Lorraine, and find out where this cabin was. Worse, she hadn't been completely certain of the exact location.

He had someone trying to call the homeowner down in Arizona, but so far they were having no luck. All they could do was hope and pray they would get there in time. Before anyone was hurt.

35

2019:

B randy was starving. The can of dog food, disgusting as it was, had been a bit of a relief that morning. She was certain that Cathy was planning to starve her.

As it was, she'd already lost too much weight. Before long, the Tensor bandage around her chest wasn't going to be necessary. It was already loose, but she hadn't said anything to Cathy. If Cathy found out, she would be forcing her to tighten it again, putting pressure against the sores that were already there.

Cathy had also not allowed her to change her diaper that morning or go to the washroom. Due to lack of water, her urine was dark and pungent.

If she'd been offered the special coffee again today, she would gladly take it. The dog treat offered after her breakfast had only served to dry her mouth out more. Even when she moved her tongue around in her mouth, she struggled to make any saliva flow.

A headache had been nagging her since the night before. Whether it was from hunger or thirst, she didn't know, but it was only growing worse.

Each of her limbs ached from being pulled so harshly. The bands around her ankles and wrists where the zip ties held her tight burned. Over time, as she'd been tied down into the trailer, her skin had been rubbed raw.

Out here in the cabin, when Cathy had let her move about more freely, they'd started to scab over. Now the scabs broke open and she could feel the slickness of blood on her wrists. She tried not to disturb them or move too much, but every breath made it ache.

Cathy hadn't been kidding about the hike she was planning to take. The sun had barely been up when she left, and now Brandy could see by the sunlight that it was quickly setting. Part of her wondered if Cathy hadn't gone on a hike, but rather just left.

It would be months before Brandy's body was discovered, if that was the case. She wondered if she'd still be recognizable, or if the flesh would have rotted away enough that they had to use DNA.

As the light got darker in the room, she closed her eyes, hoping for a bit of sleep. Rest was difficult when she couldn't move.

She drifted in and out, waking every time she heard an odd sound. It was so much quieter out here than it had been in the trailer. Now, every time the furnace kicked in or the wind rattled the windows, she was startled awake.

At one point, she thought she heard a vehicle in the driveway, but she drifted off to sleep again before she could be certain.

Finally, she woke groggily, wondering what had awakened her. It was brighter in her room. If she looked through her peripheral, she thought she could see a light under her door. Cathy was home. Rather than fear, she felt relief at the thought. She wasn't going to be left out here to starve right now.

"Jess?" came a muffled voice. She recognized the voice, but it took her a moment to place it. "Brandy?" It was her dad. Glee flooded her body along with a rush of adrenaline that put her fully awake.

"It's Dad," he said. She needed to get his attention.

She strained against her bonds, hoping to make the chains rattle, but she couldn't do anything. She screamed as loud as she could behind the tape. Through the heavy door, her father didn't hear a thing.

"Brandy?" He walked a little bit closer to her door, but then he paused. She heard him mumble something quietly to himself. She didn't know what he said, but it sounded like he was lecturing himself.

She thrashed her body around as much as she could. The zip ties dug into her wrists and ankles and blood flowed freely.

Her throat was raw from screaming.

Then the light went out. Panic set in and she moved like a wild animal that had been caged. She heard a pop as her arm dislocated and the pain was excruciating, but she didn't care. She could move around a bit.

After a moment, she was able to push a pillow onto the nightstand. She flung her body around as much as she could, and the pillow slid over into a delicate lamp. She watched as the lamp tottered back and forth.

Then it fell to the floor with a crash.

There was silence again and she began to scream once more.

The light flicked on again and she felt tears stream down her face. "Hello, who's there?" said her dad.

He moved toward the room and Brandy screamed some more. He opened the door and looked in at the scene in front of him.

Brandy felt her entire body relax and she fell to the bed sobbing. It was going to be alright. Everything was going to be okay. Her dad was here.

"Brandy, is that you?" he said, stumbling into the room. "Oh my God, what has she done?"

He leaned over her and pulled the duct tape away from her mouth as gently as he could. "Daddy," she gasped in a raspy voice. "We have to be quick. She's coming back. She has a dog."

"Sh, sh, it's okay," he said. "I just need to get you out of these chains." He crouched down beside Brandy and started fiddling with them.

When the lights went out, he swore softly. Brandy felt her body turn to ice. "She's here," she hissed. "Daddy, she's here."

"Who's here?" he asked in a low voice. "Jess?"

"Cathy," she whispered. "Maybe Jess... I don't know."

He stood up quickly and made his way to the door. It was hard to see now that the light was out. He pulled the door open quietly and then turned to Brandy, giving her a hand signal of some kind.

She saw the shadow stand up behind him before he did. "No!" she screamed.

Her dad turned at the last second and she saw his body jerk as Cathy slid a knife into him. Then she heard the soft dull thuds of Cathy stabbing him several more times.

She screamed until her voice was gone, thrashing about enough to dislocate her other shoulder.

When she was done, Cathy flicked on the light.

"Jess?" gasped her dad.

Cathy froze on the spot. "Daddy?" she whispered softly. Brandy was certain she was hallucinating now.

"I'm sorry, sweetie," he said to her.

She knelt down beside him, a keening sound now coming from her throat. She gathered him up into her arms and rocked back and forth. "Why? Why did you come now?"

"I-" he coughed and Brandy saw blood run down his cheek. "I love you, Jess."

Then his body went still.

A hoarse sound rose from Brandy, and she screamed like she herself had died. But the sound she made was nothing in comparison to her captor's.

Cathy – Jess – was hugging their dad tight and wailing.

After a moment, Jess stood and stared at Brandy with dull eyes. Then she turned and ran out the door.

***

2019:

I ran like I've never run before. I grabbed one thing from the porch and ran like the wind.

Thrasher saw me pass by him and whined after me, but I didn't turn.

It was nearly sunrise now. I couldn't miss this one.

Branches tore at my arms, my legs and my face. Some of my hair was caught and torn from me.

It didn't matter what kind of trail I left now. Nothing mattered anymore.

I reached the lake in time to see the sun first peek over the horizon. I stood there watching it with a sad smile on my face.

Once again, I had fucked everything up. Never again would I see a sunrise with my dad. The possibility of happiness was long gone. It had started disappearing the moment I had started that first fire a year ago.

I looked at the jerry can that I carried. My ending was kind of poetic. I was going to finish as I had begun.

I lifted it up and dumped the contents down over my body, reveling in the foul smell. Then from my pocket, I pulled a lighter.

I held it in front of me, my eyes on the sunrise, and then gave one last flick of my thumb.

***

1992, ten years old:

Garett watched as Jess bound down the trail in front of him, her mouse-brown hair swaying with each step. He held their fishing poles and tackle box.

"Come on, Daddy! We don't want to miss it," she said over her shoulder.

He smiled and picked up his pace, walking behind her.

They arrived in plenty of time to see the sun crest the horizon. A beautiful swirl of pink and oranges covered the sky and reflected in the stillness of the lake.

The two lawn chairs they'd left set up the day before were waiting for them. Jess sat down in one and leaned back, a look of contentment on her face.

It was a look he didn't see in his little girl very much anymore. There was too much arguing at home, and too much competition to be in the spotlight.

He would miss these days with her.

He sat beside her and set their stuff down. Then he reached into his pack and pulled out a thermos and two tin cups.

"What say we have some hot chocolate while we watch the sun come up?"

She nodded excitedly and he watched her every movement. He didn't know what the future was going to bring, but he knew this moment of peace would be one of the last for a long time.

He handed her the mug and they clinked them together, taking a sip and settling back.

"Isn't this the most beautiful thing in the world?" she said with awe.

He smiled and reached over to rub her head. "No," he said looking at her. "It's the second most beautiful thing in the world."

She blushed and took another sip of her hot chocolate.

He struggled, trying to come up with some wisdom to impart to his little girl. But instead, he decided the best thing he could leave her with was peace and beauty.

He leaned back in his chair and took a long sip from his mug. It was looking like it was going to be a beautiful day.

EPILOGUE

Hutchinson sat in his car outside of the remand centre, waiting for Walker to come out. The man had been so relieved to know that he was free. To Hutchinson, his release had been the only positive outcome of the entire case.

Never had he seen something so convoluted and messed up. This one would go down in history and he was sure he would have nightmares about it the rest of his life.

It had been unfortunate that the woman responsible for all of this pain had committed suicide rather than face the consequences of her actions. It was a coward's way out, he thought, despite the amount of pain she must have been in when she did it.

She had left a trail of tragedy and misery behind her and he wasn't sure how Brandy could ever fully recover from the experience. The remainder of the family would also need years of therapy just to get back to any semblance of normality.

He noticed Walker coming out of the door, squinting in the sunlight. Hutchinson had made arrangements to give Walker a ride home after he learned that the man had no one who was waiting for him. Walker was going from one prison life to another, and Hutchinson felt some responsibility for his predicament.

Walker got into the car with a sheepish look on his face. "I really appreciate this," he said quietly.

When he'd been arrested, he hadn't had any money on himself. He would have had to walk home, which would have been a fine thank you after what he'd been through.

"No problem," said Hutchinson. He pulled into traffic and headed toward Walker's place.

"This was a real wake-up call, you know?"

Hutchinson only nodded in response.

"I know that I didn't do anything wrong, but the choices that I've made in my life made this happen. I need to make some changes."

"That's probably a good idea," said Hutchinson. He just wanted to give the man a ride, not engage in an Oprah-style interview. He hoped that would be the end of it.

"So that woman only pretended to be interested in me so that she could frame me for her crime?"

"I thought you didn't remember her," said Hutchinson sharply.

Walker shrugged uncomfortably. "I don't really, but I still feel used and hurt. How desperate could I have been?"

There wasn't much to say to that and Hutchinson let the conversation drop. Although not another word was said, he could sense the sorrow and self-hatred coming from Walker. When he pulled up in front of the bungalow that the man called home, he reached out and put a hand on Walker's shoulder.

"Listen," he said firmly. "None of this was your fault. You were just in the wrong place at the wrong time. It wouldn't have mattered who was there that night, she would have made her move."

"You think?" Walker asked.

"It could have been anyone. She was sick and messed up. She's screwed up many people's lives. Don't let her have any more effect on yours. Just move on, make those changes and don't waste any more time thinking of her." He knew that wouldn't happen, that Walker would spend many hours both awake and asleep thinking of that woman, but it was the best advice he could give at the time.

"Thank you," said Walker. He took a deep breath and got out of the car, making his way up the pitted sidewalk outside of his house.

Hutchinson felt terrible for him. There was nobody there to check in on him and see how he was dealing with the situation. If Walker went missing, Hutchinson was certain that few would notice.

He sincerely hoped that the guy would take his advice to heart.

As for him, he couldn't wait to visit Crystal and hug her tight. No matter what inane problems she had for him, he would listen to them all intently because she was the most important thing in his world.

***

2019:

Garett's funeral was a quiet one. Only his family attended; Brandy, Nathan and his wife Jenny, Lorraine, Laura, and Lorraine's brother Daryl.

Laura had learned a lot about Garett's first family in the last few days. Lorraine, of course, hadn't been very helpful. She'd refused to speak to Laura after everything had happened.

According to Nathan, the cancer was really beginning to take a toll on her. It didn't help that she'd lost her will to live.

She turned up to the funeral wearing the engagement ring that Garett had purchased for her. Laura wasn't sure how she felt about it, but then eventually decided that Lorraine was grieving in her own way.

Emily was with them. Laura had taken the box from Garett's nightstand and brought it with her. That was a woman who deserved to be here.

They would never know what had made Jess decide to kidnap Brandy. The police had found her on the beach covered in third-degree burns. It was an attempted suicide.

She was still alive, but she was unconscious, and she passed away in the hospital a few days later.

Brandy hadn't said a word about the experience. The only thing she had insisted on was a wig for the funeral. Laura had obliged, taking her shopping for blonde wigs and a dress. None of the ones Brandy already had would fit her.

She'd lost a good fifteen pounds off of her already slim body. The doctor said a lot of it was muscle mass because she'd been unable to move for most of her time in captivity. It would take some time for her to gain back her strength.

Right now both of her shoulders were taped up and bandaged. The paramedics at the scene had done their best to not move her, but the damage to her shoulders was already done. She was likely going to need surgery at some point.

Austin had rushed to the hospital to see her once Laura had got in touch with him. He looked both relieved and distressed at the sight of his girlfriend in the hospital bed. Brandy had refused to see him. She asked Laura to break things off with him. She didn't want the reminder of her life before, she said.

That statement worried Laura. Therapists were lined up for Brandy for both body and mind. After seeing her dad being murdered and learning that she'd been kidnapped by the sister she had always wanted to meet, she would need all the help she could get.

But Laura felt that Brandy didn't want it from her. She was just another reminder of Garett.

The funeral for Jess had been the day before. At first, Nathan had decided that they wouldn't do anything for Jess, but Brandy had insisted. She was adamant that Jess be honoured and remembered.

She'd also insisted on bringing the dog with her, much to the dismay of the rest of Jess's family. Laura was surprised that she would want to keep the dog that had helped to keep her captive, but Brandy didn't want him to leave her side.

So they'd held a small gathering, consisting of the same people and Thrasher. Brandy insisted on the eulogy.

"A few short months ago, I was living a great life. The only two regrets I could name was the death of my mother and the fact that I had two siblings in the world that didn't know I existed.

"I didn't expect to ever meet them, but in my mind, I had created personas for them. My brother was a hard-working young man, he lived for hockey and was coaching his kids' teams. My sister..." She paused for a second and took a deep breath. "My sister was a strong, independent woman. She was beautiful and successful. Maybe she had married, maybe not. She'd been raised by the same dad. She didn't need a man to complete her life.

"I first met her at a nightclub. I didn't know who she was at the time, but I can tell you she was none of the things that I had imagined her to be. She was shy, insecure and she didn't take care of herself. But she was nice, and I enjoyed talking to her.

"I am angry about what was done to me. I didn't deserve the treatment that I had, but Jess, or Cathy as I knew her, did not deserve the treatment she got, either.

"She didn't kidnap me out of spite or out of any desire to harm me. She needed a companion in life, someone to love her. Her life was ridden with torment and neglect, and by the time we met, she was very ill.

"So I am angry about what was done, but not with her. If anything, I wish that I'd known she was my sister when we first met. I would've taken her into my arms and told her that she wasn't alone anymore. That she would always have me.

"Many will continue to judge her, glad that she's gone. I don't. I don't condone the choices she made, but if she had been shown any kindness in her life, we would not be here today.

"My sister deserved a life of love and happiness, just like everyone else. And today, I stand here with my bandages, my wounds, and my scars, and I say to you, Jess, 'I love you'."

What Did You Think of Burning Rage?

Thank you for purchasing **Burning Rage**.
I am extremely grateful and honored that you chose this
book to read or give as a gift.
I hope that it adds value and quality to your everyday
life. It would be really nice if you could share this book
with your friends and family by posting comments
to Facebook and Twitter.
If you enjoyed this book and found some benefit in
reading Burning Rage, I'd like to hear from you and
hope that you could take some time to post a review on
Amazon and/or my author website
www.donbanting.com
Your feedback and support will help me to greatly
improve my writing craft for future writing projects.

donbanting.com

To order more copies of this book, find books by other
Canadian authors, or make inquiries about publishing
your own book, contact PageMaster at:

PageMaster Publication Services Inc.
11340-120 Street, Edmonton, AB T5G 0W5
books@pagemaster.ca
780-425-9303

catalogue and e-commerce store
PageMasterPublishing.ca/Shop

About the Author

Don Banting has a child and youth care diploma and a teaching degree. Burning Rage is Don's second published book. Don has written four screenplays along with several short stories. Don's interests include probability, philosophy, crime and psychology. Don has always cared for the less fortunate and donates his time and monetarily to several worthy agencies in Edmonton. Don currently resides in Edmonton, Alberta, Canada.